FATAL STAR

STAR MAGE SAGA BOOK SEVEN

J.J. GREEN

INFINITEBOOK

CHAPTER 1

*C*arina faced some tough decisions, but she'd already made one. She had decided to exclude Parthenia from the meeting to discuss the plans for the voyage to Earth. Her sister was pissed off, but it wasn't for the first time and it wouldn't be the last.

Plenty of other people were attending. Jackson had come as the representative of the Black Dogs, and Hsiao, the pilot, was there for obvious reasons. Carina had also invited Justus, the sole remaining Lotacryllan, due to his knowledge of the current sector's star systems. The ship's database held some information but it was centuries out of date.

There were two more attendees: Bryce and Jace. Bryce was essential. He knew her weaknesses as a leader and would counterbalance them. Jace's presence was important too. He was probably the wisest person on the ship.

Hsiao spoke first, giving her estimation of the length of the journey they had ahead of them.

"*259 years?!*" Carina exclaimed. "I don't understand. When you showed me Earth on the star map holo, it was in the same frame as the ship's position."

"Those maps cover vast areas," Hsiao replied. "I thought you knew that. You've flown starships."

"Only a little. I basically managed not to crash them. You're sure it's going to take us that long to reach Earth?"

"I'm not making this up," the pilot said tetchily. "It'll take us a decade or so to slow down from maximum speed, don't forget."

"I know, but..." Carina was at a loss for words. She looked to the others, wondering if they were as surprised as her at the pilot's revelation.

"We knew Earth had to be very far away for its position to be forgotten," said Bryce. "And the galaxy's tens of thousands of light years across. I suppose it shouldn't come as any surprise we have a long journey ahead."

Jackson shifted in his seat, his prosthetic arm softly clunking on the tabletop. "I don't get what the big deal is. We'll be in Deep Sleep most of the time. Doesn't matter if it takes us two hundred or two thousand years to get to Earth, does it?"

"I don't want to leave the ship on automatic pilot," said Carina. "Remember the Regians? We need at least a skeleton crew up and around at all times. And now we don't have the Lotacryllans..." she avoided looking at Justus "...there are even fewer of us. How are we going to manage it so we don't all die before we reach our destination?"

"Yeah, well," said Jackson, "we *did* have a skeleton crew when the Regians attacked, and we know how that turned out."

"You're seriously arguing we shouldn't bother leaving anyone awake because it won't make any difference?" Carina asked irritably. "That we're doomed whatever we do?"

Bryce touched her forearm. "Jackson has a point. The *Bathsheba* is a prize for any outlaw spacefarers who spot her, and as we leave the more densely populated areas there are going to be more of them. Maybe our real problem is how to defend the ship regardless of how many of us are awake or in Deep Sleep. We were boarded last time and we could be again."

Jace had been silent, stroking his beard, up until this point. But then he leaned both elbows on the table and said, "You're right, Bryce, and we must remember the detrimental effects of Deep Sleep too. If we do manage to rig up an automatic defense system, we still mustn't sleep the journey away. We need a timetable of waking and sleeping periods for everyone aboard."

"Great," muttered Carina. "Now we have two problems."

The older mage smiled. "We have two opportunities. One, to give the *Bathsheba* the best defenses we can, and, two, to figure out whose company we will have the pleasure of enjoying while we're awake. As I recall, Carina, going to Earth was your life's ambition. It looks like you may achieve it, and while you're relatively young. Not many can say the same."

"Or not so young," she said. "It sounds like I'll be an old woman by the time we arrive. What do we know about the safety parameters of Deep Sleep? Does anyone know how long it's safe to stay under?"

"I can check the database for information," said Jackson, "but we know that seventy-plus year stretch nearly did Calvaley in. Though he was an old guy to start off with. That probably didn't help."

A pang of sadness hit Carina. The old Sherrerr officer had been murdered by the Lotacryllans while she was away buying starship fuel. He'd given her sage advice on commanding the ship and its crew, and according to Bryce, he'd allied himself with the Black Dogs, warning them of the impending Lotacryllan attack. At one time, Calvaley had been a hated enemy, but he hadn't deserved such a brutal, ignoble death. She wished she had the benefit of his years of military experience now.

"Let us know what you find out," she said to Jackson. "I remember feeling like shit when I came out of suspension last time. I don't think anyone, young or old, should be under that amount of time again. My guess is our bodies can only sustain maybe forty or fifty years of Deep Sleep, tops, before we suffer harmful effects."

"You should look up how long it takes to recover too," Hsiao commented. "We need to be awake at least that long before going under again."

"Got it," Jackson replied.

"How's the training with Bibik going?" Carina asked the pilot. Bibik was Hsiao's apprentice. She'd been teaching him the ropes for several weeks. Carina had taken some lessons as well, though she didn't feel confident to pilot the gigantic colony ship solo yet.

"Pretty well. He isn't a natural, but he's keen and he listens, which is more than can be said for most nineteen-year-olds. Er, present company excepted."

Carina chuckled. "As another nineteen-year-old, I don't see myself as an exception. But I hope I've been listening too."

"Absolutely," the pilot replied, also laughing.

"You sure about that?" asked Bryce.

Carina gave him a playful shove.

In truth, the need for competent people to check the *Bathsheba's* heading and progress regularly was vital. Hsiao, Bibik, and herself would be the bare minimum required to avoid a major disaster. The ship held sufficient fuel to take them the distance, but they couldn't risk traveling far off course. A mistake of a fraction of a degree meant a journey of millions of kilometers in the wrong direction.

"Could you check among the crew for another volunteer apprentice?" she asked Hsiao, who nodded.

"Good, we're making progress," said Jace. "If Jackson finds out the information we need, we can figure out the Deep Sleep schedule." Turning to the man, he added, "You might want to speak to Nahla about accessing the database. She's been digging around in there for a while."

The merc's eyebrows rose. "The kid?"

4

"Don't be fooled by the fact she's only as tall as your chest," said Bryce. "She's sharp as a tack."

"Noted," Jackson replied. "So, what about these defenses for the *Bathsheba*? Seems to me that's the most important question here, not who's going to sleep and when."

It wasn't only the most important question, it was the hardest. If even the unintelligent Regians could overcome the colony ship's armaments, it meant the weapons were inadequate at fending off any determined attack.

"Can we improve our current stock?" asked Carina. "Do we have anyone among the Black Dogs who could take a look at them?"

"Doubt it," Jackson replied. "Our techs have struggled with most of the ship's systems. I don't think anyone's even taken a look at the weapons. I can ask."

"From what I've heard," said Hsiao tentatively, "our best weapon's your brother. The youngest one, I mean."

"Darius? A weapon?!" Carina exclaimed.

"Hey!" The pilot raised her hands in a gesture of placation. "It's just what I heard. He's the most powerful one out of all of you, isn't he?"

Carina's jaw muscles tightened as she tried to frame a reply. Bryce squeezed her forearm.

"But Darius will be in Deep Sleep for most of the journey," said Jace mildly, "like the rest of us."

"I know. I just thought he could—"

"What?" Carina asked tersely.

"He could...do one of those spells you do, like maybe..." Her words trailed off under Carina's hard stare.

"Maybe you should stop digging," Justus advised.

Hsiao clamped her lips together and looked away.

"What do you think we should do?" Jace asked the Lotacryllan. "You haven't said much yet."

"I've been too busy listening. I agree with all you've

discussed so far. For my part, I'm grateful for the opportunity to accompany you all. After the behavior of my companions, it would have been understandable if you'd marooned me at the nearest habitable planet."

"You did nothing wrong," said Bryce.

"Even so. On my home world, I would have been executed for my association with the mutineers."

"You aren't on Lotacrylla," said Carina. "We aren't like that."

She was still calming down after Hsiao's suggestion that her little brother should be used as some kind of human shield.

"Fortunately for me," said Justus. He went on, "Regarding the ship's armaments, I recall my father talking about a place that specializes in them."

"An entire planet that specializes in producing space weapons?" asked Bryce.

"No, a space station. It orbits a star that lacks any naturally habitable satellites, and the star sits between three star systems at war with each other. From what my dad said, the station plies a very good trade, supplying each of the three sides with technology it develops."

"Cool idea," said Jackson. "A market that never becomes exhausted. As soon as one side gets the latest weapons tech, the other two sides want it as well."

Carina sighed. "I'm not in love with the idea of a diversion from our route and more delay. We could pay for an armaments upgrade with ember gems, I guess, but I was hoping we could set out right away."

"On the other hand," Hsiao offered tentatively, "*I* don't like the idea of going into Deep Sleep not knowing if I'll wake up."

Carina frowned. What *was* it with the pilot? They'd gotten along pretty well up until now. Hsiao seemed to want to deliberately antagonize her.

"Can we trust the people at this station?" asked Jace. "What's to stop them seizing the *Bathsheba*?"

"It would be bad for their business reputation," replied Justus. "Why would they do something unscrupulous when they're so successful?"

"Should we put it to a vote?" asked Jackson. "I like the idea of upgrading the ship's defenses. Like Hsiao says, it'll help us sleep better."

"I'm not sure it's necessary," said Carina, "but I'd rather do that than have a seven-year-old *child* as our first line of defense."

Hsiao rolled her eyes. "I only meant... Never mind."

"Let's vote," Carina said, though she was sure of the outcome.

CHAPTER 2

"When are we going to sleep?" Darius asked Carina as she entered her siblings' suite. He bounced into her arms, wrapping himself around her and nearly bowling her over.

"Hey," she admonished. "You're getting too big for this."

He certainly *had* grown. He was much bigger and stronger than the little boy she'd rescued from the Dirksens more than a year ago. More importantly, he seemed much happier too. Putting him down, she said, "We aren't going into Deep Sleep for a few weeks yet."

"Good!" Ferne exclaimed. "Oriana and I have lots of fashion design ideas we want to try out."

"Silly," said his twin sister. "It doesn't matter if we do that before or after we enter life suspension, as long as we're awake together." She turned to Carina with a frown. "We *will* be together, right?"

"Don't worry," she replied. "I know better than try to separate you two."

"We're *all* going to be together, aren't we?" asked Darius hopefully.

"The sleep schedule hasn't been finalized, but yes, we will."

"You don't have to include me," said Parthenia, a bitter edge to her tone. "I'd be fine with being awake while the rest of you are Sleeping."

Nahla looked up from the interface she'd been reading and put both hands to her face before rolling her eyes.

Carina guessed Parthenia must have been sniping at her brothers and sisters while the meeting had been going on, taking out her anger on them.

She wasn't mad at her. If anything, she felt sorry for her. Feeling hurt by her exclusion from the meeting was natural, even if it had been necessary. More significantly, Parthenia's boyfriend Kamal had been killed while she was in the throes of her first love. She had to be still working through her grief.

"We'll be in Deep Sleep together," Carina said gently. "*All* of us. The voyage will be long. It's going to take centuries to reach Earth."

"Centuries?!" exclaimed Oriana.

"Of course," said Nahla matter-of-factly. "Didn't you know?"

"Not everyone has read the entire ship's database back to front and inside out," Oriana retorted.

Carina explained, "We don't have any choice except to leave the ship to run on automatic for years at a time. There aren't enough of us to always have even a few people awake for the entire journey. We would all age and die before we reached Earth. There's no point in trying to have a mage in every group not in Deep Sleep so we might as well stick together."

"The *Bathsheba* will fly without anyone awake?" asked Darius. His big brown eyes grew wide. "Like a ghost ship?!"

"Oooh, spooky!" said Nahla.

"But what if one of us wakes up and can't go back into Deep Sleep?" Darius continued. "He would be all alone, and he would get old while everyone else stays the same age. I could be an old man by the time you woke up, Carina!"

"That's not going to happen," she said, trying to sound reassuring, though her brother's words were painting a creepy picture in her head. She gave him a hug.

Nahla asked, "If we aren't going to sleep yet, what are we going to do?. I thought we had all the fuel we needed to reach Earth."

"We're going to have the *Bathsheba* fitted with some equipment at a place called Lakshmi Station."

"Lack what?" asked Ferne.

"Lak-sh-mi," Carina repeated, more slowly.

"What a strange name," said Oriana. "Why is it called that?"

"I don't know. It's probably named after the founder. I'll explain more during din—"

"And *who* decided we're going to this station?" Parthenia interjected.

"The people at the meeting. We took a vote."

"But what if I don't want to go? What if other people on the ship don't want to go? Don't we get a choice?"

Carina sighed. "Jackson spoke for the Black Dogs, the biggest group among us by far, and he voted to go to the station, so if you're trying to make a point about democracy..."

"I'm trying to make a point about my free will!"

"We always do what Carina says," said Nahla. "She saved us from—"

"*I* haven't always wanted to do what she says," Parthenia spat. "And when I didn't, she made me."

She clearly hadn't forgotten the time Carina had been forced to Enthrall her to get her away from danger on Ostillon, and she would never forget.

"I was trying to save your life!" Carina protested.

"Don't be dumb, Parthenia," said Ferne mildly. "If you don't come with us, where will you go?"

"This isn't about alternatives," she replied. "This is about having a say."

"Well, you've had your say," said Ferne. "Now shut up and let's eat. I'm hungry."

Parthenia gave a huff of frustration, spun on her heel, and marched into her bedroom. Aboard a starship it was impossible to slam a door, but Carina guessed that was what her sister would have done if she'd had the chance.

"Phew!" said Ferne. "Now we can eat in peace."

"Don't be mean," Carina scolded. "She's upset."

Her sister was hurting, and her pain was apparently bringing all her past grievances to the front of her mind. Perhaps not allowing her to attend the meeting had been a mistake.

"Can we get some nice food at Lacks Me Station?" asked Ferne. "I'm getting tired of printed stuff. It doesn't taste the same as fresh."

"We can try, but they specialize in starship equipment, not general supplies."

After a disastrous visit to Magog, attempting to restock the ship, they'd been forced to go to Gog, a much sparser, more basic place where they could only buy fuel, not much else. She wasn't too concerned about fresh food, but they definitely needed the complex chemicals required for the nutrient solution in the Deep Sleep chambers. Ferne's question reminded her she needed to check how much of them they had in store, especially now she knew how long they would be Sleeping.

"What kind of equipment?" Darius asked.

"Uhhh, just stuff we need. Who's ready for dinner?"

* * *

LATER, as she was getting ready for bed in their private suite, she said to Bryce, "I don't know what to do about Parthenia. She threw a fit today after I came back from the meeting. She was so angry I'd excluded her, she went into her room and wouldn't come out to eat. I think I made a bad call."

"Maybe," he replied. "It wouldn't have hurt to have her there. I didn't know she felt so strongly about it."

"I knew, but I kept to my guns. I wanted to limit the numbers for efficiency's sake."

"Is that the only reason?"

"What do you mean?"

"Would one more person really have made a big difference?"

"I guess not." She frowned, confused. Why *had* she been so adamant Parthenia didn't attend?

"Do you think maybe you were trying to protect her?"

"Protect her from what?"

"I don't know. You tell me."

Carina sat on their bed. "Do you think I'm over-protective of the kids?"

"What?!" Bryce exclaimed, raising his hands in mock outrage. "No! Never."

She grinned sheepishly. "I suppose you have a point. But, to be fair, things have been dangerous and difficult for them for a long time, ever since their monster of a father took them out of their estate on Ithiya."

Bryce joined her on the bed and put an arm around her, pulling her close. "I'm only saying Parthenia has grown up over the last year or so. And even before that, from what you've said, she was older than her years. I know you love your family—our family—and you'd do anything to keep them from harm, but maybe it's time to start treating your oldest sister like an adult. It wouldn't have been a problem for her to come to the meeting, and it would have made her feel like she was being taken seriously. That means a lot when you're seventeen."

"Oh, Bryce..." she laid her head on his shoulder "...how can I be a good mother to those kids? I don't have a clue what I'm doing."

"No one is expecting you to be their mother, and you've

already been an amazing older sister. But maybe it's time to loosen the reins a little."

"Yeah, I hear you. I'll apologize to Parthenia tomorrow."

"Good idea. I'm sure she'll come around."

He touched her chin and turned it toward his before kissing her.

Together, they fell backward onto the bed.

CHAPTER 3

*C*arina was in the twilight dome when Hsiao arrived. Sitting in the shadows directly beneath an opaque section of overhead, repaired after the bomb blast, she was in a melancholy mood, thinking about the long journey ahead before they reached Earth, and didn't feel like talking. When she saw the pilot come in, she shrank into her seat, hoping she couldn't be seen. She'd been avoiding the pilot since the meeting. Hsiao's comments about Darius still rankled.

But Hsiao's sharp gaze soon found her. "Carina! I thought you might be here."

"Yeah, just hanging out."

"Can I join you?"

No.

"I guess."

Hsiao came over and sat next to her before looking upward through one of the remaining transparent areas of hull, where a field of stars glittered in the black.

"You've come to see Lakshmi Station?" she asked.

"Huh?"

"You can see it from here. Didn't you know?" The pilot

pointed in the direction of a brilliant star outshining all the others.

"I figured that's where we're going," said Carina, "but that's the sun the station's orbiting, isn't it? It can't be the station itself."

"The brightest one is the sun, and at six o'clock there's the gas giant, the biggest planet in the system. Look between the planet and the sun. There's a tiny speck. Can you see it?"

Carina squinted. There *was* a pinprick of light at the spot Hsiao described.

"Whoa," she breathed. "It must be *vast*."

"It's quite something, right? And the star it orbits is unusual too. It's spinning super slowly, and its spectrum is wild— neodymium, strontium, cesium. All kinds of heavy elements."

"Uhhh…"

"You wouldn't normally expect a star to emit anything like that."

"Okay," Carina replied. Hsiao was a bit of a nerd. Normally, she wouldn't mind listening to the pilot's monologues on obscure subjects, but today she wasn't in the mood.

Hsiao took the hint and was silent for a while. Then she said, "About your brother…"

"What about him?"

"I think you misunderstood what I was getting at in the meeting."

"You do, do you?"

"Yeah." The pilot squirmed uncomfortably. "I didn't mean he should be responsible for defending us if we're attacked. I only meant…" Her words faltered to a stop.

"What?" Carina turned to face her. "What *did* you mean? Look, Darius might be the most powerful mage in my family, and he might be able to do things the rest of us find impossible, but at the end of the day, he's just a little boy. And, more than that, what you have to understand is a lot of what he does hurts him. When we were on Magog and he guessed Kai Wei was a Dark Mage, it was because he felt the man's evilness and corruption. And when he knew the starwhale was in agony from the Regians' binding, it was because he *felt* her pain. Would *you* like to live like that?"

"No," Hsiao muttered.

"No, me neither, even if it meant I could do all the things Darius can. His abilities come at a price, and he doesn't have a choice about it. So when I hear people talking about him like he's a thing, something to be used for everyone's benefit, it pisses me off."

"All right! I get it."

Carina took a deep breath, and Bryce's gentle advice came back to her. Moderating her tone, she said, "I appreciate you coming to talk to me about it and trying to set things straight between us. I hope you understand now where I'm coming from."

"I do. I didn't know that about your brother, that he was sensitive in that way."

"I suppose, outside the family and Bryce, we don't really talk about what being a mage means. When I was growing up, I had it drummed into me that I had to keep my abilities secret, and my mother did the same with my siblings. None of us is comfortable with discussing this stuff with non-mages."

"I'd like to know more, if you're okay with talking about it. I think it's fascinating. I'd love to understand how it works."

"You and me both."

"You don't know?"

"The only explanation I've seen for mage powers is in the old documents we found on Ostillon. They were written by the mages who colonized the planet, though the stories were already ancient history at the time. They say the original mages believed they carried a genetic mutation, and the ability to Cast was unlocked when someone experimented with drinking mixtures of different substances. It does have to be something in our genes. That's how Kai Wei identified us on Magog, through the saliva samples."

"A genetic variation makes sense," said Hsiao, "but that doesn't explain *how* you do what you do. Transporting from one place to another, starting fires, healing people, locking doors so they can't be opened...none of it has any rational explanation according to the laws of physics."

"Beats me. It isn't something I think about. My grandma taught me how to Cast, the same as she taught me to read and write. Do you wonder about how you can read?"

"No, but..." The pilot's brow wrinkled. "I can explain *why* I can read. I can explain most things if I put my mind to it. I could tell you how the *Bathsheba's* engines work, for instance, and why it's odd Lakshmi Station's star emits heavy metal particles."

Carina shrugged.

Hsiao turned her gaze upward to the star field again and was silent.

Carina also concentrated on the speck that was the station, trying to guess how big it was. It had to be at least the size of a substantial moon.

After several minutes, the pilot said, "There has to be an explanation for everything, even if we don't know it yet. It took us hundreds of thousands of years to invent deep space engines, but we did it in the end. Maybe, one day, someone will figure out what makes mages different. Maybe one day splicers will be able to give anyone the same abilities."

"I certainly hope so. Life would be a lot easier."

Hsiao got to her feet. "For me too. I'd love to close my eyes and transport myself anywhere on the ship. The *Bathsheba's* way too big."

"I usually walk," said Carina, "though I can't deny it's nice to have the option of a shortcut. How long until we dock?"

17

"We've been slowing down for a while. A couple of days, assuming they allow us to dock right away."

"Why would we have to wait?"

"Lakshmi's a busy place. There's space traffic all around it. We've been picking up their advertising spiel for days too."

"We have? I didn't know."

"You should have a listen. It's illuminating."

CHAPTER 4

*L*akshmi Station was shaped like two squares superimposed, creating an eight-pointed star. The *Bathsheba* approached the upper side, in the lane of space traffic heading for the site.

Parthenia watched as the station grew gradually larger on the bridge holo, along with Hsiao and a few of the Black Dogs. The pilot would perform the maneuver to dock, but after that she would join the away party.

Parthenia wasn't going to the station. Carina had snubbed her again, but she had no interest in business meetings anyway, assuming that's what the others were doing. Father had forced her to attend too many meetings with clients on Ithiya. He'd made her Cast Enthrall on the unsuspecting men and women so they would agree to unfavorable terms. She felt sick and her skin prickled with anxiety just remembering. Participating in the process again would bring back many bad memories, though she didn't think Carina would pull the same under-handed trick to buy space weapons for the *Bathsheba*.

One of the Black Dogs, a woman called Van Hasty, quietly swore, expressing her wonder at the size of the station.

"How far away are we?" she asked Hsiao.

"An hour," the pilot replied.

"As long as that?"

"Uh huh. But we stop here. I'm reversing thrust to bring us to a standstill. When I've shut the engines down I'll fly the *Peregrine* the rest of the way. Bibik will be along soon to keep an eye on things while I'm gone."

The edges of Lakshmi disappeared and the station took up the entire view, the detail of its hull growing more defined as each second passed. Lines cut across the base of the points of the construction, channels of some kind, separating the triangles from the octagonal whole. More lines criss-crossed the main surface, creating an intricate pattern that Parthenia guessed was more decorative than practical. There would be conduits, service tunnels, air ducts, and much more running underneath the hull, but there was no reason for these to show on the outside as far as she knew. It looked quite pretty, if a space station could ever be called pretty, which was strange considering its trade

"Shit," said Van Hasty, "I wish I was going with you, Hsiao. Must be all kinds of fun things to do there."

"You'll get your turn," the pilot replied. "As soon as we've figured out what we're doing about the armaments, everyone will get their R and R."

"I could do with it," Van Hasty said. "How long has it been since we had a chance to let our hair down?"

"Stop complaining," said another Black Dog, Rees. "You went planetside with our friends the Regians. What more fun could you want?"

"Huh, *I* wouldn't call nearly being made a larva snack fun, but whatever floats your boat."

Rees's face creased as he grinned and he seemed about to fire back a quick reply, but his gaze slid to Parthenia and he hesitated before eventually saying, "You're welcome to float my boat anytime, and you know it."

"Yeah, you wish," said Van Hasty.

Parthenia inwardly sighed.

Rees was moderating what he said because she was there. The Black Dogs all treated her like a kid. Kamil had been the only one who didn't, and now he was dead. A sob welled up in her throat, but she swallowed it.

Carina treated her like a kid too, even though they were only three years apart. Her sister had apologized for not allowing her to attend the discussion about what to do next, but Parthenia knew she didn't really mean it. And she showed it when she left her out of the away party.

There had been a time when she'd thought Carina had begun to see her as more of an equal, but that was forgotten now. The next time something important had to be done, she would be excluded again.

She wished Magog hadn't been run by Dark Mages. She and Kamil could have stayed there, abandoning the journey to Earth. She could have had some kind of freedom. Now, her fate was tied up with her family's and the Black Dogs'. Whatever they did, she would be sucked into it. She had no choice and no say because everyone saw her as a child.

"Hey," said Hsiao, "listen to this."

She did something on her console and suddenly the bridge was filled with sound.

Welcome to Lakshmi Station, technology center of the sector!

What do you need? Space cannon? Mechs? The latest energy weapons? Whatever you want, you'll find it here, guaranteed! The most up-to-date, cutting-edge tech at your fingertips, all for a reasonable price.

Or maybe you're only looking for somewhere to get away from the stresses of interplanetary conflict? You've come to the right place. Bars, sim pads, leisure hotels, extra-friendly hosts and hostesses, anything and everything you need to relax and forget the war for a while.

The voice continued at a faster pace and in a more serious tone, *No personal arms allowed on site, and brawlers will be immediately and permanently expelled.*

The message began to repeat, and Hsiao turned it off.

"Extra-friendly hostesses?" Rees asked, grinning again. "I like the sound of that."

"*I* like the sound of the latest space cannon," said Van Hasty. "Waking up to a ship invasion was a nasty surprise I don't want to repeat. I hope Carina has the creds to get us the best."

"She's paying with the last of the ember gems," Parthenia commented. "I don't know how much they're worth."

"None of us does," said Hsiao. "They're a Geriel Sector thing. Never heard of them back home."

"She'd better watch out," Rees said, "or she'll get ripped off."

"Yeah," said Van Hasty ruefully, "it happens easily enough. You still up for a trip to the station after hearing that, Rees?"

"'Course. Why not?"

"Didn't you hear the bit about 'no personal arms' and 'brawlers expelled'?"

"Yeah, so?"

Hsiao laughed. "I'll explain it to him in simple terms. We're right in the middle of three warring systems, and they're all coming here to fill their weapon orders. *All* of them. What do you think the tension on the station's gonna be like?"

Rees's eyes widened and he whistled. "Holy shit. They'll be at each others' throats."

"He's got it!" Van Hasty exclaimed sarcastically.

Rees went on, "Cool. Can't wait to get down there."

"You're kidding, right?" asked Hsiao.

"Nah, who doesn't like a good bar fight?"

"Well," Van Hasty said, "you'd better not get caught or your R and R will be cut short, and you won't be getting any more."

"Yeah, I'll wait until I've spent some time with those extra-friendly hostesses before starting anything."

Van Hasty wrinkled her nose. "Ewww! Hostesses? Sex bots, you mean. What if they don't clean themselves properly between—"

Rees elbowed her, nodding at Parthenia.

Van Hasty gave her a glance and continued, "...turns?"

Parthenia clenched her jaw. "For goodness sake, I know what you were going to say. I know those words. You can say them around me without my ears falling off or my head exploding."

"Sorry," said Rees, "but you know what your sister's like. If she gets wind we've been treating you like another merc, our lives won't be worth living."

"Yes," Parthenia retorted bitterly. "I do know what my sister's like."

She stalked from the bridge.

CHAPTER 5

*T*he umbilicus snaked out from the *Peregrine's* airlock. The ship's outer hatches were not compatible with the station's, so the away party was forced to enter it via the slightly more risky method, which meant EVA suits for everyone. At the farther end, Lakshmi Station waited.

"Okay," said Carina via her helmet's comm, "let's go."

She reached for the nearest handhold and pulled herself into the tube. As she moved out of the *Bathsheba's* a-grav field, she floated forward, her momentum carrying her on almost too fast for her to grab the next bar.

The umbilicus was about twenty meters long. Glancing back to check the others weren't having any problems, she saw Hsiao, Jackson, and Justus in a line behind her. She wished Jace had agreed to come too, but he'd turned her down. He hadn't given much of an explanation, only saying he didn't know the first thing about space weapons or commercial negotiations.

The guy was a pacifist at heart and would never change.

She'd invited Bryce too, though she had to admit the invitation had been half-hearted. He'd seemed to guess she would prefer him to stay on the ship and look after the kids.

Turning a bend in the umbilicus, she saw the station's hatch opening and the light of its airlock. She pulled herself onward until she reached it. The station's a-grav quickly settled on her and she had to twist fast to get her feet under her before she hit the deck.

Hsiao and the others arrived, the hatch closed, the airlock pressurized, and the inner portal opened.

On the other side, the passageway was empty.

Carina removed her helmet and peered up and down it. "Huh?"

"What were you expecting?" Hsiao asked, tucking her helmet under her arm. "A welcoming committee?"

A muffled beeping was coming from inside Carina's suit. She unzipped it and opened the comm.

"Party from the *Peregrine* to proceed to Deck Five."

Justus said, "They want to check we aren't going to shoot the place up before they'll see us face-to-face."

"Makes sense," said Carina.

There was only one other exit from the passageway: a set of elevator doors. When they were inside, it didn't ask where they wanted to go. There was only one stop. The doors opened at Deck Five.

"Hi," said a man on the other side of a high desk. He and the desk stood behind a deck-to-overhead transparent shield. "You're from out-sector, right?"

"That's right. Uhhh, except one of us." She remembered Justus's planet, Lotacrylla, was in Geriel.

"I'm not from around these parts," said Justus. "So I'm probably not on your system either."

"Step forward one at a time for retinal scans," said the man, "and to receive your visitor ID code. From now on, if you don't show your code on request, you'll be immediately returned to your ship and your permission to enter the station will be permanently revoked."

Carina went first. After looking into the scanner, she had to present the inside of her wrist, where a laser etched a pattern. It stung a bit but didn't hurt too bad. When they'd all been scanned and received their codes, the man said, "Deposit your suits in the locker room to your left."

Carina asked, "Do you—"

"Locker room on your left."

She trudged to the room. She'd only been going to ask if there was somewhere to sell gems. Lakshmi was not Gog. It wasn't a backwater planet where people could barter for what they wanted. The traders here would only deal in creds. Heck, they probably had showrooms and pricing catalogs.

Tall lockers lined the walls in the next room they entered. Along with the others, Carina took off her EVA suit, hung it up in a locker, and closed the door. A square hole opened up in it.

"What's this?" she asked.

"You breathe into it," said Justus. "The locker records your exhaled breath signature. It'll only open if the same person breathes into it again."

Her stomach tightened. The last time her bio ID had been recorded, she, Darius, and Parthenia had been identified as mages.

"Does it collect your DNA?" she asked.

"No, just your breath chemicals, I think."

"You *think*?"

"I'm not a bio signature expert, Carina."

"It's only to be expected," Hsiao commented. "They need to use it for security."

"Yeah," said Carina, "but you know what happened on Magog."

"It's no big deal, is it?" asked Jackson.

"If they wanted your DNA," Hsiao said, "they would ask you for something different."

Carina sighed and leaned in to put her mouth to the square,

hoping the station's security didn't want anything else from them. A soft snick emanated from the locker.

Next, they had to pass through a short, brightly lit tunnel. Carina went first, followed by Justus and Hsiao, with Jackson bringing up the rear. Carina stepped out the farther side.

"Scanning us," murmured Justus as he joined her.

"Yeah," said Hsiao. "They're probably looking at our insides too."

"They don't wanna see what I just ate," said Jackson. "That—"

An alarm sounded.

A metal plate slid across the tunnel, separating Jackson from the rest of them.

"Shit!" Carina exclaimed. She banged on the metal. "Jackson! Jackson, can you hear me?"

She thought she heard some indistinct shouting, then silence.

"Uh oh," said Hsiao.

Carina turned around. When she'd exited the tunnel, there had been an open door in the chamber on the other side. Now the door was closed.

"Additional security check required," said a smooth female voice from an intercom. "Please wait."

"What the hell?" said Hsiao. "He wasn't trying to smuggle a weapon in, was he?"

"I hope not," said Justus. "We'll be screwed if he was. They don't *need* our business. If we're lucky, they'll only kick us off the station."

"What if we're not lucky?" Hsiao asked.

Justus didn't answer.

Tense seconds passed.

"Jackson isn't dumb," said Carina. "He can't be armed...can he?" As the words left her mouth, an idea about why the merc had been detained hit her. But before she could state it, the metal plate slid back, revealing Jackson bare-chested. Two people in armored suits were walking away from him.

"It was your arm, right?" Carina asked.

The man's prosthetic was extensive, encompassing his entire right shoulder as well as the missing limb. Below the elbow downward it looked like a normal arm, but above that it was covered in a dull, flexi-metal skin. The cost-cutting of the cheaper coating on the upper arm and shoulder came as no surprise. The Black Dogs' former boss, Tarsalan, had been notoriously cheap.

Though Carina had always known about the prosthetic, she'd never seen the whole thing before. Jackson must have received quite an injury to lose so much of his body. He seemed embarrassed as he hastened to put on his shirt before answering her. Pulling the lower edge down over his hips, he said, "Yeah. They wanted to check I wasn't hiding a fancy gun."

The door at the opposite end of the chamber opened.

"Looks like we're good to go," said Hsiao.

"You know," said Justus as they walked out, "that might not be such a crazy idea. Fitting your arm with a gun, I mean. Once we're out of here, of course. Have you ever considered it?"

"Never thought about it," Jackson replied.

"Or you could get a natural arm regrown," Justus continued. "I don't know about where you're from, but it was a common procedure on my world. You're stuck in bed for a couple of weeks, but after that—"

"Never thought about it," the merc repeated in a harsher tone.

Justus shrugged.

Jackson's sensitivity was a little odd. Carina had heard him crack jokes about his arm many times. She guessed it was one of those cases where it was okay for *him* to joke about it, but not anyone else.

They seemed to have finally passed the security procedures.

They stepped out into a busy thoroughfare humming with life, though not all of it was human.

In her short career as a merc, she'd come across a few alien species. Most of them had been humanoid. Evolution seemed to favor bipedal organisms for the development of intelligence. The similarity to humans made them not too hard to get used to. But the first alien she spotted at Lakshmi Station made her jump.

It scuttled like a spider, but the creature had more legs and skin rather than a carapace, and its head—what appeared to be its head—stuck up from the center of its body. It also wore clothes. Fabric draped over its body and hung down between its many legs. She wondered how long it took to get dressed and if it was confusing trying to fit its legs through the many holes.

Ten or twelve black eyes ran around the alien's head like a crown and its face contained four orifices, the largest below the eyes and three more in a line below that. Fine, short, mottled gray fur coated its body.

The alien was making a beeline for them.

"Gross!" Hsiao exclaimed, backing up.

"Shit," said Carina. The creature seemed about to speak to them, but they didn't have a translator.

It drew to a halt in front of them, swaying slightly as it poised on its claws. "Welcome to Lakshmi Station. My name is Bongo. I'll be your guide for your free introductory tour."

"*Bongo?*" Carina asked.

$\mathcal{A}$ wave of sharp anger washed over Darius. Sadness, a sense of being alone, and something else he didn't know the word for—misery?—came with it.

Parthenia was back.

Though he hadn't seen her enter the living area because he was in his bedroom playing cards with Nahla, he felt her arrival clear as day, the same as always.

He recognized all his family by the patterns of their emotions. If someone had blindfolded him, he could have picked each of them out and even made a good guess about how far away they were. The farther they went, the fainter their feelings became, until at four or five hundred meters they faded away.

He'd never let on how well he could feel his brothers and sisters' presence. He thought Mother had guessed, but he'd never talked to her about it. When he was younger, he hadn't been able to keep his face straight or stop himself from crying when a wave of emotion bashed into him. She would cuddle him, surrounding him with her love, trying to help. It hadn't helped. She was too sad. Mother's sadness had been a deep, dark well no one could ever fill. Not even him. He'd tried, but he couldn't do it.

If his family knew the truth about how they affected him, it might hurt them. They would feel sad and guilty if they knew how strongly their emotions affected him. He didn't want them to have those bad feelings. He wanted them to be happy. He didn't want them to fear or hate him.

"Hurry up," said Nahla. "It's your turn."

"Oh." He picked his next card and placed it on the pile.

Nahla was winning again. She always won, whatever game they played, but he didn't mind. He liked playing with her. Ferne and Oriana didn't spend much time with him anymore. They were busy designing and printing clothes. Nahla was often busy too, searching for information in the *Bathsheba's* database or translating the mage papers. But sometimes she agreed to play with him.

He liked Nahla best of all his brothers and sisters, except Carina, of course. He loved Carina so much it hurt. He would never forget the day she'd rescued him from the horrible Dirksen men who had cut him. Even then, before he knew she was his half-sister, he'd loved the way her feelings of care and concern wrapped around him like a big, soft blanket. Carina's pattern of emotions was strong and powerful. Every so often, it wavered into sadness, but mostly it was strong. He felt safe when she was nearby.

"I win," said Nahla, putting her final card on the top of the pile. "Better luck next time."

Darius gathered up the cards and began pushing them together to make a pack. "Do you want to play again?"

"No, I'm bored with this game. It's too easy."

"What about something else? We could play a different one."

"All the games are too easy."

"We could learn something new."

"Like what?"

"I don't know. Maybe we could find a new game on the database and learn the rules."

Nahla's face twisted as she considered his idea. Her feelings were mixed up. He guessed she didn't really want to play with him and she'd only agreed to be kind. She didn't want to say yes, and she was trying to think of a way to say no nicely.

"How about we do something else?" she asked.

"Like what?"

"Like…" She leaned closer.

He sensed a strange emotion in her—fear tinged with a little bit of excitement.

"Would you like to explore the ship with me?"

"Is that all?" Darius replied, disappointed. The odd feelings she was giving out had raised his hopes she had something interesting to suggest. "We've explored the ship lots of times. How about we volunteer to be models for Ferne and Oriana? They would like that."

Nahla wrinkled her nose. "I don't want to wear their silly clothes. And we haven't explored *all* the ship. I found some new places."

"You did?" He was surprised and excited. "Like the time you found the ember gems on the *Zenobia*?!"

She nodded. "Promise you won't tell anyone?"

"I promise."

Now he came to think of it, he had been sensing a secretiveness about her lately. "Why don't you want anyone to know? Maybe there are more jewels hidden on this ship. Carina could use them to buy us more stuff."

"You know what the grown-ups are like. If I tell them, they won't let us take a look. They'll say it's too dangerous."

"Well, it might be dangerous," said Darius, having second thoughts.

"It isn't." She frowned. "And even if it is, you could Transport us out of there, couldn't you?"

"Yeah, but..." He was still uneasy. If Carina knew they were planning on investigating a secret part of the *Bathsheba*, she wouldn't want them to do it.

"You promised not to tell anyone," Nahla reminded him. "If you don't want to come with me, that's okay. I'll go by myself. But you can't tell on me, okay?"

"I suppose so," he said grudgingly.

"Do you want to come or not?"

"Why didn't you go there by yourself already? Were you waiting until I agreed to go with you?"

"Kinda," Nahla replied sheepishly.

He didn't want to go. Starships weren't adventure playgrounds, as Carina had often said. There were garbage chutes and airlocks that you couldn't mess around with or you might end up in space. There were restricted areas near the engine that were deadly if you stayed there too long. There were boxes and machinery that could fall on you.

But if he didn't go with Nahla and something bad happened to her, she couldn't Cast to get herself out of trouble. All she could do was use the ship's comm, and the rescuers might not arrive in time. The *Bathsheba* was huge. If she needed an adult to help her, it could take too long for them to run there.

"I'll come," he said. "But if it looks dangerous, we have to leave right away."

"Okay," Nahla agreed, "but I keep telling you, it isn't dangerous."

"Let me get my elixir. Then we can go."

He hopped down from his chair and grabbed his elixir bottle from the top of a cabinet.

They went into the living area, where Oriana and Ferne were drawing a design on an interface. Parthenia wasn't there. Darius could feel her in her bedroom, a bundle of heartache and unhappiness. He felt sorry for her, but whenever he tried to give her a hug she would push him away.

"Where are you two going?" asked Ferne as they headed for the door.

"Um, we're getting something to eat," Nahla replied.

"We only ate an hour ago," said Oriana. "You can't be hungry again."

"Darius is. He's a growing boy. He needs to eat all the time."

He elbowed her. Oriana and Ferne would think he was a greedy pig. Couldn't she think up a better lie?

"Bring us something too," said Ferne. "Some of those corn crackers. Carina will be back late from her trip to Lacks Me Station—"

"Lak*sh*mi," Oriana interrupted.

"That's what I said. Anyway, we won't be eating dinner until late and I need something to keep me going."

"All right," Nahla agreed. "Corn crackers. Do you want anything, Oriana?"

"Could you get me a brother who can speak properly?"

Darius and Nahla giggled.

Ferne rolled his eyes. "There's nothing wrong with how I speak."

"Should we get anything for Parthenia?" Darius asked.

"Ugh, no," said Oriana. "No point. She's given up on eating. I expect she'll miss dinner again too. She's still upset after *you know what*."

Darius did know what. The young man Parthenia liked had died. When it happened, her feelings had hit him like a flash flood racing down a riverbed.

"Okay," said Nahla. "See you later. Come on, Darius."

CHAPTER 7

"Where are you from?" Bongo asked.

He spoke through his upper orifice. Carina guessed the ones below it were probably only for breathing, though why he needed three wasn't clear. The alien scuttled alongside her as they walked down the passageway. His head only came up to her waist, and when she looked at him to answer she didn't know which of his many eyes to focus on.

"You won't have heard of it," she replied. "We're from outside Geriel Sector." She didn't want to give him—or her—any more information than necessary. Justus might feel confident no one on Lakshmi would try to steal the *Bathsheba*, but she wasn't. She couldn't afford to be. The colony ship was all she had. That, and the little pouch of ember gems in her pocket.

"Outside the sector!" remarked the alien. "Fascinating. Well, you're all human, so it doesn't really matter. What brings you to the station?"

"We're interested in space armaments. Our ship is already heavily kitted out," she lied, "but we heard Lakshmi has some of the most advanced tech in the region."

"You heard right," said Bongo. "You won't find better within the *sector*, let alone region."

"That's good to hear. I'm glad you can speak Universal. We don't have any translators. Do all the vendors speak Universal too?" She'd presumed they would be human, but Bongo's existence had made her realize they might not.

"You don't need to be concerned about translation," he replied. "If an arms specialist can find a way to part you from your creds, he'll do it, even if it means he has to speak…" He concluded his sentence with a sound like someone gargling while at the same time trying to not throw up.

"Talking of creds," said Carina, "we don't have any."

Bongo stopped dead in his tracks and his head rotated as he scanned her with all his eyes. "Then how do you plan to—"

"We have valuable items we want to exchange. Is there a place we can do that?"

"What kind of valuable items?"

"I'd rather not say." And she certainly didn't want to pull out the gems to show him in the middle of the busy thoroughfare.

"I see. I can take you to some—"

A passerby stepped too close and caught his foot on one of Bongo's many outspread legs. The stranger stumbled, but at half his weight, the alien came off worse from the collision. He flipped right over onto his back, his head bending into his body.

"Damned spider creep!" the man yelled, getting to his feet.

"Hey, take it easy," said Carina. "It was an accident."

Bongo was struggling to right himself. The accident had drawn the attention of the crowd and a ring of bystanders was forming. Wriggling exactly like an arachnid, the alien was becoming a spectacle.

"Yuck," someone murmured. "Revolting."

Everyone watching was human, and they were having exactly the reaction most humans had when confronted with an insect or spider in distress—disgust. But Carina had always liked bugs, ever since childhood. Nai Nai had discouraged her from making friends, fearing she would accidentally reveal her mage powers, and her planet hadn't evolved large life forms she could have as pets. So she'd taken to playing with invertebrates, constructing elaborate homes for them in her room, much to her grandmother's annoyance when they inevitably escaped.

She scooped Bongo up and set him on his feet.

Meanwhile, Jackson snapped to the crowd, "What are you gawping at? Move on. Nothing to see here."

"I can manage!" the alien exclaimed. He shook himself like a wet dog and reached up with a couple of claws to adjust the cloth hanging below his belly.

"Sorry," said Carina. "I was just trying to help."

"Are you all right?" asked Hsiao.

"I'm fine," Bongo retorted irritably. "Now, where were we? Currency exchange centers, right? I'll take you to some, and I'll show you the leisure and recreation facilities on the way."

"We aren't interested in leisure and recreation," said Carina, but he didn't respond. She guessed it was his job to take them on the standard tour.

What had been a bare, pedestrian transit tunnel opened out into a commercial zone. The congestion eased in the wider space, and the air was suddenly filled with scents of food, perfumes, and other, unrecognizable things. The noise increased, sounds of talking, footsteps, and a warbling singer echoing from the three-tier-high walls and walkways.

Justus continued on, unimpressed, but Carina, Hsiao, and Jackson halted to take it all in. Stores, restaurants, cafes, offices, and establishments she didn't even recognize ranged around them and above. She had always kind of known such places existed, but she'd never seen one. The course of her life had never given her the opportunity to visit a high-end market like this. From the way they stared, she guessed Hsiao and Jackson's backgrounds were similar.

Bongo was waiting patiently for them. Justus had turned around and walked back.

"You'll have plenty of time for shopping after the tour," said the alien.

They continued on. After a few minutes, Carina realized some of the people in the throng weren't actually alive. At first, she'd thought Lakshmi Station held more than the average share of attractive folk. Several of the men and women they passed were head-turners. But when the next one came along, she noticed there was something not quite right about the way she looked. Her skin, eyes, and hair were literally flawless, and her face and body was perfectly symmetrical. The other good-lookers were the same.

These had to be the 'hosts and hostesses' mentioned in the station's broadcasted advertising. Hsiao had explained they were androids and what they were for, and it was then she'd decided Parthenia and the other kids shouldn't come to the station, at least not until she'd checked it out. In fact, so far it was tamer than she'd imagined, but they'd hardly seen any of it yet. She didn't want to take the risk of exposing them to things beyond their years, especially considering everything they'd been through.

"Mind massage," Hsiao read aloud from a sign. "I wonder what that is?"

"Externally induced meditation," said Bongo. "It's pleasant, but nothing to write home about."

"Do you have sim modules here?" Jackson asked.

The alien emitted a long stream of air from its three lower orifices, causing them to flap and vibrate noisily. The effect was something like laughing.

Bongo had holes just for laughing?

"Do we have sim modules? Sir, we have the best sim modules in all Geriel. Military, romance, sensual, adventure, historical, futuristic, theological, whatever you can imagine. We have sim modules that read your deepest fantasies and recreate them for you. And your worst nightmares too, though I wouldn't recommend that option."

"Cool," Jackson commented.

"After we figure out what we're doing about the armaments," said Hsiao, "we should get something to eat. I bet they have all kinds of weird, delicious stuff here."

"Probably," Carina replied, "but we aren't here to have fun, remember? We have a job to do."

"The Black Dogs are expecting some relaxation time here," said Jackson.

"They're in a state of nearly constant relaxation on the ship!" Carina protested. "Who started *that* rumor?"

"Uhhh," said Hsiao, "I just assumed..."

"Great," Carina muttered.

She was beginning to feel like a matriarch in charge of a bunch of demanding, whiny offspring. Didn't the mercs understand they were on a mission? It was a very long one, she had to admit, but the time for R and R would come later, after they'd reached Earth.

"I don't have any idea how many creds we'll get in exchange for the..." she coughed as Bongo's head swiveled her way. "Once we've bought the weapons and supplies, there might not be anything left over to spend on having fun."

She felt bad. The mercs had worked without pay for months. They'd joined her expedition to Earth mostly because they'd had no choice. It was either that or spend the rest of their lives hiding from vengeful Dirksens. She'd come to see them as extended family, but in reality they were work-for-hire soldiers who were working for no compensation.

An alien of the same species as Bongo approached through the crowd. As the two passed each other, they raised their legs and hit claws in a multiple high-five.

They entered a leisure and recreation area, which the alien

insisted on showing them around, though Carina tried again to explain they weren't interested. Hsiao and Jackson made a liar of her anyway, expressing great interest in every place Bongo took them, from the 'hosted' lounges to the 'soaring rooms', where you could turn off the a-grav and fly, wearing wings. The latter seemed particularly silly. Aboard starships, losing a-grav generally meant imminent disaster.

Most of the entertainments were behind closed doors, which Carina was grateful for, though they did see one section open to the public: a hot spring 'lake', where bathers lounged and lazily swam. The creators had gone to a lot of trouble to make the place appear authentic, probably shipping in the rocks from a planet. The plants looked real, from the tall ferns that overhung the water to the moss on the pebble shore.

Finally, the obligatory tour of the recreation area was over and Bongo took them to a currency exchange booth. There was only room for three people on the customer side of the counter. Or, as it turned out, one human and a…whatever Bongo was. He crawled into the booth with her, and then no one else would fit. Hsiao, Jackson, and Justus waited outside, peering in.

Was it a set up? Was she about to be ripped off?

She decided to show the assistant only one of the gems and find out how much they were willing to offer before she decided whether to go ahead with the exchange.

Another of Bongo's species stepped out into the back of the booth through a curtain.

That explained why the counter was so low.

It had to be a set up. Bongo had brought her to a friend, relation, or associate to fleece her. Was he even an official guide? The sack-thing he was wearing didn't display any words or a logo.

He spoke with the sales assistant, using their mutual language. The sound reminded her of water running over rocks.

"Hey," she said, "could you use Universal? I'd prefer to know what you're saying."

"I was explaining to my cousin you'd like to conduct a non-standard exchange. She wants to know what you're offering."

Cousin, huh?

With a sense of unease, Carina drew out her pouch and removed one of the gems before returning it to her pocket. Squatting down, she put the gem on the counter but kept her finger on it.

A second round of bubbling dialogue ensued.

She picked up the stone and folded it inside her palm. "Universal!"

"I apologize," said Bongo. "If that's what I think it is, it's the first time I've ever seen one in real life. My cousin doubts it's genuine and wants to check for herself."

"Yeah, but…" She couldn't think of a nicer way to put it. "How do I know your cousin isn't going to run off with it and disappear, or take it out the back and swap it for a fake?"

"Wow," said Bongo's relative. "Rude much? If you don't trust me, you're welcome to take your business elsewhere."

"Don't be a stupid…" Bongo scolded, using a word from his language. "When are you gonna see another ember gem?" His head swiveled toward Carina. "It's clear you're from a rougher part of the galaxy. What you have to understand about Lakshmi Station is that it's tightly, I mean *tightly*, regulated. Just last week a cafe owner was found selling coffee from a printer as the genuine article. They spaced him."

"Spaced?!" Carina exclaimed, looking over her shoulder at her companions.

"Yeah, *spaced*. What do you think they'd do to my cousin if she tried to steal your gem?"

Carina still couldn't believe him. He could be spinning her a tale.

"The gem is real," she told the exchange owner. "Assuming I let you verify that, how much will you give me for it?"

Bongo's cousin named a sum that would have made Carina's eyes pop if she hadn't been carefully trying to keep a neutral expression. She'd made a similar exchange on Ithiya for starship fuel. and now she knew how badly she'd been screwed over. She wasn't going to make the same mistake again.

Bongo had begun babbling like a brook to his cousin, who replied at a louder volume. He upped the ante some more, rising onto the tips of his claws to lean over the counter.

Were they arguing? It appeared so, but really Carina didn't have a clue.

He broke off abruptly and said, "We're going somewhere else."

"What?" asked Carina. "Why?"

"Because my cousin thinks she can retire early on a visitor's gullibility."

He crawled out of the booth, and Carina was compelled to leave too. A stream of liquid utterances from his relative followed them.

"Bongo," Carina said, trotting to catch up to the alien, "what's going on?"

He halted, rocking on his many legs. His head rotated, each of his eyes scrutinizing her before he replied, "Not many of you humans are nice to us. I get that we remind you of a creature you don't like, but we have feelings, you know? Before, when you helped me onto my feet, I was embarrassed, and I'm sorry I snapped. But I was touched by your gesture. It was a kind thing to do. To thank you, I want to get you the best deal I can, and my cousin wasn't going to give you it." He added, as he set off again, "She always was a greedy bitch."

CHAPTER 8

*S*ince the Lotacryllan men had gone away, the *Bathsheba* seemed bigger and more mysterious than ever. Darius was tempted to ask Nahla if he could hold her hand as they walked down the empty passageway, but he didn't want her to think he was a silly little kid. Instead, he held his elixir bottle more tightly. Like Nahla had said, if anything bad happened, he could easily Transport them back to their suite.

"Where are we going?" he asked.

"Deck Zero."

"Deck Zero?" He hadn't known there *was* a deck zero. "What's down there?"

"You'll see."

She gave him a quick, excited smile.

She loved knowing things other people didn't, he guessed. That had to be why she spent so long reading stuff in the ship's database and translating the mage papers. She'd kept the knowledge of the ember gems to herself for ages—actually took them and kept them for herself until the others knew about them!

Ordinarily, that would have been a bad thing. It was wrong to steal. But it had all turned out okay in the end and Nahla hadn't been punished. Maybe it was all right to steal from bad people like Lomang.

A shiver ran through him.

Lomang's feelings had been thick, dark treacle, strong and full of wants.

They arrived at the elevator. When they stepped inside, Nahla told it to take them to Deck One.

Darius protested, "But you said—"

"The elevators don't go all the way to the bottom."

"Why not?"

"I think they used to, then someone changed them."

"Why would they do that?"

"That's what I want to find out."

The elevator pinged and the doors opened.

"I'm not sure we should be doing this," Darius said uneasily as they stepped out. "There has to be a reason the elevators were fixed so they don't go to Deck Zero. What if something's living down there?"

"Nothing's living down there."

"How do you know?"

"Because it would need food and water."

"Maybe it has food and water. If it has the whole deck to itself, it could keep enough food and water to last a lifetime."

Nahla didn't like this answer. Her annoyance spread out from her in ripples. "There's nothing living there. That's dumb. Why would something choose to live there and never come out? We've been aboard the ship for months and no one's ever seen anything."

"It might only come out during the quiet shift, when hardly anyone's about. It might come out and take what it needs from our supplies."

Her sharp anger stabbed at him. "Do you want to come with me or not?"

"Ye-es," he replied. Now he'd had time to think about it, he wasn't sure he did. But if he didn't, he was sure Nahla would go there by herself. And if he told on her, he would be breaking his promise, and she probably wouldn't play with him for weeks. Then he wouldn't have *anyone* to play with. "But if we see that something must be living there, we have to leave right away. We won't look to find out what it is. We'll tell a grown-up."

"Yeah, okay."

Her mood calmed, and he felt its cool draft.

Walking along the passageway on Deck One, he wanted to hold her hand more than ever. Hardly anyone came down here. Old, broken equipment that couldn't be fixed was stored here for spare parts, as well as things kept 'just-in-case' like out-of-date medications and supplies. The place had a creepy, neglected feeling, even though he knew it couldn't really feel anything and it was just his imagination.

Nahla stopped at a hatch. "We have to climb down the rest of the way."

It was a service tunnel for techs to use when the elevators didn't work or they had to reach something they couldn't get at any other way.

A metal ladder led down into darkness.

"Lights will come on when they sense us in the tunnel," said Nahla.

"Okay," Darius replied nervously.

"I'll go first. Do you have somewhere to put your elixir?"

Darn it. He hadn't brought a bag with him. "I didn't know I'd have to use two hands."

"Can you tuck it in your waistband?"

"I guess so. I'll try."

"Whatever you do," said Nahla with a grin, "don't drop it on my head."

She climbed into the hatch and onto the ladder.

He peered down at the top of her receding head. Lights lit up the tunnel, just like she'd said.

He pushed his bottle into the top of his pants. He shouldn't be doing this. He wished Carina was here.

When he reached the bottom, he half-expected to find Nahla standing in the dark, but the lights worked the same as everywhere else.

"Hmph," she said. "Well, the sanobots certainly know about Deck Zero."

The place looked the same as the rest of the ship. He wasn't sure what he'd been expecting—dust, cobwebs?—but it *was* kinda disappointing in a way.

"Yeah," he agreed. "Maybe there isn't anything special here. The people who owned the ship decided one day they didn't need this deck, so they closed it off."

"That has to be the most boring explanation I ever heard!" Nahla exclaimed. "There has to be a better reason than that. Let's explore."

She strode off, and he had to hurry to catch up to her while also taking his elixir bottle out of his pants. It looked like their expedition was going to be perfectly safe, but he still clutched the bottle tightly, just in case.

The first room they came to was stuffed with piles of clothes. The many-colored garments were stacked high, higher than he or Nahla could reach. She grabbed the edge of something and pulled.

"Don't do that!" Darius warned.

Too late.

The pile toppled over, right on top of her. She screamed, but in a giggling, happy way. She'd fallen down, and when she stood up, she was holding onto the piece of clothing she'd pulled out. It was a sparkly dress. Nahla held it up to her chest. The dress was much too long and wide to fit her. It was for an adult.

"Look at me!" she commanded. "I'm a beautiful *lady*." She pronounced the 'y' long and drawn out, *eeeee*. "Ferne and Oriana would love this. There are all kinds of clothes here. We should choose some to take back with us."

He looked around, wondering what they should take.

"Oh!" The dress had fallen from Nahla's fingers, or rather, most of it had. She was holding a straggly bit of it between her hands. She dropped it and, reaching down, she tried to pick up the fallen pieces, but they dissolved into tiny fragments.

She pushed a hand into the mound on the floor. It collapsed into dust.

"These clothes must be really old," Darius remarked.

"Yeah, they must." Nahla frowned like she always did when she was thinking hard. "I hope that's all it is."

"What do you mean?"

She brushed the remnants of material off her hands and then brought them up to her face to look at them closely. Then she looked at him.

"Do you feel okay?" she asked.

"Yeah. I-I think so." Now that she asked, he wasn't sure he did. Or was that only because she'd asked him? "Maybe we should go."

"Maybe, but..." She kicked the dusty pile. "Let's explore just a little bit more. Once we tell the others about this place, I bet they'll never let us come here alone again. We should take our chance while we can."

"All right, but just a few more rooms. Then we'll leave. If we don't go back soon, the others will wonder what's happened to us. And Ferne is waiting for his snacks."

"Okay. Just a few more rooms."

CHAPTER 9

*H*olding her wrist under the scanner, Carina grimaced. Not that being scanned to enter the bar, the Mystic Supernova, was painful. It didn't hurt at all. Her pain was internal. She'd discovered that when she'd bought the starship fuel on Gog, she'd been royally swindled.

She was also deeply pissed off at Justus. He'd been with her when she'd made the transaction. How could he not have known the value of the ember gems? His dad had been a trader, for star's sake. Why hadn't he said something?

Hsiao must have seen her expression, as she whispered, "It's not a big deal, Carina. Get over it. We got a great price for the gems and we won't have to skimp on updates for the *Bathsheba*. Let's relax and have a good time."

Easy for her to say. *She* wasn't the one responsible for the only money they had and everyone's safety on the journey to Earth.

"*Three* ember gems," she hissed back. "I paid three whole gems, just to fill up the tanks. I can't believe I was so stupid."

She imagined the Gogian fuel supplier laughing at her behind her back. Her only consolation was the knowledge that the gems she'd given the ground dwellers on Magog would easily buy more than enough weapons and equipment to overthrow their Dark Mage masters.

"You weren't stupid," said Hsiao, maintaining her quiet tone as they were allowed through the security check. "How were you supposed to know?"

"But Justus should have known and told me. The gems are only found on his planet. Of all people, *he* should know."

"That isn't always the way, though, is it? The Lotacryllans are the wholesalers. They don't control the point-of-sale price, and they might not even know how much their export fetches in other parts of the sector. Justus said he wasn't from around here, didn't he? The station doesn't have him on its database."

It was a fair point.

"What does it matter, anyway?" Hsiao went on. "What's done is done. We have plenty left to get exactly what we need and everyone can have some fun too. I'd call that a win."

"Yeah," Carina grudgingly conceded, "I suppose so."

The volume of ambient noise increased as the doors opened and they stepped through, Justus and Jackson joining them. Wide stairs led down to an open space filled with people and dotted with bar islands.

"Just a couple of drinks," Carina announced, "then back to the *Bathsheba*. I want a good night's sleep before starting negotiations tomorrow."

The last four ember gems were exchanged and the creds deposited in an account, but she still had to decide how best to use them to fortify the colony ship against attack. The armament vendors had given a wide, varied range of options, and, as well as sleeping on it, she wanted to discuss the choices with the others.

A slide ran down to the lower level next to the stairs. She'd thought it was a gimmick, but as she began to walk down the steps, a long creature slid past her on its belly, slim, tentacle-like legs held high. When it reached the bottom, it slithered into the crowd.

"The kids are gonna have fun at Lakshmi," said Jackson.

"They aren't coming here," she replied. "Not the little ones at least."

"Aw, come on. You have to let them come to the station. When are they going to get another chance to see all the cool aliens? You could introduce them to Bongo."

Bongo had become somewhat of a friend while he'd been taking them to the currency exchanges and then on to the starship armament vendors. Carina was fairly certain his job only required him to show them the basics and then leave them to their own devices. Yet he'd gone above and beyond and offered to be their guide again when they returned.

"Bongo is one thing," she said. "What I'm not sure about is all the other things. Especially the sex bots."

"Hosts and hostesses," Jackson corrected.

"Right," she replied, rolling her eyes. "Hosts and hostesses."

"So we only have to show them our ID codes?" asked Justus, his eyes bright with excitement.

"Yeah," said Carina, "but—"

He disappeared into the crowd.

"Take it easy," she finished.

"Don't worry," said Hsiao. "He can't drink the budget. He won't even make a tiny dent in it."

"That's not what I'm worried about." She didn't want him getting himself into trouble. The story of the cafe owner who'd been spaced indicated there could be dire consequences for stepping out of line.

Just then, a man loomed up. Almost as big as Pappu, and he thrust his chest out aggressively.

"Wha' planet?" he demanded.

"Huh?" Carina asked.

"It's a simple question," he sneered drunkenly. "Wha' planet are you from?"

The long day, annoyance about being duped over the ember gems, guilt at being forced to exclude Parthenia again, and the stress of needing to make the best choices to defend the ship had all been getting to Carina *before* Justus had run off. Unprovoked hostility from this goon pushed her over the edge. "What planet are *you* from?" she spat back.

"The war, remember?" said Jackson softly. "He wants to know what side we're on."

"This section's only for Quintonese," slurred the man. "You're not from there, are you? Leave, now! 'Fore I help you on your way."

"No, we're not Quintonese," Carina declared, rearing up and glaring at him. "And we're not from Marchon, or the other side in your goddamned conflict, whatever the hell it's called. We're from out-sector and we're here to have a quiet drink, so get out of my face!"

"Selan," said another bar patron, pulling on the big guy's arm. "You'll get yourself thrown out. Leave them alone."

"Yeah, leave us alone, *Selan!*"

"Carina," said Hsiao, "cool it!"

The drunk grinned lopsidedly. "S'okay. Thought you were Marchonish. Your clothes are funny. But a Marchonish wouldn't have those balls."

His companion succeeded in pulling him away. Selan staggered off.

Jackson's heavy prosthetic hand landed on Carina's shoulders. "What were you saying to Justus? Something about taking it easy?"

"Carina has balls," joked Hsiao. "Who knew?"

"Bryce, probably," said Jackson.

"Let's get that drink," Hsiao said. "*Someone* needs to calm down."

CHAPTER 10

*W*hen they returned to the *Bathsheba*, Bryce was waiting for them at the airlock. He was pale and sweaty, and he looked at Carina with dread in his eyes.

Before she could ask him what was wrong, he said, "I need to talk to you."

He took her to one side while Hsiao, Jackson, and a somewhat unsteady Justus passed by them, walking into the ship.

"I'm not sure how to put this," said Bryce.

In all the time Carina had known him and through all the life-threatening situations they'd faced, she had never seen him looking so scared.

"Stars, just say it!" she urged. "You're worrying the hell out of me."

He swallowed. "We can't find Darius or Nahla."

"*What?!*" A wave of icy fear hit her. "What do you mean you can't find them?"

"They left their suite about an hour after lunch, saying they were just popping out to get snacks, but they didn't come back. Oriana and Ferne didn't notice until a couple of hours later. They were too engrossed in what they were doing. And

Parthenia didn't leave her room until the alarm was raised. Everyone's been looking for them ever since, but there's no trace of them."

Carina felt numb. The mood in the *Peregrine* on the journey back had been so good. The visit to Lakshmi Station had been a great success. They had an account fat with creds and access to the latest defensive tech the sector had to offer. They would be able to sleep peacefully the rest of the way to Earth, safe and secure. But none of it meant anything if something bad had happened to her brother or sister.

"But…" A realization broke through the tide of terror rising in Carina's heart, creating an overwhelming sense of relief. "It's fine. I'll just Cast Locate." She reached for her elixir bottle. "I don't know why Parthenia and the twins didn't think of it. Darius and Nahla are probably hiding somewhere, enjoying the idea of us searching for them. You know what little kids are like."

"They tried that," said Bryce. "Oriana, Ferne, and Parthenia. They've all tried it over and over again. I told you, we can't find them."

"They can't find them with Locate?" she asked dazedly. "That's not possible. Even if they were…" she couldn't bring herself to say it "…Locate would always find them."

"Unless they were out of range," said Bryce. "That's what Parthenia said."

"Yes, but…" Her mind was whirring. She couldn't think straight. How far did Locate operate? "The *Bathsheba* hasn't changed position since we left, has she?"

"No, or if she has, it's just a little from gravitational effects."

"Then the only way Darius and Nahla could move out of range would be—"

"Carina!"

It was Oriana. She ran down the passageway and hugged Carina tightly. Her eyes were red in her puffy face. "We can't find them!" she sobbed. "We tried everything. We looked and looked. I'm so glad you're back. Can you think of something else we can do? There has to be something else."

She was gazing up hopefully.

Carina tried to look calm. In truth, she was barely holding it together herself. It was up to her to be strong, to figure out a solution, to find the way out of a sticky situation, again. But she had nothing. She had no idea what could have happened to her little sister and brother or how to find out where they'd gone.

Ferne and Parthenia appeared. Ferne's expression was downcast, and Parthenia looked like Carina felt—utterly distraught.

"Let me think," Carina said. "I need to think."

She began to walk, though she had no destination in mind.

"I'm sorry," said Parthenia. "I should have been watching them."

"No," said Bryce. "It's my fault. I should have stayed in the suite with you guys."

"It's nobody's fault," said Carina. "Neither of you could be expected to watch all the kids every second. They're old enough to look after themselves, and they should be smart enough to not put themselves in danger."

"They *should* be," muttered Parthenia.

"No other ship approached while I was gone?" asked Carina. It was a dumb question. Bryce would have told her if that was the case, but she had to get the possibility of a kidnapping out of the way.

"Absolutely not," he replied. "Bibik and I searched all the scanner data three times. Nothing has come anywhere near the *Bathsheba* except the *Peregrine*. Even if a ship could avoid scanner detection somehow, the computer would have registered an airlock opening. There's been nothing. Not even a garbage evacuation."

"So they can't have left the ship," said Carina. "Which

means they must be here somewhere, and that means they must be in range to Locate." She halted and swung toward Parthenia and the twins. "Is it possible your elixir is the problem?"

"I made it the other day," Parthenia replied defensively. "I've never got it wrong before."

"Okay, but let me try with mine. It's from an earlier batch. Does anyone have something of the kids' to use?"

"I have some of Nahla's hair from her brush and Darius's playing cards," said Oriana, taking them out of her pocket and handing them over.

Carina walked to the bulkhead and leaned her back on it. She unscrewed the lid on her bottle and, holding Nahla and Darius's personal items in one hand, took a swig. Closing her eyes, she concentrated. Casting under pressure was hard. It required focus, which was nearly impossible to achieve when you were worried something terrible had happened to people you loved.

She pushed away the black cloud of fear and went down into her mind. Locate was a seven-stroke character. Carefully, she wrote each glowing stroke in the darkness and sent it out.

She waited.

If the Cast worked, she should begin to sense her siblings, bright spots in the gray field of mental space.

Time stretched out, measured by each thump of her anxious heart.

She continued to wait, longer than she should have, past the moment she knew, deep down, she had failed.

Tears filled her eyes as she finally opened them. Unable to speak, she shook her head.

The four mages and Bryce stood silently in the passageway.

A flash of hope hit Carina, though as she spoke she realized it was irrational. "What about Jace? Has he tried to Cast for them?"

"Yes," Parthenia replied. "He tried many times. He gave up and joined one of the search parties."

Despair descended again.

If Jace could not Locate them, no one could. Only Darius was a better mage than him.

"Has Casting ever not worked for you before?" asked Bryce.

"Plenty of times," Carina replied, "when I was a kid and learning. But you can sort of feel if you did it wrong. Even if that wasn't so, it isn't possible that we're *all* doing it wrong. It can only mean they aren't here and searching for them is pointless."

Another idea occurred.

"Did the scanners pick up anything strange? Is it possible the *Bathsheba* was hit by something similar to what killed Lomang and Mezban?"

"We checked for that too," he replied. "There was nothing out of the ordinary the whole time you were gone."

Dammit.

"They have to be here!" she exclaimed. "I can't explain why we can't Locate them, but they must be somewhere on the ship." She didn't add the final part of the sentence that sprang to her mind: *dead or alive.*

"If they're here," said Bryce, "we'll find them eventually. The *Bathsheba's* big but she isn't infinite. We won't stop looking until we've found them."

"Do you two remember exactly where they said they were going?" Carina asked Ferne and Oriana.

"All they said was they were going to get something to eat," Ferne replied. "Which to me meant the galley on our deck."

"If they wanted something that wasn't there," Oriana chipped in, "they would only have to go to the printer on the deck below. They should only have been gone half an hour at most, but it took us longer than that to notice they hadn't come back." As she spoke, her cheeks flushed.

"Look," said Carina, "I don't want any of you to blame your-selves." Yet she could empathize with how they felt. What had happened wasn't her fault either, yet she couldn't help feeling somehow it was.

"They must have gone to another place," she went on. "How could they have gone missing between your suite and the galley or the printer? There's nothing dangerous in those areas, not even an airlock. They had to be going somewhere different and they didn't want to tell you because they knew you would try to stop them."

"That *does* sound like something Nahla would do," Oriana agreed. "I love her, but she can be sneaky."

"And Darius would go along with it because he wanted to please her," said Parthenia. "He wants to keep everyone happy."

"That's right," Carina agreed. There was no need to state the reason Darius needed the people around him to feel happy. "What were they doing before they left?"

"Playing cards," Ferne replied. "The cards were on the bed when we looked into their room to check they hadn't come back without us noticing."

His answer was no help. Carina couldn't see how playing cards could have led the two children to lie and go somewhere forbidden.

"Has anyone checked Nahla's interface?" she asked.

"I did," Ferne said, "but there was no activity on it for the last couple of days."

"Doesn't sound like Nahla," said Carina.

Bryce commented, "I checked it too. He's right."

"There's no way she didn't use her interface recently. She must have wiped the history to cover something up. What about the ship's database? Anyone check what she's been doing on that?"

CHAPTER 11

$\mathcal{T}$he old schematic of the ship Nahla had been looking at before she disappeared showed an extra deck that didn't exist on the more recent plan. Deck zero.

Why had its existence been hidden? Carina couldn't think of any good reason why the ship's previous occupants would want to make a secret of an entire deck.

She peered down the service tunnel on Deck One. It disappeared into darkness, but that was innocuous. The lights were probably motion-activated the same as everywhere else.

"They're down there!" Oriana exclaimed, leaning over Carina's shoulder. "They have to be."

She launched herself at the opening, but Carina grabbed her and held her back. She understood the impulse. There was nothing more she wanted to do herself than to shoot down the ladder and find her siblings.

"Let me go!" yelled Oriana.

"She's right," said Bryce. "Hold on. We need to be careful. We don't know what's down there. If it's only another deck, why haven't Darius and Nahla come back yet?"

Fear and anxiety gnawed at Carina.

Stupid, stupid, kids.

If they were okay, she would ground them for a month.

If they were okay.

"What worries me most is that we can't Locate them," she said. "The only thing that can block a Cast is another mage, but usually you would feel it being blocked. I didn't feel a thing when I Cast earlier."

Bryce asked, "You're sure it would work even if they're..."

"Yes!" she snapped, then immediately regretted it. He loved those kids as much as she did.

"Yes," she repeated, more softly, touching his arm. "No matter what's happened to them, it would work."

Except...

She remembered cremating Ma's body in a shuttle's engine flare. You couldn't Locate someone if there was nothing left of them.

She comm'd Jackson. "Bring five Black Dogs and pulse rifles to Deck One ASAP."

"Pulse rifles?" asked Ferne. "What do you think is down there?!"

She turned to Bryce. "Could some of the Lotacryllans have re-entered after you spaced them?"

"It would be a miracle," he replied, "but I have to admit I didn't check the logs. I don't know if any of the other airlocks were activated."

"Could we be carrying Lotacryllan stowaways?" asked Parthenia.

"If the Lotacryllans do have Darius and Nahla," asked Oriana, "why haven't they said anything? They would have asked for a ransom or...I don't know. It just seems weird they would keep quiet about it."

Carina could think of a dark reason why the men might have

said nothing. They might be perfectly content with their situation, moving around the ship during the quiet shift, stealing enough food to survive, waiting for an opportunity to sneak away—perhaps waiting until everyone went into Deep Sleep. Then they could take over the ship and fly wherever they wanted. All they would have to do to ensure they never met any opposition was to turn off the life suspension system.

If her guess was correct, the arrival of Darius and Nahla would have thrown a spanner in the works. It would be in the Lotacryllans' interest to silence the children, permanently.

The elevator doors opened and six Black Dogs emerged, all in full armor and carrying rifles.

"You suited up," said Carina. "Good idea."

One of them replied, his helmet comm switched to external, "No harm in being cautious."

It was Jackson. He peered into the service tunnel hatch and whistled. "You think the kids are down there?"

"Yeah, and I think they might not be alone."

"It'll be a tight fit in our suits, but I think we can do it."

"I'm coming too," said Carina.

"I didn't bring a spare rifle."

"I have my elixir. I'll be okay."

"Better to let…" ventured Bryce.

Carina gave him a hard stare, and he didn't finish his sentence.

"Let's go," she said. "We've wasted enough time."

Jackson managed to persuade her to allow himself and the other Black Dogs to climb down the service ladder first. After the last merc entered the hatch she followed. As she descended she listened for sounds of fighting, but there was nothing. At the bottom, she climbed out into a passageway the same as the others on the ship, empty except for the mercs.

"Carina," said Jackson, "you've gotta leave. My HUD's reporting low O2."

"Huh?"

"Get back up the ladder, or you'll be unconscious within a couple of minutes."

"But—"

"I don't wanna have to carry you *and* those kids. Leave. Now."

With great reluctance, she returned to Deck One. By the time she reached the top of the ladder, she'd begun to feel a little woozy. She climbed out and sat with her back to the bulkhead.

"Did you find them?" asked Oriana excitedly.

"No, I had to come back because the oxygen's low down there. It was lucky Jackson suited up. His HUD warned him."

"So that's why Darius and Nahla didn't come back," said Bryce.

She shared a look with him.

"What does it mean?" asked Ferne.

"It means there aren't any stowaway Lotacryllans," said Carina.

Oriana exhaled heavily. "Thank goodness for that!"

"But if you came back right away," said Parthenia, "that means the atmosphere must be really dangerous if you aren't wearing armor."

"Let's not speculate," said Bryce. "Let's wait and see what the mercs find."

Carina was holding it together the best she could. She didn't want to lose hope or upset her siblings by showing how she really felt, but a scene kept playing through her mind. She could see Jackson emerging from the hatch, carrying Darius, lifeless, in his arms. Another merc appeared carrying Nahla, her body limp, her skin blue, her chest still.

Carina sank her head into her hands.

Bryce sat beside her and put his arm around her shoulders.

Seconds crawled past as they waited.

Her confusion about why the Locate Cast hadn't worked

didn't matter anymore. All she could do was hope the inevitable wasn't true.

It couldn't be true.

"Someone's coming!" Ferne announced.

She leapt up and leaned in next to her brother at the open hatch. She saw the top of a helmet—a child's form rested over the merc's shoulder.

"He's got Darius!" Ferne yelled. "They found him!"

Carina backed out and pulled Ferne with her. "We have to make room." She took the lid off her elixir and put the bottle down, ready to Cast Heal.

When the merc reached the level of the hatch, she called out, "I'll take him!" and reached into the tunnel to lift Darius off the man's shoulder.

She laid the small figure down.

He was so tiny! So young.

"Is he breathing?" whispered Parthenia.

Darius was deathly pale. Carina put her ear against his chest.

The thump of his heart sounded. It was quiet and slow, but it was there.

A dam broke within her and tears flooded her eyes.

"He's alive," she gasped. "He's alive."

Distantly, she heard Oriana announce, "They've got Nahla too!"

"Heal her, Parthenia," she said.

She was already sipping elixir. She placed a hand on Darius's chest and squeezed her eyes shut. With a great effort, she managed to control her ragged emotions and Cast Heal.

She opened her eyes, expecting her sweet brother's eyes to open in a moment too.

They did not.

Nothing had changed. He remained unconscious and just as pale. She thrust her ear against his chest again. His heart beat at the same slow rate.

Next to her, Parthenia had done the same.

"It isn't working!" her sister wailed over Nahla's still form. "Why isn't it working?"

CHAPTER 12

*C*arina's understanding of the dreadful situation was confirmed by Jace later in the sick bay. Before he mentioned the problem, however, he asked how Darius and Nahla were doing.

"They're alive," she replied, her throat tight. "That's the main thing. The doc says it's going to be hard to tell how the oxygen deprivation has affected their brains until they wake up. She's put them under sedation to help them recover. We'll know more tomorrow when she begins to withdraw the treatment."

The children looked better than they had when they'd been found. As they lay in the sick bay beds with oxygen masks on their faces, their skin was pink and plump as normal. But they'd been unconscious for hours, the oxygen-depleted atmosphere slowly sapping them of life. Black Dog medics had hooked them up to life-sign monitors, which displayed their steady heart-beats, respiration, blood pressure, and other figures on bedside interfaces. The screens provided the brightest light in the quiet room.

"I heard they were found on a deck no one knew existed?" Jace asked, sitting down.

"Deck Zero," she replied. "It must have been abandoned decades ago. The *Bathsheba* is centuries old, and at some point the atmosphere management system began to struggle to maintain safe oxygen levels down there. So whoever was running the ship closed the deck off. I doubt even Lomang knew about it."

"But why isn't there a warning somewhere?"

"There is, on the computer, but the database is in the original colonists' script, remember? Some of it is converted to Universal now, but not all of it. Nahla must have found out about Deck Zero but she didn't fully understand what she was reading."

"No signs outside the service hatches?"

Carina shrugged. "There are no signs anywhere on the ship. Maybe the colonists didn't use them, or they were taken down. Who knows? It doesn't matter now."

Jace ran a hand through his hair. "Thank the stars they didn't die."

She nodded. "According to the doc, they wouldn't have lasted much longer if we hadn't found them."

Then Jace brought up the second awful event on both their minds. He said quietly, "You tried Casting Heal, didn't you." It was a statement, not a question.

She nodded again. The suffocating blanket of alarm and fear she'd been feeling tightened around her.

"It didn't work, right?" he said.

She shook her head. There was nothing else to say.

"I've tried them all," he went on. "Every Cast I know. Rise, Fire, Break, Obscure, Transport, Lock, and the rest."

"None of them worked?"

He looked down. "Not one."

Carina tried some Casts too. She tried to Lock the sick bay door and Cast Rise on the water in the beaker next to Darius's bed. These were simple Casts a child mage could do. Her experience mirrored Jace's.

A pause stretched out as the significance of their failures expanded between them.

"Have you ever heard of this happening before?" Carina asked.

"Never." He met her gaze. "You remember Magda?"

"Of course." How could she ever forget the old Spirit Mage?

"I listened to all her stories. I never heard a single one about mages losing their abilities."

She stroked the back of Darius's hand.

What did it mean?

She'd never imagined there might be a time she could no longer Cast. Mages retained their abilities until death, only losing the capacity in old age in the same way that old people's minds didn't work so well.

Even with the evidence staring her in the face, she couldn't imagine no longer being able to Cast. She couldn't wrap her head around it. Her ability was a part of her, like talking, eating, and walking. Losing it felt like having a limb sawn off.

"Do you have any idea what might have happened?" she whispered.

"I'm as much in the dark as you. How have Parthenia and the others taken it?"

"We were all shocked when neither she nor I could get Heal to work. While we were waiting for the medics, we realized that might be why no one had been able to find Darius and Nahla by using Locate, that it was because the Cast hadn't been working. Then the medics arrived, and after that...it's all a blur, honestly. I was so worried Darius and Nahla were going to..."

Jace put a hand on her back.

"I comm'd Parthenia to tell her what the doc said but I haven't spoken to her or anyone else since," said Carina. "I don't know how they're doing. Bryce is with them."

"Would you like me to talk to them?"

"Please. Bryce loves them like his own, but he isn't a mage. He won't understand what this means or how they'll be feeling."

"I'm not sure I do myself yet," Jace commented. "It's hard to take in."

"You can say that again."

He rose to his feet. "Darius and Nahla were found alive. That's something to be grateful for. Tomorrow will bring us more good news, hopefully. They're young and healthy, and that will help with their recovery."

"That's what the doc said. And today I discovered the ember gems are worth an absolute fortune. If I have to use it all to pay for medical treatment at Lakshmi Station I will."

"There are hospitals there?"

"They have *everything* there." She sighed. "I was so happy when I got back, looking forward to telling everyone about our good luck and deciding the best ways to protect the ship. And then *this* happens." She looked up at her towering friend. "Do you think it might be only temporary? That we'll get our abilities back?"

"Your guess is as good as mine. If it had happened after you'd returned from your trip, I would have wondered if you'd brought back a virus that had infected us. But the effect began earlier than that. My Locate Casts didn't work while you were gone. To find out whether the problem is temporary, we need to discover what's causing it, and at the moment I don't have any ideas. But I'll think about it. That's all we can do."

"That, and get used to being normal."

"You said it. I'll go and talk to the kids."

"Thanks," said Carina as he left.

Normality. To be like 99.9 percent of the rest of humanity. It was a weird feeling.

There had been many times she'd considered her magehood to be more of a curse than a benefit. It had caused so much pain in her life. Ma had suffered years of torment due to it, and for

Carina herself it had meant living with loneliness and constant fear of discovery.

Yet it was also a fundamental part of her identity, like the color of her eyes or her interest in bugs. It was *who she was*. If she could never Cast again, she would feel like a different person.

And what did it mean in terms of the journey to Earth? The reason she wanted to go there was to try to find a home where she and her family could live safely. She hoped things were different there now, thousands of years after mages had departed. But if none of them was a mage anymore, was there any point in making the long voyage? Might it not be better to find a quiet, backwater planet and live out their lives like regular people?

CHAPTER 13

*C*arina was in a long, dark tunnel. The air was humid and stuffy, and thick cobwebs stretched from wall to wall. She turned, trying to find a way out. At one end was impenetrable darkness, at the other, a pinprick of light shone.

How had she come to be here? She couldn't remember.

All she knew was she had to get out.

She pushed through a sticky web, breaking it apart. Thick threads clung to her face and hair as she walked toward the light. She tried to pull them away, but they stuck to her skin and trailed behind her.

Another web, and another effort to break it and pass through. At this one, something unseen scuttled away along the ceiling. The spot of light grew larger.

She was hot, sweating in the still, warm air. Her legs were already growing weary, though she didn't think she'd gone very far. Perhaps this was a high-g planet. She did feel heavier than usual. Or maybe there was something different about the air. It felt thick and syrupy.

Figures were moving in the light, silhouetted by its brightness. They were moving toward her slowly, shuffling. She could see four distinctly, but there might be even more behind, judging from the gray shadows in the brilliance.

She turned and looked back. Might it be better to retreat into the dark? But what lay that way was unknown. The least she could expect was more of the webs and the creatures who had made them.

She went on.

As the light increased, it grew softer. A cool wind blew from the same direction, drying her sweat.

She could make out the first figure. It was a woman wearing a dress that fell to her feet, her long hair arranged carefully on her head.

Carina gasped.

Ma!

She ran into the woman's arms and hugged the thin woman tightly. She felt so small, so frail, Carina was frightened she might hurt her. She let go and stared into her mother's deep brown eyes.

"What are you doing here? Are you okay?"

Ma didn't answer, only smiled sweetly and pointed behind her.

Ba was here too!

He raised a hand in greeting, but before Carina could run to him she saw someone else she recognized farther down the tunnel.

Hobbling forward, hunched over by age and long years of gathering semi-precious stones, was Nai Nai.

Tears sprang to Carina's eyes. She couldn't believe it. Here were three people who meant so much to her. Who to speak to first? She hadn't seen Ba since she was three years old, and Nai Nai had raised her, dedicating her life to protecting her and teaching her how to be a mage.

Then she saw the others.

Behind Nai Nai walked ranks of other people, all appearing

familiar. She could see Nai Nai's, Ba's, and Ma's features in their faces. These were her family's ancestors, going back down the ages. Mages who had lived before her in different places and on other planets across the galaxy, all the way back for thousands of years to the people who had fled Earth.

"Carina," said a quiet, high-pitched voice.

She opened her eyes.

She was sitting down, bent forward, resting her upper body on a bed—Darius's sick bay bed.

She sat up.

He was awake and watching her. "Were you dreaming?"

"I think I was. How are you feeling, sweetheart?"

He looked healthy, and the fact he'd spoken to her was a good sign.

"I thought you were dreaming," he said. "You were talking. I think you said *Nai Nai*."

"I was dreaming about our family."

The family who had been mages for hundreds of generations. Was the line going to stop with her and her siblings?

"How are you?" She stroked his hair. "I've been so worried about you."

He began to cry. "I'm sorry, Carina. I'm sorry I was bad."

"Hey," she said softly. "It's okay. We found you. That's the most important thing. What do you remember?"

"I was with Nahla on Deck Zero and—" he sat bolt upright. "Where is she? Is she—"

"She's still asleep," said Carina.

Nahla's unconscious form hadn't moved while they'd been talking.

The sick bay door slid open and a medic appeared.

"How are my young patients?" he asked cheerfully, adding, "One's awake I see. Excellent."

"He seems to have fully recovered," said Carina.

"I certainly hope so," the medic replied. "You are looking

chipper, young man. If your sister would kindly step outside, I'll do some checks."

"No," Darius protested, "I want Carina to stay."

"It'll be fine," she said. "It's just for a few minutes, right?" she asked the medic.

"That's all." He leaned down and fake-whispered in Darius's ear, "And I have candy Carina won't approve of."

Darius giggled.

"I'll see you soon," said Carina, stepping out.

While she waited, she rested her back on the bulkhead and folded her arms. Closing her eyes, she wished she could Send to Parthenia to tell her Darius was awake and was apparently okay. She could comm her, of course, but there was something special about Casting Send. It was a more emotional, meaningful act, in the same way an embrace felt different from hearing the words *I love you*. And Casting was something that drew them together.

All that appeared to be gone now, perhaps forever. If she could never Cast again, she would need to learn a new way of being, like learning to walk again.

She comm'd Bryce.

"Fantastic," he said when she told him her brother seemed okay. "I haven't slept all night, worrying."

Guilt niggled at Carina. She'd left Bryce to look after her siblings again. She relied on him so much.

"How about Nahla?" he asked.

"She hasn't woken up yet. There's a medic in with both of them at the moment. I'll see what he says, but if Darius is all right I think Nahla must be too."

"Good. Let me know, okay?"

"Of course. What's been happening there?"

Bryce paused before answering, "Jace came over to talk to the kids and…" he paused again "…they haven't taken the news they've lost their mage abilities very well."

Neither have I.

"I guess it's only to be expected," said Carina. "It's a big shock for all of us. I never imagined this could happen."

"It's a bummer," he said, "but it isn't *that* big a disaster, is it? You're all still healthy."

"It's more than a bummer, Bryce. I don't think you really understand what this means to us."

"You're right. It *is* hard for me to understand. Oriana hasn't stopped crying since Jace told her and Ferne's acting like he just got hit by a truck. Parthenia hasn't left her room, though to be fair she hasn't left it much at all lately. Is it so bad to be an ordinary non-mage person like me?"

"No, but..."

"What?"

"I'm sorry. I can't explain right now."

The medic emerged from the sick bay room.

"I'll talk to you soon," Carina told Bryce before cutting the comm. "What did you find out?" she asked the medic.

The man's expression stopped her heart.

"They're going to be okay, right?" she asked nervously.

"I performed cognitive function checks on Darius, and he doesn't seem to be suffering any major impairments." The medic looked down for a second before continuing, "Nahla woke up while I was working with her brother, so I ran the basic tests on her as well. The doc will be along soon to run more advanced checks, but it seems clear the hypoxia caused some brain damage."

"What?" Carina breathed. "What kind of brain damage?"

"She's suffering memory loss and her gross motor skills have been affected. We'll be able to tell you more after the doctor's seen her."

"No! Poor Nahla."

"It's still early days," said the medic. "We'll begin treatment right away and do everything we can to help her regain her abilities."

"Will she ever be the same again?"

"It's hard for me to say," he replied, though his tone implied he was only trying to be kind. "The doctor will be able to give you a prognosis for her recovery."

"Thanks," said Carina quietly. "Can I see them now?"

"Go ahead."

CHAPTER 14

"*A*t last," said Parthenia sarcastically. "A gathering I'm invited to."

Carina bit back an equally acid reply. They were facing their greatest challenges yet, and her eldest sister had to make it about *her*.

"A very important gathering," said Jace. "Let's get started."

Carina had invited the older mage to the kids' suite to lead the discussion on what they would do to face the latest developments. Bryce was present as well as the mages and Nahla, who had curled into Jace's side on the sofa, sucking her thumb.

It was hard to look at her. Nahla had sucked her thumb sometimes in the earliest days Carina had known her. It wasn't hard to guess why the little girl had retained the baby habit. Her father had been a monster and their Dark Mage brother, Castiel, had mercilessly manipulated and later tortured her. What was harder to understand was the amazing resilience and adaptability she'd shown as soon as she was free of these two terrible influences on her life. The thumb-sucking had stopped as the little girl bloomed.

Nahla had developed into a very smart, savvy child, despite

all the trauma she'd endured, and her discovery of the ember gems had saved them all.

Now her little escapade had resulted in brain damage that was probably irreversible, according to the doctor. She'd lost a lot of memories and cognitive ability, leaving her with the mental capacity of a child half her age. She also struggled with walking, using a knife and fork, and operating an interface. When the doc had shown her a screen, she hadn't even seemed to understand what it was for. She could still speak, but with a limited vocabulary.

With treatment, the doc had said, she should make some progress, but it was most likely she would never return to the sparky, quick-witted youngster she'd once been.

The advanced tests on Darius had revealed he'd escaped his sister's fate, possibly due to his younger age or another factor they didn't understand. His brain seemed unaffected.

"Do you know why this has happened to us, Jace?" Oriana asked plaintively. "Why can't we Cast anymore?"

It was a pointless question. Everyone already knew what he would say, but Oriana appeared to hope if she asked again she might get a different answer.

"I'm sorry," he replied patiently. "I don't know."

"Which means," said Ferne, "we might get our ability back. If we've randomly lost the ability to Cast, we could randomly regain it."

"Being a mage isn't random," said Carina. "It's genetic. That's what I always guessed, and we found out for sure on Magog. They knew we were mages after they'd taken DNA samples."

"Then has something gone wrong with our genetic code?" asked Ferne. "Can that happen?"

"I talked to the doctor," she replied. "He said space radiation damages DNA but the ship's hull and the EVA suits protect us from it. And if there had been a radiation breach, alarms would have sounded."

"True," said Bryce. "Anyway, Carina, you were away when whatever happened to you all happened. If it was due to radiation on the *Bathsheba* you wouldn't have been affected."

"Are we sure it happened while Carina was visiting Lakshmi Station?" asked Jace. "We didn't notice the effect until we were searching for Darius and Nahla, but we could have lost our abilities before then. It will help to pinpoint the event if we all try to remember the last time we Cast successfully."

Carina thought back. It was hard to bring to mind the last Cast she'd made. She definitely hadn't done any Casting at Lakshmi for fear of being noticed. Before that... She frowned.

"It's so hard," said Oriana. "I can't remember. I don't do it very much anymore. There's no need to Cast on a starship where everything's close at hand and all we do is mess around all day."

"I remember," said Parthenia. "I Cast Locate five days ago for something I'd lost. It worked then."

"So," said Jace, "sometime in the last five days, we all lost our mage ability."

Silence settled over the room. Nahla snuggled closer to Jace, who wrapped a protective arm around her.

"I know it must be hard for you all," said Bryce, "but looking at it over the long term, does it really matter? Carina, you've told me so many times how hard it is to be a mage, always living in fear of discovery, facing the threat of slavery and torture. If this thing that's happened is permanent, you aren't at risk anymore. No one has a reason to capture or hurt you. Surely that's a good thing?"

"No, it isn't a good thing!" Oriana snapped. "How would you feel if I cut off your leg and told you how much fun you'll have hopping?"

"Cool it, sis," said Ferne. "Bryce is only trying to help us feel better."

"I'm sorry," Bryce said. "I'll shut up."

"Please don't," said Jace. "Your opinion is valued and welcome. We need to discuss this calmly and figure it out."

"Is there a lot to figure out?" Carina asked. "We don't know why this has happened so we don't know how to put it right."

"I've been wondering if it is related to our genes," said Parthenia, "but not in terms of damage, more like a genetic clock counting down. I don't know how it works exactly, but maybe mages' powers have been ticking down over millennia until now, and suddenly they're gone. No mages are able to Cast anymore. It's over."

"You mean it could have affected all the people we left behind too?" asked Ferne. "None of the mages back home can Cast now?"

"I'm just speculating," she replied.

"My most urgent concern," said Carina, "is what it means in terms of traveling to Earth. Is there any point now? Bryce was right when he said we have nothing to fear any longer—or at least no more to fear than regular people—so why should we continue our journey?"

As she spoke, the dream she'd been having when Darius awoke sprang to mind. Ma, Ba, Nai Nai, her great grandparents, great-great grandparents, and on and on, back in time, farther into the light. They all had one thing in common, but she didn't share it with them anymore.

Mentally dragging herself back to the present, she asked, "Why spend the money from the ember gems on fitting out the *Bathsheba* when we could use it to settle down somewhere?"

"You mean you want to give up everything you've worked for all this time?" asked Oriana.

"When you put it like that," replied Carina, "I want to say no. But going to Earth was my idea. I feel like I've hauled you and the Black Dogs along with me. I don't know if that was right. What's happened has made me rethink everything. It's all a mess in my head."

"Kamil and I might have settled down on Magog," Parthenia blurted. *He* wanted to, anyway. I wasn't sure. He wanted me to give up being a mage, abandon the voyage, leave all of you behind, and live there with him." She finished with a croaky voice, and a fat tear ran down her cheek. She wiped it away with the back of her hand.

So that's what you two were arguing about, thought Carina, remembering their time on the planet. "I'm glad you didn't," she told her sister. "I would have missed you."

"We all would have," said Ferne quietly.

Parthenia's confession subdued everyone to a second silence.

After a few minutes, Jace said quietly, "We have another item to discuss today. Nahla."

She'd fallen asleep, her thumb still in her mouth.

"What's wrong with her?" Darius asked timidly.

Carina realized she hadn't told him anything about his sister's medical status. The news had been a shock she hadn't quite recovered from herself, without the additional necessity of explaining it to her brother.

"She's...sick," she replied. What else could she say? How to explain to a seven-year-old that his sibling would probably never be the same again.

"Her brain is hurt," said Jace gently. "That's why she's acting differently."

"Oh," said Darius. "Did it happen when we fell asleep on Deck Zero?"

"Yes, that's right,"

"When will she get better?"

"We don't know," replied Jace. "Maybe never."

"Oh no!"

"Nahla's going to need our help from now on," said Carina. "We'll have to be patient as she learns how to do things again."

"I can teach her," said Darius.

"I'm sure you'll be a great helper." Carina turned to the

others. "I don't know how useful this discussion has been. We don't have any idea what to do to get our powers back, and I guess it's too soon to accept they're gone forever. Until we know that, we can't decide if we want to continue on our journey to Earth. But I do know one thing. We have to pour our resources into helping Nahla. At Lakshmi Station they have the most up-to-date medical facilities in the sector. I propose that I take Nahla there tomorrow and find out what they can do for her."

"I think we can all agree on that," said Bryce.

CHAPTER 15

*P*arthenia hadn't spent much time aboard the late Mezban's ship, the *Peregrine*, and she wasn't in a mood to explore it now. Sitting on the bridge reminded her of the time Kamil had taken her to the *Duchess*, the Black Dog's crippled military ship that remained attached to the *Bathsheba*. He'd frightened her by not telling her where they were going, and she'd had to explain to him what being a mage really meant.

He'd seemed to try to understand how she had to be constantly vigilant to protect herself, though she wasn't sure he really had succeeded. It wasn't something easy for others to comprehend. Unless you grew up as a mage, unless you'd lived it, day in, day out, it wasn't possible to know how it felt.

Nor was it possible to understand how it felt when it was all taken away from you.

"Parthenia," said Carina, "I think you should know some things about Lakshmi Station. There are androids there called hosts and hostesses, and—"

"I know what you're talking about. You don't need to explain."

She'd been tempted to reply, *The sex bots? Oh, I know all about them,* just to embarrass and annoy her sister, but Darius and Nahla were on the bridge with them.

"You do?" Carina asked. "How come?" She was holding Nahla on her lap, though she barely fit, while Darius was sitting next to Hsiao, who was showing him the ship's controls.

"Some of the mercs were talking about them."

"Oh, okay."

Her sister looked worried and concerned.

"For goodness sake," Parthenia said irritably. "I'm not twelve. You don't have to protect me from that kind of thing. Do you really think that after growing up with Mother and Father I don't understand what happens between adults?" She was tempted to say more, about the times Father would stare at her with a certain look in his eye, or when he would stand too close and touch her too much and in the wrong places, but she didn't want to burden Carina with the knowledge. She didn't hate her *that* much.

Her sister looked deflated. She stroked Nahla's hair and replied, "I'm sorry. I was forgetting."

"Lucky for you. *I* can't forget so easily."

Carina sighed. "What I'm trying to say is, when we get to the station, be careful to stick with us. The place is huge and confusing and it's easy to get lost. It's also full of all kinds of people, mostly visitors from the three warring systems. There are strict penalties for breaking regulations, but I'm sure plenty goes on the station officials don't know about, or at least they don't find out about until it's too late."

"Yeah," said Hsiao, speaking over her shoulder as she sat at the controls, "Carina nearly got in a fight on our last trip. Jackson and I had to hold her back."

The pilot was clearly trying to lighten the atmosphere, but Parthenia wasn't in the mood for it. Carina seemed to feel the same.

After registering their looks, Hsiao gave a small cough and

faced her console again. "So, Darius, do you want to take a turn?"

His jaw dropped. "Me? Fly the ship?"

"Sure, why not? I can trust you not to do anything stupid, right?"

"I won't, I promise!"

"Then scooch over and sit here." The pilot got up, and Darius just about leapt into her seat.

Hsiao opened a shipwide comm. "Belt up, everyone. Trainee pilot at the controls." Then she leaned over Darius to swipe the screen, stating, "Switching to manual."

As she fastened her safety harness, Parthenia smiled. She was touched by the pilot's kind gesture and sensitivity. Darius hadn't said much, but he'd been quiet and glum since finding out about his sister's problems. He probably felt guilty, and Hsiao was doing a great job of taking his mind off it.

Carina moved Nahla to her own seat and strapped her in. As she secured her own belt, the *Peregrine* suddenly dipped and Parthenia's stomach seemed to rise above her head.

"Whoops!" said Darius, giggling.

Hsiao reached forward and gently moved his hands from the console. "Take it easy, speedracer." A swipe of her finger brought the ship level again. "Did you think you were training to pilot a fairground ride?"

Nahla had squealed at the sudden movement, but then she started giggling too. "That was fun! Do it again!"

"No, thank you," said Hsiao. "Straight and steady, Darius, like I showed you."

He bent his head down as he concentrated on the controls. The ship continued on with small swerves and jumps for a few minutes. Then Darius's legs began to kick, which was a sure sign he was either bored or needed the bathroom. Hsiao appeared to recognize the signs too, as she said, "Is that enough for now?"

He nodded and closed his fingers, causing the *Peregrine* to swoop again. An alarmed yell came from the passageway. Someone had decided to ignore the pilot's order to strap in.

"Whoa," said Hsiao. "Switching to auto."

Darius unfastened his harness and jumped out of his seat before running to Nahla. "Did you see me flying the ship?"

"Yeah, that was really cool!"

"Did you see me Carina, Parthenia?"

"We did," Carina replied. "Do you want to be a pilot when you grow up?"

"Maybe. Nahla, do you want to..." The boy's voice faltered and his face fell.

"What's wrong?" Carina asked.

"I was going to ask Nahla if she wanted to look around the *Peregrine* with me, only..."

He didn't need to say any more. Everyone knew what had happened the last time he'd gone exploring with his sister.

"It's okay, sweetheart," said Carina. "As long as you stay out of restricted areas, there's nothing here that can hurt you."

His features brightened. "What about it, Nahla? Do you want to come with me?"

"Uh huh."

Nahla tried to undo her belt but she couldn't manage it. Darius leaned in and did it for her. She hopped down from her seat, and Darius took her hand. Together, they walked out.

Parthenia saw Carina's sad gaze following their youngest sister. Nahla now walked unsteadily with a pronounced limp. It was heartbreaking to watch her. She knew exactly how Carina felt.

Parthenia said, "Maybe we'll find someone to help her at Lakshmi."

"I hope so." Carina looked drained and tired. She'd spent the entire night in the sick bay after they'd found the children, and she probably hadn't slept much since. "Maybe Bongo can help us."

"Bongo?" Parthenia asked.

"He was our guide the first time we went to the station. Nice guy. You'll like him."

* * *

ARRIVING AT LAKSHMI, Parthenia was under-impressed at first. The place seemed bare and boring. Yet the mercs who had accompanied them for their *R and R*, as they called it, weren't fazed by its appearance. As they completed the entry procedures they bantered with each other excitedly. The Black Dogs reminded her of big kids sometimes. Big, muscled, lethal children.

She had to have an ID code etched on her wrist, which was mildly painful, and then she passed through a scanner. When she stepped into the main area, her illusion about the station fell away. Sound and light crashed in on her. Lakshmi Station was humming with life and activity.

"It's quite something, isn't it?" asked Hsiao, raising her voice. "Have you ever been anywhere like it?"

"No, never," she answered.

The closest comparison Parthenia could make was the spaceport at Ithiya. That had been thronged with hundreds of people too. It had been there Darius had spotted Carina and run up to her, thus revealing her existence to Father, who had taken her captive.

What would have happened to them if Darius hadn't seen their sister?

Carina had rescued them from the Sherrerrs, escaping their flagship, the *Nightfall*. Would they ever have broken away without her help? Mother was already very sick by then, and Father had refused to have her transferred to a planet for treatment. After Mother died, they would have been stuck aboard the ship indefinitely.

With a heavy heart, she was forced to admit to herself that without Carina, she and her siblings would probably still be enslaved to her father's clan, Casting to help Sherrerr businesses and military offensives, imprisoned forever in their gilded cages.

"Here he comes," said Carina.

"Are you sure that's him?" asked Hsiao.

"Yep, I'm sure."

"How can you tell?"

Carina shrugged.

Parthenia peered into the crowd of people and aliens, trying to see who they were talking about. From among the sea of bodies, an alien ran straight at them on many legs, its claws tapping the floor tiles.

She took a backward step. Was it going to attack them? Where was the guide Carina had mentioned? Could he make the creature go away?

"Hey," said Carina as the creature reached them. "Thanks for meeting us."

"Hello again," it replied. "I got your comm. I have a few medical centers lined up. Wanna make a start?"

"Yeah. I brought Nahla's information from our ship's doctor."

She and Hsiao began to follow the alien, Carina holding Nahla's hand while Hsiao held Darius's.

This was Bongo?

Carina looked over her shoulder. "Are you coming, Parthenia?"

CHAPTER 16

"*H*ey, Bryce," Jackson said, approaching him in the refectory. "Fancy a spacewalk?"

He put down his fork. "Now?"

"After you finish eating. Me and Justus were thinking we need to get visuals on the damage the Regians did when they boarded the ship. The diagnostics can only tell us so much. If we're going to upgrade her, we need to know what we're facing."

"Sure," Bryce replied. "But you should know I've never spacewalked before."

"That's what I thought. It won't hurt for you to get some practice. You can never tell when stepping into the black might come in handy. If it's an emergency, you don't want to be doing it for the first time."

"Okay. Sounds good."

"Meet you at Airlock D, this deck."

As Jackson left, Bryce shoveled the remains of his rice and beans into his mouth. His first spacewalk would be a good distraction from the current situation. He'd come to the refectory to get a break from Ferne and Oriana, who had taken the loss of their powers badly. They'd given up their usual activities and spent all their time lying around listlessly, occasionally attempting a Cast. When it didn't work Oriana would burst into tears and Ferne would stomp into their bedroom dramatically and throw himself on the bed.

Bryce was sympathetic, though he knew he couldn't properly empathize with the teenagers. But being around them brought him down too, and he was already upset about Nahla. He'd needed a breather.

Jackson and Justus were suiting up when he arrived at the airlock. The two men seemed in a good mood, laughing about something. Bryce edged past them to lift a suit out from the store. As he did so, he caught a whiff of alcohol.

He halted. "You two been drinking?"

Jackson replied, "I had a beer with lunch. Is that a problem?"

Bryce said, "I thought we aren't supposed to drink before going outside."

"Man, you sound like your girlfriend," Jackson joked. "Carina's no Cadwallader, but damn that woman's a hard ass. No offense."

"He's got a point," said Justus. "It *is* a little soon to go out after having a drink. Maybe we should wait a couple hours."

"Says the guy who could barely walk when we got back from Lakshmi."

"That was different. I wasn't planning on stepping into the black then."

"I had one beer!" Jackson exclaimed. "I've lost count of how many spacewalks I've done. If I can't be trusted at the end of a tether after a single beer I might as well shoot myself."

Justus seemed to debate with himself for a moment before saying to Bryce, "Don't worry. It'll be okay. We're only taking a look around out there. If we were doing some work it would be different. But if you're not comfortable, you can join us another time."

The two older men continued to fasten up their suits.

They'd worked on starships most of their adult lives, whereas Bryce had only ended up on the *Bathsheba* by accident. He couldn't remember what his ambitions had been while growing up on Ithiya, but he knew they hadn't involved space travel. It was only after meeting Carina the idea of leaving his home planet had crossed his mind. But now this was to be his way of life for the next few years, he supposed he should learn all the ropes.

"No, it's fine," he said. "I'll do it."

Starship a-grav didn't extend to the hull. You couldn't successfully walk on a ship's exterior if you were constantly pulled toward her 'base'. To compensate for the lack of gravity, EVA suit boots could be made magnetic so the wearers' feet clung to metal surfaces, and tethers could be pulled from the waist to attach the suit's wearer to the hull. Additionally, if spacewalkers became separated from their vessels, nozzles at their elbows and back could expel pressurized gas to control movement. A final safety measure was the constant positioning signal emitted.

Providing you didn't somehow end up very far from the ship, you could usually be picked up in time to save your life even if your suit sprang a leak.

In short, it was very hard to die on a spacewalk.

As he looked out into the cold, dark, airless expanse beyond the airlock's outer hatch, Bryce found these facts comforting. Yet it didn't change his impression of how vast, empty and *dead* it was out there. He'd become used to living aboard the

Bathsheba, forgetting that only a few meters of hull separated him from—

"Comm check," came Jackson's voice inside his helmet.

"Check," said Justus.

"Check," said Bryce.

"You need to check your suit's levels too, Bryce," said Jackson. "Everything in normal range?"

He studied his HUD, mildly annoyed. He'd trained as a space soldier. He wasn't a complete greenhorn at wearing an EVA suit. "Yep."

"Okay, let's start aft and work our way forward. As well as the D airlocks we can reach airlocks C and E on Decks Three, Four, and Five. I'll take Five. Justus, you take Three, Bryce, you cover this deck."

"What am I looking for?"

"I expect we'll see acid damage from the Regian attack, but look for any kind of wear and tear too. Your helmet will pick up heat leaks. The computer is telling us the lasers are fully functional but this ship's damned old. Who knows when they were last checked?"

"Got it."

Jackson pulled the tether out from his waist, reached beyond the airlock and clipped it onto the hull. Then he grabbed the edge of the hatch, hauled himself through it, twisted sideways, and moved out of sight as the a-grav lost its grip on him. There were two clunks as his boots stuck to the metal.

"You're next," said Justus.

Bryce copied Jackson's movements and soon found himself looking at the outside of the *Bathsheba* for the first time. A metal plain stretched far and wide beneath his feet and 'above' it hung a void peppered with points of white diamond. The hull was also peppered, but with dents and scorch marks. Long scratches had been gouged from it too. The results of encounters with space debris over the centuries, he guessed. An aura hung around the edges of the ship, brightening the black—light from Lakshmi Station's star on the ship's far side.

"Give it a minute before you move around," said Justus as he emerged. "Helps to steady yourself and get your bearings."

He must have given the command to close the hatch, for it slid shut. Darkness closed over them like a blanket, alleviated only by the diffused light from the nearest star. Bryce's helmet switched to night vision and his view took on a steely tint.

Jackson was already several meters away, walking the high-stepping, long-striding gait imposed by magnetized boots. Justus also set off.

Bryce waited the advised minute, surveying the small laser weapons several meters distant from him, pointed toward the airlock. Their purpose was to defend against boarders. In the Regians' case that had been a bust.

He scanned for heat loss, but none showed. It was time to take a closer look.

He lifted a foot to break the magnetized contact. Weightlessness seized him and he wobbled. His sense of balance was all over the place until his foot met metal again.

Four lasers surrounded the airlock, mounted and angled to point at an edge of the square portal. The first laser Bryce checked didn't appear to have anything wrong with it though, despite Jackson's advice, he wasn't sure what he was supposed to be looking for. He connected with the ship's computer and searched for the device's schematics. When the image representing the laser's exterior came up it matched what he was seeing.

He moved toward the second laser.

"*Arghhh!*" Jackson cried out. "*Help! Help!*"

Then Justus's voice sounded in Bryce's helmet. "What's wrong? What's happened?"

Jackson yelled, "I accidentally activated one of the las —arghhh!"

He sprawled on his side, attached by one boot to the hull.

Bryce began to sprint in the direction of his injured shipmate…except he couldn't sprint. Each movement of his legs required breaking the magnetic hold, slowing him down to little more than a fast walk.

Should he use his pressurized gas pack to get him to Jackson's side faster? Justus was heading for their shipmate at a similarly restricted pace. He couldn't see exactly what was wrong with Jackson, but he must have been hit by a laser, which meant a suit leak. If they didn't get him inside quickly he would suffocate.

Bryce de-magnetized his boots and his feet lifted a fraction off the hull. The smallest push would now send him floating away from the ship. He checked his tether and then fired a small spurt from the nozzles at his elbows and on his back. The effect was far greater than he'd anticipated. Within less than a second, he was tens of meters from the hull. The *Bathsheba* continued to recede from him at an alarming rate, the downed Jackson and run-walking Justus reduced to dolls on the expanse of pockmarked metal.

He adjusted the direction of the nozzles and angled his body forward before firing a second spurt of gas, even smaller than the first. He moved headlong this time, traversing a line parallel to the colony ship. That was better. His tether looped out below him, a reassuring link to safety.

Justus had almost reached Jackson.

Bryce cursed. He should have walked, not attempted this ridiculous effort.

Turning his head toward his companions, he fired a third burst of gas.

By slow maneuvering and several corrections, he managed to bring himself back to the hull nearby Jackson. To Bryce's confusion, the man was standing by the time he reached him and acting normally. He didn't seem to be hurt.

Bryce realized he hadn't heard anything from either of his shipmates for a minute or so.

Then laughter exploded into his helmet. Jackson and Justus had cut their comms to him. They'd been laughing all the while he'd been making his way over to them.

When Bryce's boots finally snapped to magnetic contact with the hull, Jackson slapped him on the back. "It's good to know I can rely on you in a crisis."

"I haven't seen anything so funny in a long while," said Justus, gasping for air. "Thanks for that."

"Come on, fellas," Bryce remonstrated.

But he knew there was no use in saying any more. The mercs loved to have fun at others' expense, even if it cut close to the knuckle sometimes.

He asked, "Did you set me up right from the beginning or was this a last-minute joke?"

"Right from the start," Jackson replied. "Even gargled a mouthful of beer just so I could breathe it out on you." He leaned closer. "Word of advice. Don't *ever* go spacewalking with someone who's been drinking. Not even *just one beer.*"

"Okay," Bryce said ruefully, "I get it." It was a hard lesson but well-taught. "Did you make up the part about checking the lasers too?"

"No, we do need to do that. Take a look at Deck Four C lock. I'll carry on checking this one."

Justus continued to chuckle as he high-stepped toward another set of lasers.

Bryce began the slow walk to Deck Four C.

He hadn't gone far, however, before Jackson exclaimed, "Holy shit!"

Half-expecting another prank, Bryce turned to see what he'd found.

Jackson was bent over a laser, pulling at something.

There was a blinding flash, momentarily wiping out Bryce's night vision. When he could see again, Jackson was collapsing and an object was floating away from him, spinning lazily in its own orbit.

It took Bryce a second to realize the object was an arm.

CHAPTER 17

*N*ahla looked glum, and Parthenia knew exactly how she felt. This was the fifth medical center they'd visited, accompanied by the strange alien-spider creature Bongo, and at each one her little sister had been questioned, prodded, poked, scanned, and tested. She didn't seem to understand what was going on, but she had to be exhausted. Parthenia only had to watch and wait as the medics did their work, and *she* was exhausted.

Nahla's prospects didn't look good. After an hour or longer of investigation, the conclusions of the doctors at the previous four establishments had been the same: there wasn't much they could do. While medical science had cracked the problems of regenerating every other human tissue and organ, triggering the brain into repairing itself still eluded it.

"You can expect to see *some* improvement," said the head of the latest center, "if you follow our treatment program. Nahla is young and her brain is still developing. Some of the functions that were lost in the hypoxia incident will be taken over by the remaining healthy areas. But will she ever return to her former state? I would say, according to what I've seen, it's unlikely."

"It would be hard for us to stay here for a long course of treatment," said Carina. "I was hoping something could be done for Nahla over the short term."

"Out of the question, I'm afraid. Your sister requires months of therapy to make any progress. I think perhaps you're underestimating just how much brain damage she sustained."

"But Darius was deprived of oxygen over the same period," Carina protested, "and he seems fine."

"With respect, you don't know that. I could run some tests..."

"No. No more testing." Addressing her siblings, she said, "Come on, let's go."

"Uh," the doctor murmured, "there's the small question of payment for—"

"Don't worry, I haven't forgotten," Carina replied irritably. "I'll pay on the way out."

"I'm sorry we couldn't help you."

Carina didn't reply as they left the office.

At the receptionist's desk, she held her ID code to the scanner for the center to extract their fee from her account. Parthenia saw the figures on the screen. It was a drop in the ocean of the amount they had available, but creds weren't worth much when they couldn't help Nahla.

"If we could just Cast Heal," Carina muttered.

"What now?" Parthenia asked.

"Find Hsiao and Bongo. I want to talk to some weapons suppliers and get a feel for what we should buy for the *Bathsheba*."

"So we're still going to Earth?"

Carina sighed. "Honestly, I don't know. I don't know what the hell we should be doing anymore. But it won't hurt to explore our options."

Hsiao had balked at attending Nahla's fourth round of

testing and had gone to find her merc buddies. Bongo had left them when they'd arrived at the fifth center, though he'd said he would be back soon. Carina had purchased the local comm and translation devices on her previous trip, and Parthenia waited, holding Nahla and Darius's hands on the busy thoroughfare, while her sister contacted the missing members of their party.

Bongo was the first to appear, dodging between the many pedestrians with ease. He was clearly accustomed to it, even avoiding the people who jumped in random directions, startled by his approach.

"Any luck?" he asked.

"Nope," Carina replied.

"Sorry to hear that. Do you want to try another place? There are a few—"

"No. There's no point. They're all going to say the same thing."

"You're probably right," replied the alien. "The medical centers compete for custom so they're all pretty up to date on the latest treatments, though I would say they're best at combat injuries. Where to next?"

"Military equipment suppliers, I guess," said Carina. "Starship defense armaments."

"Um," Parthenia demurred.

"What?"

"The children are hungry and tired, and so am I. How about we find somewhere to rest and eat?"

"Yeah, you're right." Carina rubbed her forehead. "I was forgetting."

"If food and relaxation are next on the program," said Bongo. "I know just the place."

* * *

"Is Hsiao meeting us here?" Parthenia asked when they arrived at the restaurant, Etheric Edibles.

"I can't raise her," Carina replied. "She isn't answering her comm."

"What about the other mercs? She must be with them."

"Yeah, you're right. I'll try Van Hasty."

Bongo was speaking to the maître d'–another, different, alien. This creature was humanoid but extremely tall and thin and completely hairless. After a short conversation where Bongo explained all the humans were from out-sector, she—Parthenia had the impression the maître d' was female—beckoned them with a long-fingered hand and led them between the occupied tables and chairs to the rear of the restaurant. Her movements seemed full of effort, as if she was struggling with the local gravity.

"I can give you an hour and a half," she said. "I have a booking for this table."

"Thanks," Carina replied. "We won't be here that long."

"Did you manage to speak to Van Hasty?" asked Parthenia as she sat down.

"No." Carina ushered Darius and Nahla onto the bench between her and Parthenia.

Bongo dragged over a low seat with a hole in the base and squatted on it, announcing, "I recommend the fungus and larvae. I've eaten it here before and it's delicious."

"The..." Parthenia swallowed. Table manners, especially when dining with guests, had been ingrained into her from a very young age. She smiled politely. "Is that a local specialty?"

"It's a Marchonish dish. Very tasty."

"Are you from Marchon?" she asked.

"Stars, no!" A bubbling sound came from the alien's orifices as he appeared to laugh. "My species' home system is a long way from here, and our culture is peaceful. We would never end up in a conflict like the Three System War."

"Fungus and larvae, hm?" Carina asked, scanning the menu screen.

You aren't serious? Parthenia mentally questioned her sister, but she didn't want to offend Bongo by speaking aloud.

She was about to ask their guide about the war when Carina continued, "The larvae *are* dead, right?"

"Well, they're frozen," Bongo replied. "So, technically—"

"Yeah," said Carina, "you're not exactly selling it. I think I'll pass." Her head down, she carried on reading the menu.

Parthenia was also reading it, trying to find something Darius and Nahla wouldn't reject out of hand. One of the noodle dishes seemed a fair bet. She made the suggestion.

"I want to choose for myself!" Darius exclaimed.

"I want what Darius wants," said Nahla.

"Fine," said Parthenia. "Let Carina know what you decide."

She wasn't particularly hungry herself. As she waited for the others to pick their dishes, she decided to try an experiment. She'd brought her elixir along. Carina hadn't wanted her to, but the small bottle of liquid hadn't triggered any alarms. She wanted to try a Cast. It could be something aboard the *Bathsheba* that was preventing them from working, or something in the ship's vicinity.

After checking no one was watching, she took the bottle from its bag at her waist and unscrewed the lid. Carina looked up at precisely the wrong time—from Parthenia's viewpoint— and saw what she was doing. Her sister gave her a severe frown and shook her head sharply.

"Is something the matter?" Bongo asked her, his many-eyed head swiveling from one sibling to the other.

"No, nothing at all," Parthenia replied, taking a sip of elixir while meeting Carina's hard stare.

She closed her eyes. A small Cast would do for a test. Something simple.

She wrote the Send character in her mind, followed by a message *You don't own me, Sis* and then released it.

From the lack of reaction on Carina's face it was clear the Cast had failed. Her heart settled like lead in her chest. Even at Lakshmi Station, she no longer had her special ability.

I'm no longer a mage.

The words in her head sounded unreal. It seemed impossible they were true.

Perhaps reading her expression, Carina's look became sorrowful and sympathetic.

Darius and Nahla called out their meal choice, which was something that sounded deep-fried and very unhealthy. Parthenia said she wouldn't be eating anything.

The food took only a few minutes to arrive. The center of the table retracted into a slot and the steaming dishes rose on the flat top of a column, into the gap. Bongo reached over the tabletop with two limbs and picked up a bowl of something looking suspiciously like chopped up fungus peppered with frozen maggots. The maggots were rapidly thawing and beginning to wriggle.

He placed the dish in front of him, scooped out a handful, or, rather, a clawful, of food and put it underneath his chair. When the claw reappeared it was empty.

That explained the hole in his seat. The orifice he used for eating had to be somewhere in his belly.

Parthenia was deeply pleased she'd decided not to eat.

Thankfully, Darius and Nahla were too occupied by their own food to notice and make a rude comment. Carina, if she'd registered what the alien was doing, didn't react.

After waiting a few minutes, Parthenia asked, "Bongo, can you explain about the Three Systems War? How long has it been going on and what's it about?"

"Ah, do you want the official story or the truth?" he asked.

"What do *you* think?" Carina asked in return.

"I'll give you both, seeing as one kind of explains the other. But don't ever repeat what I tell you to a Marchonish, Quintonese, or Gugongian. You'll get yourself banned from the station, or worse."

CHAPTER 18

*J*ackson had lost an arm but gained a Regian one. He was staring at the alien limb stupidly while his severed prosthetic dripped fluid.

"You need to get out of your suit," said Justus as the airlock's outer hatch closed and atmosphere hissed in.

Jackson raised his head. "What? Oh, yeah."

Bryce had expected the man to be in a worse condition by the time he and Justus had reached him, but his suit had only lost pressure to the top of the remainder of his arm. A seal in his suit had activated, preventing air from escaping and providing a tourniquet to slow blood loss.

"You know what this means?" asked Jackson.

The airlock's inner hatch opened.

Justus removed his helmet. "You fancied trying a different kind of arm?" He began to unfasten Jackson's suit for him.

The merc was clearly in shock, which wasn't surprising. Amputation via laser beam would shock the most hardened veteran, even when the limb in question wasn't made of flesh and blood.

Justus removed Jackson's helmet, and his voice switched

from comm to natural as he said, "It explains how the Regians got around the laser defenses."

As if suddenly hit by revulsion, he dropped the insectoid appendage. Black and shiny, it lay on the deck. The limb must have been stuck in the laser emitter ever since the Regian attack. It had traveled along with the *Bathsheba* all the way to Magog and Gog and the millions of miles the ship had voyaged afterward.

"They swarmed them," Bryce said. "The Regians threw themselves at the lasers to give their buddies time to crack the airlocks."

"Yeah," agreed Jackson. "Their usual offensive tactic: overwhelm your opponent by sheer force of numbers, whether the enemy is another species or a weapon."

"Sick bastards," muttered Justus. "Step out," he ordered. He'd removed Jackson's suit down to his knees.

"Hey," the merc protested, apparently only just noticing what Justus had been doing, "I can do it." He pushed the legs of his suit down with his remaining arm and lifted his feet out of the boots. "I'm not a freaking kid."

"Does your arm hurt?" asked Bryce, wondering if the prosthetic had a biofeedback linked to Jackson's brain.

"Nah," he replied. "It stung a little when the beam cut it, but the pain sensors closed down after that."

"Well, one thing's for sure," Justus commented, beginning to remove his own suit, "we've gotta replace all the lasers. They shouldn't misfire like that, even if someone's tugging at them like you did to pull that thing out. But we would have to get rid of them anyway. I've never seen such antiques. They must be centuries old."

"Assuming we're still going to Earth," said Jackson, "and we need defenses."

"Why wouldn't we?" asked Justus.

Bryce explained, "Carina's reconsidering the options since

she and her brothers and sisters lost their powers. She's not sure there's any point in continuing our journey anymore."

"That's news to me," said Justus. "Don't we get a say? If we don't go to Earth, I'm not sure where I'd go. Lotacrylla's closed to me now. I can't go back there after what happened to my old shipmates. I'd be tried and executed for desertion."

"But you didn't desert," said Bryce.

"Doesn't matter. In my culture, it's all for one, not every man for himself. I'm expected to defend my company or die trying."

"No need to fret," said Jackson. "You're a de facto Black Dog now. Wherever we go, you come too."

"Says who?"

"Says me." Jackson patted his shoulder.

"Thanks. That means a lot. So, I guess you'll have to get that arm replaced now?"

"Yep. Another item on Carina's shopping list."

While the two men talked, Bryce had been taking off his suit and helmet and stowing them. Jackson's prosthetic continued to drip on the deck.

"Another antique to be replaced," he said, noticing the fluid loss. His brow wrinkled and he lifted the short stump that was all that remained and peered at the end. "Feels weird. Never thought I'd lose it like this."

"How long did you have it?" asked Bryce.

"I don't know. Long time. So long it felt—"

Bryce's ship's comm bleeped an 'urgent' signal. He slapped it. "What?"

"You have to come to the bridge!" Oriana cried. "Right now! The ships are firing."

The three men sprinted down the passageway.

What a time for an attack! Hsiao, their only experienced pilot, was on Lakshmi with Carina. Would Bibik be able to perform evasive maneuvers? Could the mammoth *Bathsheba* even move evasively? Bryce assumed the other Black Dogs had been alerted and someone had taken charge of the ship's weapons, such as they were.

"Why the hell are they firing at us?" Jackson asked breathlessly. "We don't have anything to do with their stupid war."

"You'd think they would give us a warning at least," gasped Justus.

They reached the bridge and the doors slid aside, revealing Oriana, Ferne, Bibik, and a couple of mercs watching a holo playing in the center of the room.

"What's happening?" asked Jackson. "Have we taken any hits? Did you put up the force shield, Bibik?"

"Why would I do that?" the young merc replied mildly, raising his eyebrows at the newcomers' out-of-breath state.

Jackson said, "To defend the..." He paused and studied the holo closely. "Wait. They're not firing at *us*."

"No," said Bibik. "Oriana, I told you they would get the wrong idea from what you said. Sorry, guys. I think she got over-excited."

The scene playing out on the 3D image was of two fleets in battle—with each other. Pulse bolts streamed across space as the ships appeared to crawl slowly to new positions, though in reality they were moving fast.

"Sorry," said Oriana sheepishly. "I thought you would want to see it, Bryce."

"I do, but maybe explain what you mean a bit more clearly next time?"

"It's so cool!" Ferne exclaimed. "I think the one on the left is winning."

"Not so cool when you're in the middle of it," said Jackson. "Don't you know that? You must have been in some space battles in your time, youngster."

"Yeah," Ferne replied, "but this is different. It's like a vidgame."

"It's not a game when your life's at risk. You'd do well to remember that."

Jackson's expression became serious and contemplative. Bryce wondered how many battles he'd taken part in. It had to be a lot, considering the grizzled man's age, and the fact that he wasn't even sure how long he'd had his prosthetic arm.

Carina had told Bryce once that Jackson had taken part in the first attempt to rescue Darius from the Dirksens. How many of that team of Black Dogs were still alive? Not the captain, Speidel, certainly. Carina had spoken sadly of how he'd died in the second, successful attempt. Others had died since—Atoi, who had lost her life to the Regians, and Halliday, who had perished in a glider crash on Magog.

He guessed Jackson and Carina might be the only remaining survivors from the original rescue team. Mercenary life was generally short and brutal. If the old merc made it to their journey's end, where he could live out the rest of his life in peace and safety, that would be something.

CHAPTER 19

"So," said Bongo, adjusting his position in his seat as if getting comfortable, "the official reason for the conflict between the governments of Marchon, Quinton, and Gugong is a territory dispute. There's a rogue planet roughly equidistant between the three systems, and each sovereignty claims it as its own."

"What makes the planet so valuable?" asked Parthenia.

"Nothing, as far as I'm aware, and I've done a fair bit of research into it. It's a small place, barely bigger than a moon."

"Nothing at all?!" exclaimed Carina.

"*Shhh!*" Bongo gestured downward with a claw. "This is a sensitive subject around here. You never know who you might offend. We..." he made a burbling sound "—that's the name of my people—we have to be careful to remain neutral about the war. Feelings run high, even after eighty Standard Years of fighting, maybe because of eighty years of fighting."

"They've been at war for eighty years?" Carina exclaimed again, equally loudly.

Bongo's head swiveled as each of his eyes glared at her in turn.

"Sorry," she said, continuing more quietly. "They've been at war for *eighty years?*"

"Eighty-three, to be exact."

"Over a worthless rogue planet?"

"He's already told us that," Parthenia reminded her.

"I'm just checking," replied her sister. "It is a real war, right?" she asked Bongo, "with people dying and everything?"

"The estimated death toll passed into the hundreds of millions decades ago," said the alien.

Parthenia asked, "How long have *you* been here?"

"This will be my fourteenth Standard Year at Lakshmi. I'll probably make it a round fifteen before heading home. I'll have saved enough by then to retire, providing I'm frugal. That's not to say I haven't enjoyed my work here, but you can only listen to the same biased, dogmatic opinions from each side for so long, you know? I can't tell you what a relief it was to hear you guys were from out-sector."

"I suppose it must be hard to stay out of the argument when you're right in the middle of it," Parthenia commented.

"You don't know the half of it," said Bongo. "To keep the war going, the governments on the three planets feed their populations all kinds of propaganda, and the people believe it because, well, why wouldn't they? They never get to meet each other except here at Lakshmi, and then they segregate themselves. Most service jobs are carried out by non-humans. Prior to the recruitment drive for workers from other areas of the sector, the fighting on the station used to be a lot worse, I've heard."

"What do their governments tell them?" Parthenia asked.

"Oh, all sorts of nonsense. That the other side beats their children, practices slavery, creates human/animal mutants, is planning to take over the sector, and so on. I forget who says what about the different sides. It's all bullshit, but there's no point in reasoning with them. They've been told this stuff all their lives. It's best to not get involved. They're in too deep."

"But they must interact with each other at least a little," Carina said. "We were accused of coming from the 'wrong planet' in a bar the other day, so it happens. It's kinda hard to believe they see and speak to the people from other planets and yet never question what they've been told."

"Some probably do question it," said Bongo, "but they don't dare to say anything. It must be hard to speak out when the war's gone on so long and everyone you know believes the propaganda."

"I think I understand," Parthenia commented. "They've been fighting for generations and the war has become a part of their identity. They're all invested in it. And every family must have people who died in the fight. Propaganda aside, that gives them a reason for hating their opponents and continuing the war. They want revenge."

"What an identity to have," said Carina. "I'm glad ours isn't like...wasn't..." She stopped speaking, firmly closing her lips.

Parthenia guessed exactly what her sister meant and what she'd nearly said. The same thought had sprung to her own mind. From what she'd come to learn about mage culture, they were essentially pacifistic, like Bongo's species. It was a far better identity to have than to belong to a warlike society, but were they even mages any longer?

Speaking softly to Bongo, she said, "You mentioned something about the real reason for the war."

"Ah yes," he replied before making his strange burbling sound again. "Now I'm wishing I hadn't."

He tapped the two claws of his limbs that rested on the tabletop before continuing, "You must promise me you'll never mention this to another soul at the station, or to anyone among your crew who can't be trusted to not speak of it. You must *especially* promise me that, if you do mention it by accident, you never tell anyone it came from me."

"We promise," said Carina.

"Yes," Parthenia said, "we'll never speak of it." She checked Nahla and Darius, who definitely couldn't be expected to keep any such promise, but they were playing a game with the condiment bottles, oblivious to the conversation.

"Perhaps I don't actually need to tell you," said Bongo. "You seem like intelligent people. I'll give you some facts, and you can draw your own conclusions. I told you the war began eighty-three years ago, didn't I? Do you know how old Lakshmi Station is?"

"Eighty years?" Carina guessed.

"Wrong," said Bongo.

She tried again. "Seventy-five? Construction must have begun after the war started. Someone saw an opportunity to make money selling weapons to the three sides, and so they built the station."

"Wrong again," Bongo said.

"Oh!" Parthenia moved her hand to her mouth as the realization began to hit.

"Seventy?" asked Carina.

"No," Parthenia said. "Lakshmi isn't younger than the war, is it, Bongo? It's older, right?"

Her sister frowned. "But why...?" The frown disappeared and was replaced by open-mouthed horror. "Stars! You don't think—"

"The owners of Lakshmi Station are fabulously wealthy," Bongo interrupted, "and so are the arms dealers, medical professionals, and everyone else who services the war machine, including the governmental leaders."

Tears pricked Parthenia's eyes. "You said hundreds of millions have died?"

"The figures are probably into the billions by now, and that isn't counting all the injured, permanently disabled, orphaned, and bereaved."

Could it really be true? Could the war between the three

planets only have come about in order to make a small group of people rich? She guessed some high-ranking individuals from Marchon, Quinton, and Gugong must have worked together to hatch the plan. They must have begun to build Lakshmi in preparation. Then when the time was ripe, they'd whipped up the planets' inhabitants into a frenzy of xenophobic hatred and staged an incident to trigger the start of the war. She'd known some terrible people in her time—such as her own Father—but she'd thought people like him were rare. She'd been wrong. Lakshmi Station had to be making money for lots of people.

Carina echoed her thoughts. "Do you think everyone who profits from Lakshmi Station is aware of what's going on?"

"I can't say," Bongo replied. "I've never talked about it to anyone outside my own kind, and if you weren't from out-sector I wouldn't be talking about it with you, either. If the conspiracy was revealed and the populations turned against their governments, a lot of powerful people would lose everything. They would never risk it by allowing a blabbermouth to live." He bent his head forward conspiratorially. "That's the real reason I want to leave. *I* profit from Lakshmi Station along with everyone who works here and it makes me uncomfortable."

Parthenia murmured, "And by buying weapons here, we're complicit too."

"Don't be dumb," said Carina. "We didn't know about the reason for the war before we arrived, and we still don't for sure. Bongo could be wrong." She addressed him. "You don't know this for sure, right? You're only guessing."

Before he could answer Parthenia retorted, "It's a damned good guess. Think about it. What other reason could there be to go to war over a useless lump of rock floating in interstellar space?"

"Then the people are stupid for not figuring it out and doing something about it."

"Stupid, or brainwashed?"

"Same thing."

"How can you be so callous?" Parthenia asked her sister, nearly rising from her seat in anger.

Darius and Nahla, who had been happily chattering as they played their game, fell silent and looked from one sister to the other.

"I'm not callous," Carina said, "I'm just not interested in other people's wars. I have a family to take care of, and if it means striking deals with self-serving warmongers, that's what I'll do."

They were back to the old argument they'd had on Ostillon. Carina didn't feel the same responsibility toward her fellow human beings as she did. Her anger eased. It was only to be expected. Carina had been alienated from non-mages for most of her life. She saw ordinary folk as different from her, with the possible exception of Bryce and Nahla. She didn't really care about other people and probably never would.

"Well, I think we should complete our business transactions and leave at the earliest opportunity," said Parthenia. "Now we're here, we don't have much choice about buying what we need, but I don't want to be a part of what's going on any longer than we have to."

"You won't hear any argument from me about that," said Carina, "but I wish we could do something for Nahla."

"Oh dear," said Bongo. "This is bad. This is very bad."

"Um, what?" Carina asked.

"Your companions are in deep shit."

CHAPTER 20

*A*n hour earlier, Hsiao had found Rees, Van Hasty, and the other mercs enjoying their R and R in the Nebulaooze on the upper level of Deck Thirty-Two. Why they'd chosen this place was beyond her. Compared to the rest of Lakshmi, it was a real dive.

Most of the bartenders were Bongo's species, and they certainly needed their plentiful legs to serve the customers who crowded at every bar. The men and women looked like the lowest class of Lakshmi visitors—starship maintenance crews or space fleet grunts. Their clothes were the cheapest prints and were falling apart even so, their was hair shaggy and unkempt and some bore visible scars. Skin repair was cheap and widely available, so they were either too poor to afford it or were substance addicts, preferring to spend their limited funds on their kick.

The décor matched the clientele. The furnishings were shabby and dirty, and the only decoration on the walls were stains and scuff marks. Underlying the smell of alcohol and the smoke of narcotic herbs were the odors of sweat and bad breath.

"What are you doing here, guys?" she asked when she reached the mercs' table, raising her voice over the hubbub.

"What's wrong?" Rees asked. "Don't like the atmosphere? Seems pretty cool to me."

His pupils were dilated, and Hsiao didn't think it was only due to the low lighting.

"It's a dump," she replied. "Come on, let's go somewhere else."

"Relax," said Van Hasty. "Sit down and have a drink. I'll get you one. What do you want?"

"They don't have table service?"

It was another indication of the bar's poor quality. There were three standards of service in bars and restaurants: staffed by trained, professional servers (the highest standard), entirely automated, and staffed by low-skilled, badly paid migrant labor. This place clearly fell into the last category.

"It's not a problem," said Van Hasty. "I like seeing those spider-things pouring drinks. You know they can serve three people at once? It's like watching a show at the fair."

"I don't think we should stay here," said Hsiao. "There must be a million better bars than this. Why'd you pick it?"

Rees shrugged. "We just wandered in. If you don't like it, we can leave."

"Great. Let's go."

"Just have one drink while we finish ours."

Hsiao relented. One drink wouldn't hurt. "Okay. I'll have whatever you guys are having," she told Van Hasty.

The merc left the table and shouldered her way through the crowd. The patrons were tightly packed, but she was a tall, powerful woman and had no trouble in forcing a passage through the throng.

Hsiao pulled out a stool from under the table and sat down.

Rees turned to the merc sitting next to him and said something Hsiao didn't catch. He was smirking and his head wobbled as if he was under the influence of something.

Dammit.

The Black Dogs hadn't had a chance to unwind in months, and they'd come close to dying horrible deaths at the hands of the Regians. She knew from her years working with them what was coming next. They were going to really let loose and have a blast. Most likely they wouldn't be able to make their own way back to the *Peregrine*. They would have to be carried.

Though she wouldn't do the same herself, she didn't have a problem with it per se. The men and women risked death while they were on a job. It made sense that they lived their lives to the full while they still could.

But they were at Lakshmi Station.

Carina had lectured them on the severity of the laws here, but Hsiao had a feeling the mercs hadn't taken her as seriously as they should. Carina had a rep for being a hard ass, and the Black Dogs were used to bending the rules when out of sight of their commander. Cadwallader's iron-fisted leadership style had kind of trained them to it. That, and the fact the average merc had the mentality of a teenager, spelled trouble in a situation like this.

Van Hasty returned with her drink. Steam or smoke curled from the bright violet liquid. Hsiao checked the glasses on the table. They were half full of the same cocktail.

Oh well, I got what I asked for.

She took a sip and winced as the sour, viscous fluid slipped down her throat.

Then it hit.

The room swam before her and took on a different hue.

She grabbed the edge of the table with her other hand. "What the hell is in this?"

"Who knows?" Van Hasty replied, lifting her own glass to her lips. "It's called Sudden Death."

"Sudden Death, huh?"

Hsiao carefully put her drink down.

A woman sidled up to Rees and placed an arm around his neck before bending low to whisper in his ear. Her large breasts performed a gravity-defying miracle as they remained inside her dress.

Hsiao took a double take. It wasn't a woman, it was a hostess, and not an expensive model. Even in the bar's dim lights her skin's sheen appeared artificial and her long, curly, chestnut hair looked fake. Rees reached up and cupped one weighty breast while his other hand disappeared behind her, or rather, it.

Van Hasty and Hsiao shared an *Ewww!* look.

In another moment, Rees was up on his feet and staggering off into the crowd, one arm around the hostess's waist.

"Seriously?" Hsiao asked Van Hasty.

"I know!" she replied. "I think he has a fetish."

A group of youngsters standing near the mercs had been edging closer to the table since Hsiao had arrived, pushed in by the sheer number of people jostling for space. The young people looked different from the rest of the patrons. They were well-dressed, their clothes intricately made, and the women wore jewelry that appeared authentic. They seemed oblivious to their encroachment on the mercs' space.

What were they doing here when they could obviously afford to patronize more upmarket bars? Perhaps, like Rees, they had a fetish for sleaze.

The crowd pressed closer, and a young man in the group stepped backward, bringing his behind right up to one of the mercs' heads.

She yelled, "Hey, I can smell ass!" Standing, she tapped the man on the shoulder. "I don't feel like sniffing your butt today. Find somewhere else to shove your backside, okay?"

In response, he grinned and grabbed her before grinding

against her and saying, "If you don't like my backside, how about my front?"

The woman's elbow shot back and she landed a punch that had his eyes rolling up as he collapsed into his companions.

"Cut it out!" Hsiao hollered. "You'll get us all in trouble."

But she might as well have shouted into the void for all the notice anyone took.

Another man in the group leapt at the merc who'd hit his friend, but Van Hasty was already on her feet and in his way with her fists up. The three remaining Black Dogs weren't far behind, and neither were their antagonists. Before Hsiao could say another word, a full-on brawl was taking place.

Rees reappeared from nowhere and dove into the combatants. The bar's other patrons drew back, forming a circle of gawkers. The man who'd been punched unconscious lay at the fighters' feet, heedless of what he'd started.

Hsiao hesitated. Should she stay to help pick up the pieces when the mercs inevitably beat the rich kids to a pulp? Or should she leave and let them deal with their own problems? From what she understood of Lakshmi, there would be severe repercussions for the fight.

Loyalty made her stay.

CHAPTER 21

*B*ongo's species was apparently telepathic. While Carina had been talking with Parthenia about the war, he'd received a tip off from a friend, warning him the mercs had been taken into custody and were in danger of being spaced.

Leaving Parthenia to look after Darius and Nahla, Carina raced with the alien to the security center where Hsiao, Van Hasty, Rees, and four others were being held.

"Why didn't I receive a comm about this?" she asked Bongo as they ran, dodging the ever-present crowds.

"You would have, eventually, but maybe not until it was too late. That's the way they do things around here. They inform the relatives and friends after the sentence has been carried out and pay compensation if the accused is found innocent on appeal. They call it retroactive justice."

"That's a hell of a system."

"It certainly keeps most everyone under control."

"Not the *Bathsheba's* crew, obviously. They don't know about the law around here."

"Well," said Bongo, "they just found out."

"I don't get it. Some meathead nearly started a fight with me the first time I was here. Why would he do that if the laws are so draconian?"

"It was probably all show. There's plenty of audacious talk goes on in those places, especially when people are buzzed, but hardly anything ever comes of it. Most visitors aren't that dim-witted."

The Fifth Point Justice Office where the Black Dogs were being held was kilometers away. Carina had to take the metro with Bongo for an hour and a half, changing trains twice, to reach it. Along the way, she'd asked him if there wasn't a faster way to travel.

There was.

A second network of tunnels for autocars connected all the areas of the station, but it was only available to a minority of Lakshmi residents, not visitors or migrant workers.

By the time they arrived at the relevant district, Carina was a frazzled mess, out of her mind with worry she would be too late to save the mercs.

She still hadn't received a communication from the authorities that her companions were under arrest. To be on the safe side, she'd comm'd Parthenia, telling her to take the kids to the *Peregrine* and wait there. She couldn't risk them accidentally contravening the station's strict regulations. She wouldn't have time to fix a second problem.

This district was far quieter than the commercial zone. The metro car had been nearly empty as it pulled into the station at the end of the line, and the platform all but deserted. Carina immediately had a creepy feeling as she stepped out of the train. Overhead, the ceiling was so high it was lost in darkness, the lights on the walls too weak to penetrate it.

"It must cost a fortune to heat this place," she commented, partly to alleviate her anxiety as they entered the exit tunnel.

"It costs hardly anything at all," he replied. "Lakshmi derives its power directly from its sun, with minimal energy loss in the process. The invention of the technology was one of the things that made the building of the station possible."

"Did the inventors share the knowledge with the local systems?"

"Guess."

"No, of course not."

"It's one of the station's best-kept secrets."

When they left the metro, before the barrier would open Carina had to hold out her wrist for her ID code to be scanned. Bongo seemed to have a free pass because his barrier opened automatically.

Outside, she stumbled and almost fell. For a second, she'd felt as though she was suddenly walking on a planet surface. A blue sky stretched wide above them, looking entirely authentic. It even had clouds.

"Is that real?" she asked, wondering if the distance between them and the 'top' of the station was so great the blueness was created by the depth of atmosphere and the local star shining through it.

"No," Bongo replied, "it's an illusion, but a good one as I understand. Is that what the sky looks like on your home planet?"

She thought back. It had been a long time since she'd left the planet where she'd been born. "Yes, but it wasn't so blue."

"The Justice Office is this way," said Bongo.

Carina wondered what color the sky was on the alien's world, but she was too nervous and worried to have the discussion comparing birth planets usual between new acquaintances.

Only a few pedestrians walked the streets, which were lined with trees and shrubs, some in flower. The differences between here and the zone built for visitors continued to make their impression on her. Long-term Lakshmi residents had created a pleasant home for themselves.

She swallowed as she remembered it had all been built with the blood of billions.

She wished Bryce was here. She was afraid that when she met with the justice officers she might fly off the handle and ruin everything.

A tall, wide building of pale cream stone occupied center stage in the street. Pillars supported an overhang at the top of its steps, and beyond them stood a series of open double doors. Bongo led the way up the stairs, his many legs making short work of the climb. They walked through a set of doors into a huge lobby.

Despite the size of the space, there was only one counter and one officer sitting behind it. A line six or seven people long had formed.

"Shit," Carina blurted as they joined the end of it. "This is fucking ridiculous."

"Calm down," said Bongo. "Losing your temper will get you nowhere here. If we're lucky they'll only turf you out, but that'll be the end of your chance to help your friends."

She took his words to heart. While they waited, she closed her eyes and recalled the techniques Nai Nai had taught her to steady her mind and body before making a Cast in difficult circumstances. She took control of her breathing and mental focus as the minutes passed and they moved closer to the front of the line. By the time they reached it, most of her tension had eased and she could address the person on the other side of the desk composedly.

"Some of my companions were brought here, and I'd like to see what I can do to help them."

"Names?" the officer asked, not looking up from her interface.

Carina began to state them. Before she was halfway through, the officer interrupted, saying, "Yeah, they're here. They have some pretty serious charges. Causing a fracas, disturbing the peace, assaulting a justice officer. You're lucky you arrived in time to see them before their sentence is carried out. They're due to be spaced in fifteen minutes." She looked up. "You want to see them, right? Say a final goodbye and hear their last wishes?"

"No!" Carina yelled, the calm demeanor she'd worked to achieve falling away in an instant.

The officer frowned and reached for a button on the counter.

"Sorry," said Bongo. "Please, there's no need to summon anyone. We aren't here to make any trouble. What my companion means is yes, we would like to see them very much. I understand there's a fee involved?"

"But can't we..." said Carina, the sound of her blood pulsing in her ears. "Isn't there anything...?"

Something hard and sharp touched her hand. She looked down. Bongo had put one of his claws on it. Was he trying to calm her, or console her?

"Yes, there is a fee," said the officer. "Let me see. It's per person, and there are seven in custody. Do you want to see all of them?"

"I, er, I don't..."

What a question. Of all the mercs who had gotten themselves into trouble, the only one she knew well was Hsiao. Did she want to see them all only to say farewell before they faced an excruciating death?

"Yes," she replied, "all of them."

Fuck.

Numbly, she held up her wrist to the scanner as the figure appeared on the screen.

"Through there," said the officer.

A door opened in the wall to the rear of her desk. Carina trudged toward it, every step leaden as she dreaded what lay beyond. Bongo scuttled beside her.

"Hey," called the officer, "she only paid for herself, not you too."

The alien hesitated.

"Ah, what the hell," the officer said. "Go ahead. I'm feeling generous."

CHAPTER 22

*T*he *Peregrine* felt silent and empty to Parthenia, despite the racket Darius and Nahla were making as they raced up and down the passageway outside the bridge. She'd never been the only adult aboard a starship before. It had been stressful enough finding the way to the right exit and getting the children into their EVA suits and through the umbilicus by herself.

What if something went wrong?

Carina had seemed very anxious when she left the restaurant with Bongo. The mercs were in trouble and Hsiao was with them. What if Carina couldn't help them? Bongo had said they might be spaced. Carina had said Lakshmi law was extremely strict, but Parthenia hadn't known it was *that* strict.

If she had to take her siblings back to the *Bathsheba*, she didn't have a clue how to fly the ship. Darius probably knew more than her. If she had to resort to allowing him to take the controls, who knew what he might do?

The children had been playing for ages, and she'd been growing more and more irritated by the noise they were making. She was tired, and she felt nauseated as well, as if she'd eaten something that didn't agree with her, though she hadn't had anything at the restaurant. Maybe that was the problem. Maybe she should have eaten something.

She strode to the open doorway to tell her brother and sister to be quiet, but what she saw changed her mind. She'd thought they were having a regular running race even though Nahla's limp would slow her down. But in fact Nahla had an arm over Darius's shoulder and he was helping her, not very successfully, which was causing them to giggle and shriek as they staggered along.

A lump rose in her throat.

"What's wrong, Parthenia?" Darius asked, picking up on her feelings right away.

There was no point in telling him she was fine. He knew she wasn't, and he would be hurt or confused by the lie.

"I'm wondering what's happening with Carina and the Black Dogs on the station."

Darius and Nahla had drawn to a halt. Her brother said, "Why don't you ask her?"

"Lakshmi comms don't work outside the station."

"Oh. Then why don't you Send to her?"

"I can't."

Didn't he know?

"Why not? Did you forget your elixir?"

"No, I have some, but...Darius, we can't Cast anymore. Didn't anyone tell you?"

The little boy's eyes grew round. "No, no one told me. How come?"

"We don't know. It just happened. That's why it took us so long to find you when you and Nahla were on Deck Zero. We were Casting Locate, but it wasn't working."

It seemed remarkable Darius wasn't aware the mages had

lost their ability, but when she thought about it, it made sense. He'd been unconscious when they'd realized what had happened, and since then he'd been recovering with Nahla. He must have missed the discussions they'd had or he hadn't been listening properly.

"That's bad," he commented. "I like Casting."

"So do I," said Parthenia.

"Will it come back?"

"No one knows. Maybe one day. I hope so."

"You're like me now," said Nahla.

"Yeah," Darius replied, crestfallen. "I don't feel like playing." He stepped out from under Nahla's arm.

"It's okay," said Nahla. "Don't be sad. Let's run again."

But Darius walked away from her, heading for the bridge.

"Darius!" Nahla called. "I need you to help me run."

"I'll help you later. I want to rest." He passed Parthenia and sat in the copilot's seat.

"Will you help me run, Parthenia?" Nahla asked.

"Of course."

She took her sister's hand. For a few minutes she trotted slowly alongside as Nahla hobbled up and down, but then Nahla said, "I want to stop. I'm tired."

Parthenia suspected she wasn't actually tired. She guessed she didn't find her older sister half as much fun to play with as Darius.

"Okay," she said. "Why don't you go sit down for a while?"

"Is Carina coming back soon?" asked Nahla.

"I think so."

When *would* Carina return? It had been hours since they'd parted ways. Surely she must have fixed the problem with the mercs by now. Not being able to Send to her was frustrating.

As she stepped into the bridge, Parthenia was confused to see Darius head down with his eyes closed and his lips moving silently. He appeared to be Sending to someone, though she knew that was impossible. She helped Nahla to sit down and opened the interface for her to give her something to do.

Darius continued to have a private conversation in his head.

Then she noticed her elixir bottle on the console in front of him. The cap was off and a few drops sat on the surface. He clearly hadn't believed her when she'd told him the mages could no longer Cast and he'd wanted to try for himself. Poor Darius. He was suffering the same shock and unhappiness she and their siblings had experienced over the last couple of days. It would take time for him to get used to the fact.

He opened his eyes and looked up. "Carina says hi."

Parthenia froze. "What?"

"I *can* Cast. You were wrong."

"Darius, I…"

He *had* to be deluded.

"Darius, are you sure—"

"It's okay. Carina was surprised too."

Was it possible? He seemed very confident, and it wasn't like him to lie.

"Well, goodness!" Parthenia sat down.

No one had tested him. When they'd learned they'd lost their abilities, everyone had been so devastated, no one had thought to check if the same applied to their youngest brother. Even Jace hadn't suggested it. And Darius hadn't been aware of the news so he hadn't tested himself. But it was possible he was the odd one out. As a Spirit Mage, he was different from everyone else.

"You really Sent to Carina?"

"Uh huh."

"That's wonderful. I'm so happy you can still Cast."

What she said was true, but she couldn't help feeling some-what jealous as well. What was worse, she knew Darius was aware.

"Me too!" he said. "Now I'll be able to Cast for everyone, so it won't be so bad for you after all."

"Thanks, that's kind, Darius. What did Carina say when you spoke to her? Is she on her way back with the mercs?"

"No, she didn't talk about that. Parthenia, she was really sad, but she wouldn't tell me why."

CHAPTER 23

The guard opened the cell door. Bongo said he would wait for her outside as Carina went in. The Black Dogs were a sorry sight. Rees had a black eye and a busted lip, Van Hasty's nose and knuckles were bleeding, and though Hsiao didn't have a scratch on her, Carina had never seen her look so down.

Did the mercs know they had about ten minutes left to live?

"Five minutes," the guard said. "That's all you get."

"But—"

"That's it. We need time to get them to the airlock. Gotta keep to the schedule, or there's hell to pay."

He closed the door and the lock faintly hissed as it shut.

"What did he say?" Rees asked. "Something about an airlock?"

They didn't know.

"Thank the stars you're here," said Hsiao. "What took you so long? Can you get us out?"

"Or can you get us separate cells at least?" asked Van Hasty. "There isn't room to spit in here."

"What the hell were you all thinking?!" Carina yelled. "Didn't you hear the warning I gave you on the *Peregrine*? Hsiao, I can't believe you let this happen! You were with me on the first visit. You know how strict they are here."

"I know," the pilot winced. "I tried to stop the fight, but things got out of hand. When the guards arrived I kept my distance, but the bar patrons pointed me out and said I was with them."

"Great. Just great."

"Is it really bad?" asked Hsiao. "Do you know our sentence? Are we going to be here a long time?"

"No, you're…" Carina choked up.

Her chest heaved as she fought not to cry. She'd had her fallings out with Hsiao, but she counted the woman as a friend, one of the very few friends she'd ever made. And though she wasn't close with Rees, Van Hasty or the other mercs, they were like extended family.

Why oh why had she come to Lakshmi Station? The trip had turned into a disaster. The mages had lost their powers, and now seven mercs were about to die, including the only experienced pilot they had.

"We're *what*?" Hsiao asked. "Carina, what's wrong?"

"We could apologize to the guys we scrapped with if it would help," Rees offered.

"I'm not apologizing," said Van Hasty. "They started it."

Carina was tempted to ask what had happened. Where were the people the mercs had fought? Were they going to be spaced too? Or were the Lakshmi authorities picking on the outsiders?

But there was no time. They had only a few minutes left.

She took a deep breath. "Guys, there's no good way to say this, but your sentence for what you did is execution. You're going to be spaced very soon. If there's anything you want me to tell anyone, any message you want to pass on, you have to say it—"

Her words were lost in the mercs' cries of dismay and

outrage. Rees got in her face and demanded she do something to save them. Van Hasty began wailing, while Hsiao only looked blank with disbelief.

"Shut up!" Carina shouted. "Shut up!" She pushed Rees's chest to get him away from her. "There's nothing I can do. I told you! I warned you. And then like a bunch of dumb morons you go ahead and get into a fight anyway. What did you think would—"

"Carina?"

The voice came from inside her head, and it was very familiar.

"Darius?!"

The mercs continued to holler and sob. A couple of them were banging on the cell door, demanding to be released.

"Hey Carina," said Darius. "What's up? Where are you?"

"I'm...Darius, you can Send?"

"Yeah, I can. Parthenia said we can't Cast anymore, but I thought I would try anyway, and I can! It's great, huh?"

"Yeah, it's great." She swallowed, grief and dread over the mercs' impending deaths at war inside her with wonder and relief that Darius hadn't lost his mage ability.

"You don't seem very happy," he said. "Is something wrong?"

"Yes. No. I mean, I can't talk to you now. I'll see you later, when I get back, okay?"

"Okay. The Cast is fading now anyway. See you soon, Carina."

He was gone.

The mercs were quietening down, the reality of what was about to happen no doubt settling on them.

"How long do we have?" asked Hsiao, pale-faced.

"A couple of minutes at most."

"That's it?" the pilot's voice was a whisper.

"I'm sorry," said Carina.

It was all too much. The tenuous grip she'd been holding on

herself broke and tears overflowed her eyes. "I'm so sorry. If there was anything I could do…"

Silence descended except for Van Hasty's quiet sobs.

"No," said one of the mercs. "*I'm* sorry. I should have kept my cool when that guy grabbed me."

"No point in going over it now," said another merc. "What's done is done. I never thought I'd go out like this. Thought I'd get killed in a battle, or my ship would get blown up, and that'd be it."

"I always knew the black would get me in the end," another muttered.

The cell door opened.

"Time's up," said the guard.

"Can't we have just another minute?" asked Carina, still weeping. None of the mercs had told her their last wishes yet.

"Time's *up*," repeated the guard. "Unless you want to step outside without a suit too?"

"Stars," Carina said, "I'm going."

She found herself suddenly enveloped in a tight hug.

Hsiao had grabbed her. "I'm sorry for what I said about your brother."

"It's okay," Carina cried into her shoulder. "I forgave you days ago."

The guard coughed.

"I have to go," she said.

"I know," said Hsiao, releasing her. "It's been good knowing you, Carina."

"And you."

"I hope you make it to Earth."

Carina took a final look at the seven men and women before leaving the cell.

Bongo accompanied her as she plodded toward the exit from the jail section. The other cells appeared empty, unsurprisingly. Other visitors to Lakshmi weren't so stupid as to get into a bar fight. But the mercs must have fought other people. Where were they? Why weren't they going to be spaced too? Or had they already been executed?

"What's happened to the others who took part in the fight, Bongo?" she asked. "Do you know?"

"No, but I guess they or someone they know paid the fine. Like I was saying at the restaurant, the people who profit from Lakshmi are fabulously rich, and it's usually only those types who get into—"

"*What?!*"

Carina had been so deep in despair, the sense of what the alien had said took time to filter through to her. "What fine?! No one told me there was a fine! Why didn't you tell me?"

"Oh, it's very expensive. You probably don't want to—"

"Where do I pay? Do I still have time?" She picked up her pace. "Where do I go? Tell me where to go!"

"The accounts section is…let me see…I'm not sure if I remember."

Swiveling to face the alien, she scooped him up and held him at eye level while his many legs uselessly windmilled in mid-air. "You'd better remember, fast. If my friends die, you're the next one who'll be spaced!"

CHAPTER 24

*T*hough Bongo's culture was pacifist, his species didn't give a shit about each other, not if money was involved. He hadn't imagined for a second Carina would be willing to spend more than half the large sum she possessed to buy her companions' freedom, so he hadn't bothered suggesting it. His omission had almost cost the mercs their lives, so it was with mixed feelings she said goodbye to him when she left Lakshmi Station for a second time.

As she pulled herself through the umbilicus to return to the *Peregrine* with the mercs, Hsiao spoke to her over the comm. "He really didn't tell you until after you left our cell?"

"Of course he didn't," replied Carina. "Do you think I would have let you all believe you were going to die as a joke?"

"It's just hard to understand," said the pilot. "I mean—"

"He's a different species. You can't expect him to think like us."

"I know, but he seemed nice."

"He *is* nice, but remember how his cousin tried to fleece us? Money has an even higher value to them than to us."

"You'd think after living all that time at the station he would understand humans better. You said the other people in the fight had their fines paid too, so he's seen what we do."

"I asked him about that. He said that amount of money is nothing to rich Lakshmi-ites."

Hsiao whistled. "Holy smoke. I didn't realize the quantity of creds washing around that station even existed in the galaxy."

Carina reached the *Peregrine's* airlock and hauled herself inside. Van Hasty, Rees, and the other mercs were already waiting.

"You don't know the half of it," she said to Hsiao. "Wait until I tell you where the rich got their money."

Her boots hit the deck.

When Hsiao arrived, Rees shut the outer hatch and activated pressurization.

"Where?" the pilot asked.

At the same time, Darius spoke in her head. "Carina? Are you back?"

"Yes, sweetheart. See you in a minute."

Her HUD showed normal atmosphere. She removed her helmet. "I have to see the kids," she told Hsiao. "I'll talk to you later."

"Uhhh..." said Rees. He was holding his helmet awkwardly.

She paused. "Did you want to say something?"

"Yeah," said Van Hasty, her head down. "We're...uh..."

"We're sorry about the fight," said Rees.

"Yeah, we're sorry," Van Hasty echoed. "And we want to thank you for paying all that money to save us from..." She faltered.

"It's not a problem," said Carina.

In fact, it was. With more than half their funds gone, they were now restricted on fitting out the *Bathsheba* with defensive weapons. The mercs' stunt could cost everyone their lives in the long run, but they knew that.

"Well, thanks anyway," Rees said.

The other Black Dogs nodded in agreement.

Carina quickly removed her EVA suit and set off to find Darius, Nahla, and Parthenia. Darius hadn't said where they were, but she guessed they would be on the bridge.

It turned out she was right. Darius greeted her with a hug and so did Nahla after she'd limped over. Carina's heart ached at the reminder that the visit to Lakshmi Station had been a disappointment on another level. It was hard to face the reality that her little sister would never be the same as she'd been before her accident. In many ways she hadn't changed. She was still cheeky and adventurous, but she'd lost that spark of brilliance that set her apart from everyone else.

"Isn't it wonderful that Darius can Cast?" Parthenia asked, apparently unable to keep the note of envy out of her voice.

Carina knew how she felt. She was happy for their brother yet she couldn't help feeling a little jealous too. "Yes, it is." Turning to Darius she said, "You always surprise us with what you can do. I'm glad we still have one mage in the family."

Another child his age would have taken her words at face value, but Darius felt the emotions underlying them. He smiled sadly. "I wish you could Cast too. Maybe you'll be able to again one day."

Parthenia put a hand to her head and squeezed her eyes shut.

"Are you okay?" Carina asked.

"Not completely. I've been feeling ill since we got back."

"Go and lie down. Hsiao will be here in a minute to fly us to the *Bathsheba*. One of the ship's doctors can take a look at you."

"Yes, all right."

It wasn't like Parthenia to agree so easily. Carina looked at her more closely. She *did* look pale.

After the episode with the mercs, she didn't feel so great herself.

"What happened at the station?" Parthenia asked, halting in the open doorway. "What took you so long?"

"That's a long story, and not one for telling in front of the kids. I'll fill you in another time, but you should know we're not as rich as we were."

"Ugh, that's a shame. I hope we can still afford some treatment for Nahla."

* * *

WHEN CARINA ARRIVED at the *Bathsheba*, she discovered another disaster had occurred in her absence. Jackson's prosthetic arm had been severed in an accident with the lasers on the hull.

"I don't believe it!" she exclaimed when she found out. "I can't leave you guys alone for two minutes without something terrible happening. What'll it be next time I step out of the ship? Is she going to blow up? Is someone going to fly her into the star? Or invite the Regians to a party?"

"Calm down," said Bryce. "He only lost his prosthetic. It could have been a lot worse."

"It *is* a lot worse," she retorted. "I haven't told you what happened on Lakshmi yet."

"Yeah," said Jackson, "what went down over there? Van Hasty and Rees look like someone stole their puppy."

"Before you tell us," Bryce said, "you should know the second bit of bad news. It's probably better to get it all out the way now."

Carina pressed her palms to her face and said between her hands, "Are you sure I need to know?"

Bryce patted her shoulder. "Don't worry. No one's died."

"Thank the stars for that. Things were touch and go for a while on Lakshmi. I don't think I could stand another life and death crisis."

"Jace is in sick bay," said Bryce.

Carina's hands dropped to her sides. "Oh no! What's wrong with him?"

"The docs don't know. They're still trying to figure it out. I went to see him and found him in bed. He didn't want to bother anyone. Kept saying he'd be okay after a good sleep. I called a medic to take a look at him and she recommended sick bay right away."

"Shit."

Parthenia was also feeling unwell. Was it related? She would have to tell her sister to get checked out.

"Is that it?" she asked. "No other catastrophes to report?"

"That's it," Bryce said. "You can tell us what happened on Lakshmi now."

"Well…" said Carina, wondering where to start.

Then everything went black.

CHAPTER 25

$\mathcal{C}$arina opened her eyes. She was lying on her back in a bed, and the air smelt faintly medicinal.

Sick bay?

She moved to sit up.

A thousand hammers instantly beat on her skull and the room lurched. Her stomach began to force its way up into her throat. Swallowing hard, she lay down. She remained motionless, recovering, though her head didn't stop hurting.

The second time she tried to move, she only ventured to look to one side.

Parthenia was in the neighboring bed, her eyes closed.

This time, it was Carina's heart that lurched as she feared the worst. But her sister was only asleep, breathing regularly and gently. There was a pink flush to her skin.

She didn't attempt moving again. It only made the hammers beat harder. As she watched her sister, she went over what she remembered prior to her lost time. She'd been talking with Bryce and Jackson. Jackson was missing his prosthetic, and Bryce had said something about...she frowned. Jace. He'd said Jace was in the sick bay.

Now she and Parthenia were here too.

Three mages all sick at once? It was too much of a coincidence. Something heinous was going on. It couldn't be anything to do with Lakshmi because Jace hadn't been there, and no one on the station knew about him. It had to be the work of someone aboard the *Bathsheba*.

Was that why they'd lost their ability to Cast? Had someone discovered a substance that would take away their abilities?

It seemed unlikely. As far as she knew, no one understood how or why mages could Cast, so it should be impossible to know how to affect the process.

Plus, their sickness had begun days after they'd discovered they'd lost their abilities. The two things weren't related, or only tangentially. Everyone knew what had happened to the mages. It was possible their enemy had only decided to make their move because they felt safer now. Not that she or anyone else would have Cast to hurt them anyway, but they probably didn't know that.

Perhaps the person had spiked their food or drink with something poisonous. That might explain why Darius and the twins hadn't been affected. They tended to choose and print their own food.

She began to mentally run through the people who had the opportunity to adulterate her meals or drinks. It was a short list. If the water dispenser in the galley nearest her suite had been contaminated, it would have affected far more people than just her. And she usually ate with Bryce. If their dishes had been poisoned, he should be in sick bay too.

An impossible idea began to form in her mind. Surely it couldn't have been—

Bryce walked in. "The doc comm'd me to say you'd woken up. She said she'll be in soon. She's waiting for some test results. How are you feeling?" He drew up a chair and sat down beside her.

"Like shit," she replied. "What happened?"

"You fainted. Jackson caught you one-handed. It was pretty impressive."

"Fainted, huh?" Come to think of it, she hadn't been feeling great for a while. The farce with the mercs at Lakshmi had distracted her. "And what were you doing while this was going on?"

"Watching in wonder." He was smiling, but then his expression turned serious. "You gave me a fright. The docs don't seem to know what's wrong with you."

"How long have I been out?"

"An hour or so."

"What about Parthenia? And Jace? Did the doc say anything about them?"

His expression grew more serious. "You can add Ferne and Oriana to the list. They're in another room."

"The twins as well? Damn. Darius?"

"He's fine."

"Thank the stars."

"The docs think you all have the same problem, whatever it is."

"Makes sense." The throbbing in her head surged and she let out a groan.

Bryce gently laid his hand on the side of her face. "It's really bad, isn't it? Parthenia was saying she felt like buffaloes were stampeding through her brain before her sedative kicked in."

"She did? That's why they put her out?"

"Yeah, they said it would help her to get some rest. Carina, Darius told me he can still Cast. Is that right?"

"It is. He Sent to me when he was on the *Peregrine* and I was in Lakshmi. What a bunch of idiots we were to not check with him. I could have sworn I'd asked him to try a Cast, but apparently not."

"But if that's so, can't he Heal you all?"

"It doesn't work like that. Heal fixes injuries, like cuts, wounds, burns, and broken bones. It doesn't cure diseases. Don't you think I would have cured you when you had Ithiyan plague if I could? It would have been easy for me. And I would have Healed Ma in a heartbeat. You know that."

"Of course. I wasn't thinking."

She didn't go on to tell him Heal also couldn't save people who were near death, but she didn't. It wasn't strictly true. A Spirit Mage could do it, but only at the risk of killing themselves in the process. Darius had done it for her once, and she didn't want him to ever be put in the same position again. It was better to not remind Bryce of the fact.

She looked at her sleeping sister. They'd had their differences, but she didn't know what she would do if anything bad happened to her.

Watching her watching Parthenia, Bryce said, "Have you ever considered the fact she might be your full sister?"

Carina almost sat up in surprise at his comment but managed to stop herself just in time. "What makes you say that?"

"You look incredibly alike. No one who saw you wouldn't guess you were related. And though I only saw your mother a little, I'd say you both resemble her closely. I can't see anything of Stefan Sherrerr in Parthenia."

Carina had been three years old when Stefan had tricked Ma and Ba into revealing themselves as mages and taken them prisoner. She didn't know the exact dates it all happened, but it was possible Ma had already been pregnant before Stefan began raping her. She might not have known it, or she might have kept the fact secret the rest of her life, fearing her tormentor would kill Parthenia if he found out.

"Stars," she said quietly, "you could be right."

"Something to think about. You share similar traits too."

"What kind of traits?"

"Oh, I'll let you figure that out."

Huh. They were both stubborn, argumentative, and sometimes difficult to get along with. It was definitely something to think about.

Though Bryce spoke in a teasing tone, his face remained full of concern.

"I'll ask the doc to give you a painkiller," he said.

He began to get to his feet, but at that moment Dr Asher arrived.

The Black Dogs had two military doctors: Asher and Baxter. Dr Asher was a woman in late middle age who had worked for the band ever since Carina could remember, and Baxter was a man in his twenties who had joined just before Carina reconnected with the band. He was young for a merc. Most had completed a few tours by the time dishonorable discharge, mental instability, or a traumatic event drove them to pursue professional soldiering.

To Carina's knowledge, Baxter had never explained why he'd chosen the more haphazard, riskier life among the Black Dogs over a space fleet career and guaranteed pension. And, as was usual, no one had asked him.

Carina preferred Dr Asher. She wasn't exactly what you would call motherly, unless motherhood entailed barking at people with any non-life-threatening ailment that they needed to get over themselves. But if she took your injury or ailment seriously, you could trust her to do her level best to help, and she never treated the kids with anything less than her utmost care and concern. Whereas Baxter was always distant and offhand, regardless of the severity of his patient's condition.

"I have to hand it to you, Carina," Asher said as she walked in, "you guys have us stumped."

"You don't know what's wrong with us?" she asked, grimacing at her headache.

"Not a clue. You're hurting, right?" Asher held up a pressure syringe.

Bryce helped Carina sit up.

"This won't knock me out, will it?" she asked as Asher lifted her sleeve. "I want to talk to you."

"No, it won't knock you out. It'll just take the edge off."

A cool blast from the syringe spread through her veins. The pain in her head eased. She could still feel it but the medication also made her care less about it.

"You really have no idea at all what's wrong with us?" she asked again, lying down.

"I know what you *don't* have," Asher replied. "You don't have any of the hundreds of viruses our antivirals can tackle or a bacterial infection. You don't have cancer and you aren't suffering from radiation sickness. The tests didn't show any genetic abnormalities only manifesting now either."

Carina found her last comment interesting. Whatever was different about mage genes, it didn't show up as abnormal. "I was wondering if we'd been poisoned."

The doctor's eyebrows rose. "You too, huh? A tox screen was the first test I ran. Zilch."

"That doesn't mean we weren't poisoned though, does it? Only that the test didn't pick it up."

"Isn't that a little paranoid?" Bryce asked. "Who would want to poison you?"

"It was the first test she ran," Carina protested.

"It was, but I have a complete lack of faith in humanity," Asher countered. "It seems I'm not alone."

"So what happens now?" asked Carina.

"We continue to monitor you, and Baxter and I will rack our brains to try to figure out what's wrong. We haven't exhausted all the possibilities yet, only ruled out the most common ailments."

"How are the twins and Jace doing?"

"About the same as you, only Ferne and Oriana complain more."

"Does the order we fell ill in mean anything?"

"Not necessarily. You all exhibited symptoms within twenty-four hours. That's a standard range, given the variability of the human response to illness."

"Do you think it has something to do with losing our mage powers?"

"The correlation would certainly be worth investigating if we knew the first thing about what you do—or used to be able to do. But unfortunately we don't, so we'll be ignoring that for now. Unless, of course, you can shed some light...?"

Carina shook her head. "I'm as much in the dark as you."

"That's what I thought."

CHAPTER 26

*C*arina had been in sick bay a week, and she was going out of her mind.

"Carina," Parthenia snapped. "Would you please stop huffing and puffing? It's bad enough being stuck in here as it is without having to listen to you all day."

"I can't help it. Something's happening but I don't know what. Bryce hasn't been in to see us today and I heard a commotion outside this morning. Since then, it's been silent. Why hasn't anyone told me what's going on?"

"Because you're sick. They don't want to bother you."

"It's more of a bother *not* to know. Why the big secret? Why would knowing what's happening hurt me?"

"Because you would fret and worry and get annoyed when they won't let you stick your oar in for once."

"I wouldn't be sticking my oar in. I'd be giving them the benefit of my advice. Anyway, I'm the unofficial leader of the mission. If something important happens I should know about it, even if I am sick."

"Oh, it hurts to be left out?" Parthenia asked archly. "Who would have thought?"

Carina cast a glance at her sister. She wasn't looking at her as she spoke. She was watching something on an interface, propped up in bed.

They were both on high doses of painkillers, anti-nausea medication and other medicinal treatments that counteracted their ever-worsening symptoms. If it hadn't been for the meds, neither of them would have been able to function at all. As it was, watching endless hours of mindless entertainment was about all they were capable of. That, and sniping at each other.

More than once, Carina had contemplated asking the docs to transfer her to another room. Spending time with Parthenia only added to her problems in dealing with this disease. She guessed they'd been put in the same room so they could keep each other company. What a great idea that had been.

She'd thought about Bryce's guess that they were full sisters. As the days had passed, she'd begun to believe he was right. At certain angles, Parthenia looked like a slightly younger version of herself. If they'd had the same hairstyle their similarity would have been even more apparent.

Personality-wise, their characters were not quite so alike, despite Bryce's hints, but their differences could be explained by their upbringing. Parthenia was far more fussy and particular than her, especially about things like manners and decorum. Carina couldn't have been more different. Spending your adolescence on the streets and then living among mercs didn't exactly teach you the refinements of polite society.

Their greatest difference was Parthenia seemed to feel responsible for the welfare of all humanity, while Carina—she freely admitted to herself—only really cared about people she knew. That could be explained by their upbringing too. Parthenia had grown up the eldest child in a very dysfunctional family. She'd probably had the concept of duty to others drilled into her, whereas Carina had been trained by Nai Nai to look after herself and trust no one.

"Do you *have* to do that?" Parthenia asked, apparently aware Carina was watching her.

"Sorry." Carina turned away. She hadn't mentioned Bryce's guess about their shared parentage and she wasn't sure she should. It might make her sister dislike her even more.

"What are you thinking?" asked Parthenia.

"I'm still wondering what's happening out there."

"For goodness sake! If that matters that much, why don't you go and find out?"

"You know, I think I will."

"No, I didn't mean it. We have to rest. That's what Dr Asher said."

"And it's doing us a lot of good, isn't it? We're getting sicker and sicker every day, and every day they up our doses. What's going to happen when they can't increase them any more? I can't stand lying here passively like an animal waiting to be slaughtered. I'm going to find out what's going on or die trying."

Even she had to admit her words were melodramatic. She didn't think they were close to death yet. She hoped they weren't, not for her own sake but for Jace and her siblings. But her current situation was beyond frustrating. She felt helpless and useless. She had to act.

Pushing back her covers, she swung her legs over the side of the bed.

"Carina, cut it out. Stay where you are or I'll call the medic."

Carina had argued with the docs over their constant surveillance of her and her sister. Being watched all the time made her uncomfortable. She'd made them agree to turn off the monitoring when at least one of them was awake and able to sound the alarm in a sudden crisis.

"Why do you have to be so damned prim and proper all the time?" she asked her sister. "It's okay to break the rules now and then. That's what they're for."

"That isn't what rules are for and you know it. Look what happened on Lakshmi when the Black Dogs broke the rules."

"Parthenia, my dearest sister, would you please *shut up?*"

Carina had eased herself down from her bed while they bickered and was now standing unsteadily next to it. Her prolonged inactivity had made her weak. Coupled with her illness, she could barely stand. She felt like getting back into bed and having a long nap, but it would seem like she was obeying Parthenia, and *that* would only happen over her dead body.

She pulled on a robe lying over the bed and shuffled toward the door.

"Come back!" Parthenia called. "You're sick. Go back to bed."

When Carina didn't respond, she continued, "You look pathetic. You're making a fool of yourself."

Carina winced. Not because the words stung, though they did a little, but because they weren't something Parthenia would ordinarily say. She had to be echoing her monstrous father. Stefan Sherrerr probably said exactly that kind of thing to Parthenia and her siblings while they were growing up.

Not her monstrous *father*, Carina corrected herself. Her monstrous step-father.

As she reached the door it slid open. She stepped out into the triage room, which was empty. In the center of the floor were a few spots of blood. Someone had been hurt!

Increasing her pace to a slow walk, she crossed the room to peer in at the twins' and Jace's windows. All were sleeping. Relieved it didn't appear any of them were injured, she continued her journey, sneaking past the staff office and out into the passageway.

Her legs were already aching and her surroundings seemed to be underwater, moving to and fro as if in a choppy current. Propping herself with one hand on the bulkhead for support, she went on.

If only she could Cast Transport. The *Bathsheba* was so

goddamned big and she wasn't sure where to go. She couldn't comm anyone to ask them. They would only alert the medics about her escape.

A little voice at the back of her head that sounded suspiciously like Nai Nai's scolded her for being dumb, but something drove her on. She couldn't let others take over the running of the ship. What might happen to her siblings if she wasn't there to protect them? Ma had entrusted them to her care. She wasn't going to let her down.

She stumbled and fell.

The effort to get back to her feet threatened to take the last of her strength but she managed it. As she became upright once more, she heard distant voices. There seemed to be a lot of them. The Black Dogs must have got together for some reason. Were they fighting? That would explain the blood on the triage room floor.

It would be odd if the mercs were attacking each other. Though they weren't the most stable people, they'd generally gotten along pretty well since they'd escaped the Regians and dealt with the mutiny attempt of the Lotacryllans. Adversity had bonded them more than ever, she'd thought. But maybe the trouble with Van Hasty, Rees, and the others who had nearly been executed had divided them. The seven mercs were responsible for losing over half the ship's funds. That wouldn't sit well with the rest of the Black Dogs.

Weakness was overcoming her. She knew if she tried to make it back to the sick bay and act like nothing had happened, she would never make it. Better to press on and hopefully find out what was being hidden from her.

The voices were growing louder. She was heading in the right direction. She could even hear snatches of conversation.

"I've already explained," someone said, "this isn't a commercial venture."

Bryce.

"We understand," another voice replied. "We're here to appeal to your sense of human decency. Won't you at least consider our request? We have so much to offer you. Skills, creds, healthy females for breeding."

Healthy females for breeding?!

Carina let out a gasp of shock. The deck seemed to rise up at her, and that was the last thing she remembered.

CHAPTER 27

"**Y**ou have to stop making a habit of this," said Bryce as she came around for the second time.

She was back in sick bay.

It was like she was living a waking nightmare: passing out, waking up in a sick bay bed; passing out, waking up in a sick bay bed.

Yet it was better than not waking up.

"What's happening?" she asked groggily. "Am I going to be used for breeding?"

"*What*?!" Bryce put a hand to her forehead. "Are you getting another fever? You don't feel hot. Ohhh…" His features cleared as he understood. "You overheard the leader of the party from Marchon."

"Marchon?" Carina mumbled. Brain fog was clogging her thinking, but it still sounded wrong that people from Marchon were aboard the *Bathsheba*.

"I was going to tell you about it after we dealt with them," Bryce explained. "I didn't want to worry you unnecessarily."

She was about to say something similar to what she'd told Parthenia earlier, that she worried more when she *didn't* know what was going on, but she couldn't utter so many words all at once. All she managed was, "What's happened?"

"We have visitors. Jackson and Justus are with them now. I wanted to check you were okay after the medics got you back into bed. You know, if I hadn't heard you fall in the passageway you could have been lying there a while before someone found you. Please don't do that again. I'm sorry, but I have to go now."

Her head was beginning to clear a little. She touched his arm. "Tell me what's going on."

He hesitated. "It would take too long to explain. Jackson and Justus need my input to sort this problem out. But you can see it all on the security vids. I'll find them for you."

Dr Asher burst into the room, her expression full of fury. "I'm reliably informed you were found unconscious in a passageway a hundred meters from here." As she spoke, she marched to Carina's side. "So you repay all my hard work in treating you by leaving your bed and wandering around the ship, hm?" She pushed up Carina's sleeve to her shoulder and pressed the cool steel head of a pressure syringe into her bicep.

The relief from confusion and aches and pains that spread from the injection was blissful.

"Listen to me, young lady," said Asher, leaning close. "As it apparently wasn't obvious to you that you need to stay put, I'm making it an express order. You've been warned. Defy me at your peril. I'll be back soon to see what damage you've done to yourself. One of my more deserving patients needs me right now."

She stomped out.

"Well, that's *you* told," Bryce remarked. "Seriously, Carina, that was a dumb stunt you pulled. You're not invincible, and you're not vital to the running of the ship. We can cope without your input and we want to. Everyone wants you to get better, not kill yourself."

He reached for the interface next to the bed and gave commands for it to bring up the relevant vidfeeds.

"Can you sit up?" he asked.

She nodded.

He helped her to a sitting position and swung the screen around on its arm so it faced her.

"Take it easy," he said. "I'll come back and update you as soon as I can." He bent down to kiss the top of her head, and then he was gone.

While all this was going on, Carina hadn't been able to see Parthenia's reaction. Predictably, her sister was giving her a hard-eyed stare. As soon as their gazes met, Parthenia curled a lip in disgust and turned away.

A heavy weight settled on Carina's chest and her ribs felt constricted. She struggled to breathe, but it wasn't anything to do with her illness. Blinking away the blurriness in her vision, she told the interface to play the vids.

The first was a recording of the outside of the ship. Another ship was approaching—a battered, pockmarked craft far smaller than the *Bathsheba*. Most starships were. Her thrusters reversed and the ship slowed to a stop.

Frustratingly, there was no audio with the recording. The foreign starship must have hailed the *Bathsheba*. Carina would have liked to hear the conversation that took place afterward, but her mind was too befuddled to find the recording made on the bridge.

The colony ship's weapons were old and inadequate to protect her from a sustained attack, but no one aboard her would have gone down without a fight. No pulses had been fired, however, which meant the Black Dogs had agreed to meet the visitors.

A short, rigid umbilicus extended from the newcomers' ship and disappeared out of view as it attached to the *Bathsheba's* hull. The recording showed nothing more. The umbilicus wall was opaque, but the visitors must have crossed it and come aboard.

What had happened in the triage room? Who had dripped blood on the deck?

Bryce had found the vid for her.

She watched the sick bay doors draw apart and men pour in. A few were Black Dogs. Bryce was there too, but most of the rest were unfamiliar. Dressed in leathers, rough-shaven and shaggy haired, the men looked nothing like the people from neighboring systems she'd seen on Lakshmi. She guessed only soldiers or wealthy citizens could visit the station. These men were different.

They were clustered around an individual who sagged, supported by his companions, his arms over the shoulders of two of them.

Dr Baxter appeared from the staff room.

"Please help," said one of the men. "His bleeding won't stop and our blood generator's broken."

"All right," said Baxter. "Put him over there."

But as the men moved the patient slipped from their grasp. There were too many people around him to see what happened, but Carina heard the thud of him hitting the deck. They gathered him up quickly and carried him to the bed. Conversations went on between the visitors and Bryce and the Black Dogs while Baxter did his work, but there were too many and the voices too indistinct to hear what was said.

She watched intently. Where had the Marchonish man gone after Baxter treated him?

With surprise and alarm, she saw him carried into a room.

So he was still in the sick bay?!

Ferne and Oriana were here, and Jace too. They were all ill and they could no longer Cast. What if the stranger tried to hurt them?

She pushed the interface out of the way and moved to get out of bed.

"What are you *doing?*" Parthenia demanded. "Don't tell me you're going to get up again!"

"Someone's here, in the sick bay."

"What are you talking about? I think you're getting delirious. I'm calling Dr Asher."

But there was no need. An instant later, Asher walked in.

Her eyes took in Carina's position, half out of bed. Her lips pursed and her eyes narrowed. "Am I going to have to permanently sedate you, Carina Lin?"

"That man they brought in," she said. "The Marchonish man. Where is he? Is he still here? Is he under guard? Who's protecting the mages?"

"How did you...?" Asher's gaze drifted to the interface. "I see." Her expression lost some of its rigidity. "You don't have anything to worry about."

"I really wish," Carina said through her teeth, mustering the little energy she had, "people would stop telling me to not worry."

After giving an exasperated sigh, the doctor said, "The man from Marchon isn't currently in a position to do anyone any harm, considering he is under general anesthetic while having a damaged artery repaired. Does that answer your questions?"

Carina flopped backward onto her pillows and closed her eyes.

"Honestly," Asher went on, "your lack of confidence in others is alarming. Do you think you're the only person capable of doing anything around here? Or that we would put your siblings and friend at risk of harm?"

"No," Carina murmured, lifting a weary hand to rub her eyes. "I just feel so useless."

This seemed to soften Dr Asher's attitude somewhat. "Baxter and I are doing everything we can to get to the bottom of your illness, but you have to let us do our job and stop making things harder for everyone, okay?"

"Okay."

"Good. Now stop worr—" Asher paused and smiled, tight-lipped. "Remember, everything is under control on the ship. You should get some sleep. Would you like something to help you drift off?"

"No, I'm fine."

When Asher had left, Carina pulled the interface in front of her again.

CHAPTER 28

*D*arius peeked around the edge of the door into the mission room. The Marchonish men were lounging around, sitting on the tables resting a foot on a chair or leaning against the walls. A couple were lying stretched out on the floor.

They were waiting for something.

Bryce, Justus, and a few Black Dogs had gone into another room and closed the door. Darius guessed the visitors were waiting to be told something, and Bryce and the others had to decide what to tell them. Maybe it had something to do with the weapons Carina wanted to buy at Lakshmi Station. Maybe the men from Marchon wanted to offer them a better price.

He didn't like them.

They felt dark and dangerous, kind of like Castiel and that man on Magog, Kai Wei, but not quite the same. The darkness in the Marchonish men was cloudy and murky, while Castiel and Wei's had been hard and sharp, like a black diamond.

Nahla giggled behind him. "I want to see too," she whispered.

"Okay," Darius replied. "Swap places."

He let Nahla go in front of him to take a turn at watching the visitors.

He wasn't sure they were supposed to be here, but on the other hand, no one had told them to stay away. Everyone had been busy for a few days. First, they'd been talking about Carina and the others being sick, and now they were talking about the men who had turned up and asked to come aboard.

He hadn't been able to hear everything they said, but he thought they wanted to come with them to Earth. Their leader had said something about them being tired of the war, and wanting to start a new life somewhere else.

They'd spotted the *Bathsheba* near Lakshmi Station and so they'd come to find out who owned her.

He didn't think any one person owned her. Everybody owned a little bit of her, even him and Nahla.

Nahla looked over her shoulder and whispered, "They're so big and ugly."

That was a bit rude, and he didn't join in her giggles. But Nahla couldn't help it. She'd been different since the accident on Deck Zero. It wasn't only her body that was different—she couldn't walk properly anymore—*she* was different too. She wasn't interested in finding things out and she was always happy to play with him now.

Before, she'd only played because she wanted to be kind. Now, he felt like *he* was the kind one.

At first, he'd been glad he didn't have to keep asking to get her attention. It was fun to have a full-time playmate. But then he'd felt bad. She was like that because she'd had an accident—an accident that was partly his fault. If he'd been thinking better, he would have Transported them out from Deck Zero before they fell asleep. Then Nahla wouldn't have been hurt.

He still loved her, but he wanted the old Nahla back, even if it meant returning to being lonely sometimes.

"Hey," said a gruff voice, "we have a little spy."

"What? Where? Oh, yeah. I see her."

Oh no! Nahla had been spotted.

"Come here, little one. We won't hurt you."

Darius grabbed the back of her shirt. "Don't go in," he hissed. She didn't understand the men were bad.

"I want to!" Nahla protested. She pulled her shirt out of his hand and limped into the room.

"That's it," said a voice. "What a cutie."

Darius didn't know what to do. Should he tell Bryce what Nahla was doing? They probably shouldn't be here. It was like Deck Zero all over again.

Clutching his elixir bottle, he followed her.

This time, he wouldn't let Nahla down.

She was smiling up at a tall man. This one looked older than the others, and though his friends' muscles showed on their stomachs and arms—they weren't wearing shirts, only vests, for some reason—the man Nahla was looking at was softer and flabbier. His gut overhung the top of his pants. If he'd been a Black Dog, the mercs would have teased him about it.

"What's your name?" the man asked Nahla.

"There's another one!" someone called out. "This place is a nursery. Kids everywhere."

"It'd be good if they'd let us fill it with our kids," someone else grumbled.

"I'm Nahla," Darius's sister replied, "and he's Darius."

He wanted to tell her to be quiet and to get out of here, but now he was in the room the men would hear him.

"Nahla and Darius," said the tall man. "Nice names. And you're a pretty little thing." He put a finger under Nahla's chin and tilted it up to look at her face more closely.

Darius didn't think anyone had ever told Nahla she was pretty. His family didn't talk much about how people looked, unless they were commenting on Ferne and Oriana's new clothes designs. Nahla seemed to like the compliment because she smiled wider.

"Take another turn about," said the man.

Nahla frowned. She didn't understand, but Darius did. He clutched his elixir bottle tighter.

"Damn, I wish those mercs would hurry up and come to a decision," said a Marchonish man.

"I don't," someone replied. "They can take as long as they like, as long as they say yes."

"What do they have to talk about?" said the first man. "We made them a great offer. Men, supplies, female companions. This is a colony ship but it's damn near empty from what I can tell. They need us. They need more bodies if they want to survive."

"You're right," his friend agreed. "How many have we seen? Ten, twenty? And all the time we've been waiting, we've seen no one else except these brats. Ship's damned near rattling like a pod with only three peas."

"You know, we might even outnumber them," a third man commented.

This drew a pause from the group.

Again, Darius knew exactly what was going through their minds. He would have to tell Bryce what he'd heard, but he wasn't going anywhere without Nahla. He wouldn't leave her alone with these men.

"Kid," the tall man said, appearing to remember her presence, "I said take a turn about."

"I don't understand."

"Walk around the room. Show us what you got."

Show us what you got?

Darius was confused too.

Frowning, Nahla stepped away from the man.

She'd walked badly ever since the accident. One of her feet dragged because her leg didn't lift it high enough and she had to rise up on the other leg. It made her go up and down when she walked. She looked a bit strange, but Darius had never said anything about it.

The tall man laughed. "This one's defective, guys. They should send her back to the shop." The other Marchonish men joined in his laughter.

Nahla halted and turned. She wasn't as smart as she used to be, but she wasn't so stupid she didn't know when she was being laughed at. Her hands clenched and she looked like she was going to cry.

"Be quiet," said Darius to the men. "Don't be mean."

"Aw, she your sister?" asked the pudgy. "It's okay. We're just having fun."

"Come on, Nahla," Darius said. "Let's go."

She hesitated, but then set off toward him.

The men burst out laughing again.

Darius thought it would all be over when Nahla reached him near the door and they would go, but one of the men walked in front of her, blocking her path.

"Don't leave us, honey. We love to watch you. Walk over there." He pointed at the corner of the room.

Nahla tried to step around him, but he was too quick. Everywhere she tried to go he was there first.

His friends were laughing loudly now.

Nahla's face crumpled and she began to sob.

"Leave her alone!" Darius shouted.

He ran over to grab her hand and drag her away, but the man thrust a hand into his chest and forced him back.

"Probably shouldn't do that," the tall man said. "They won't mind us messing with *her*, but it'll piss them off if we hurt one of their sons."

But the man blocking Nahla didn't take any notice. He pointed at the corner again. "Over there with your funny walk, little girl."

"No!" she yelled, her face red and wet.

Darius couldn't stand it any longer. He should probably go and find Bryce or someone else and tell them what was happening, but that would mean leaving Nahla alone, and who knew what the horrible visitors might do to her while he was gone?

He didn't have a choice. He had to protect his sister.

He unscrewed the lid from his elixir bottle and took a sip.

he Black Dogs had taken the men from the visiting
ship into the mission room. That's where they'd been
when she'd heard them talking. The security vid showed the
mercs telling the men to sit down and explain why they were
here. Thankfully, this vid had audio.

"Isn't it obvious?" a man who had introduced himself as
Porcher asked. He was taller and older than the rest, though far
less fit. He seemed to be their leader. "The same reason as you."

"Which is?" asked Van Hasty. She'd mostly healed up since
the bar fight on Lakshmi, only the cut on her nose remaining.

Giving her a dismissive look, Porcher addressed his reply in
the general direction of the male mercs. "We're colonists too.
We want a better future for our sons. As it is, they'll have to
choose between dying in battle or making a miserable living in
a munitions plant or mine. We plan on leaving Marchon and
settling somewhere else, preferably a virgin planet, but we're
open to suggestions."

"What happened to the guy in sick bay?" asked Jackson.

"A disagreement that turned into a fight, that's all," Porcher replied. "Tensions are high on Marchon. Our government's been pushing for another assault on Gugong. Some of us want to stick it to them, others want peace, saying the war's gone on too long. People are going crazy. We're at each other's throats. The man responsible for the injury apologized when he'd cooled down, but we couldn't stop the bleeding. We're grateful for your help."

"You say you're colonists," said Van Hasty, "but you didn't come here in a colony ship."

Again, Porcher acted as though a male merc had spoken, focusing on them for his reply. "That's what we've come to discuss with you."

Van Hasty's eyebrows rose and she held a hand in front of her face, as if checking she existed.

Carina smiled.

Porcher's weird behavior hadn't gone unnoticed among the Black Dog men either. Jackson's gaze met Van Hasty's before he returned his attention to the Marchonish leader.

"Let me guess," he said. "You want to be colonists but you're missing one essential requirement—a colony vessel. So you're here to hitch a ride."

With an abashed grin, Porcher nodded. "We spotted your ship ten days ago, but it took us a while to gather everyone and make our way to you. We've been planning this for years, though to be honest at times it seemed like an impossible dream. We've brought plenty of supplies as well as equipment for settling the new planet. Soil-breakers, seeds, water purifiers, generators, medicines, dwelling kits, the lot. And we're young and strong. We didn't bring anyone over fifty. I barely made the cut off myself." He smiled again and ran a hand over his hair.

"Over the years, as we talked about leaving Marchon, the biggest problem was we didn't know where to go. We're at war with the nearest habitable planets. We would never be accepted there. And, to be honest, we aren't exactly sure what the other options are. All we knew was we needed a bigger, more powerful ship than we had if we wanted to go anywhere else. And then you guys turned up. The galaxy's a big place, right? There has to be a better world, a better life for us somewhere."

Carina stopped the recording. She felt a smidgen of sympathy for the would-be colonists, despite their odd attitude to women. Decades of war must have taken its toll on their world. Rather than working to improve the general standard of living for all their citizens, their labor had been hijacked to increase the wealth of a small elite.

Stars, their *lives* had been hijacked, sacrificed in bloody, pointless military campaigns with enemies who were just as hoodwinked and ignorant.

But the Black Dogs didn't know that. She hadn't had a chance to tell anyone what Bongo had said. She'd fainted before she got the words out.

"Parthenia?"

"What?" her sister replied sullenly, not looking at her.

"After we got back from Lakshmi, did you tell Bryce or anyone else about the real reason for the Three-Systems War?"

"No, I was too busy vomiting. Should I have?"

"I was just wondering. You know about the Marchonish visitors?"

"I'm right next to you, Carina. How couldn't I overhear what Bryce said?"

A simple 'yes' would have been enough, but she let it go. "They want to join the ship. What do you think?"

"Join the ship to go where? We haven't decided if we're still going to Earth, remember? Personally, I'll be happy to survive another couple of weeks."

"You think you're going to die?!"

"No, I think *we're* going to die. You have the same disease, don't forget. We've been getting sicker and sicker, and no one knows why. Asher and Baxter are good doctors, but even they can't figure it out. What does that tell you?"

Parthenia had been focused on her interface for most of this speech, but she turned to Carina as she asked her question with fear in her eyes.

"It tells me..." Carina bit her lip before continuing hastily, "We shouldn't worry about things we can't control."

"Nice cop out, Sis."

Carina rested her head on her pillows. *Were* they going to die? If they died, Oriana, Ferne, and Jace would die too. Bryce would have to raise Darius and Nahla by himself. Darius would be alone as a mage.

Strike that.

He was already alone as a mage. But with his brothers and sisters around, at least he would have people near him who knew what it meant.

The idea of Darius and Nahla losing their entire family was too painful to contemplate. She decided to concentrate on the problem of the visitors from Marchon. Two groups occupying the same ship for a long voyage had been a recipe for disaster in the past. The Lotacryllans had mutinied and murdered Calvaley, and they could have killed Jace too. But, thinking about it, the idea of living alongside the men from Lotacrylla had been doomed from the start. The mercs' introduction to them had been a hard-fought, bloody battle. How could anyone have imagined the two sides would ever get along?

The Marchonish colonists didn't have any history with the Black Dogs, and they would be coming along willingly, unlike the Lotacryllans, who'd had little choice in the matter.

As she saw it, the biggest sticking point was Marchon culture. Their dismissive behavior toward Van Hasty and the comment about 'females for breeding' were telling. If they did join the *Bathsheba*, she could foresee difficulties ahead as their poor attitude toward women came up against Van Hasty's fist.

A wistful pang hit her as she remembered Atoi. What would *she* have made of the Marchonish men? Something broken and bloody, probably.

But, maybe, if they were willing to accept a different way of thinking, it could work.

It would certainly solve some of the problems she and the Black Dogs faced with manning the ship during her long journey. Greater numbers meant less time spent with the *Bathsheba* flying on automatic.

Was it worth the risk?

"What are you thinking about?" Parthenia asked.

"What we should do about the party from Marchon."

"You want to let them join us?"

"I haven't decided. What do you think?"

"Why should we help them? They're stupid, aren't they? They deserve everything they get."

Ugh. Parthenia was referring to their conversation at the restaurant on Lakshmi Station.

"I didn't say that exactly."

"Yes, you did. You said the people from the planets at war should just rise up and take over their governments, and they were stupid for not doing it."

Carina was silent.

"But things aren't so simple, are they?" Parthenia asked.

"Okay, I admit you have a point," Carina conceded. "Seeing them and hearing them speak throws a different light on things. So what do *you* think we should do with them, smartypants?"

"I think we should leave it to the Black Dogs to decide. They're the majority here, and since we lost our mage powers there's nothing special about us to give us any greater say in the decision-making." She sighed. "All I want to do is get better.

Whether the Marchonish group stay or go, I only want to be well again."

Carina held out her hand across the gap that separated their beds. Parthenia looked at it for a moment before grasping it.

"Me too, Sis," Carina said. "Me too."

CHAPTER 30

*D*arius opened his eyes. He was in the twilight dome, and Nahla was with him.

She hugged him tightly. "Thank you, Darius! Thank you for taking me with you."

"Of course I took you with me. You're my sister."

She released him and looked down. "I'm different from you, though. I can't Cast like you."

"You're not different anymore. I'm the only one who can Cast now. I'm the one who's different."

Nahla looked up and smiled brightly. "It doesn't matter. Those men were horrible, weren't they? I thought it would be fun to talk to them, but they were nasty."

"Yes, they were." Darius thought for a moment. "Let's stay here a while. I don't think it was a good idea to Cast in front of them, but I didn't know what else to do. If I'd left you there, they might have hurt you."

"I'm glad you didn't." She turned her gaze upward to the starscape shining through the transparent sections of overhead. "Look, it's so pretty."

Darius nodded. "Uh huh."

The old Nahla would have told him the names of the stars and planets, and probably what types and how far away they were too. All the new Nahla saw was their prettiness.

It hurt.

He sat down and tried hard to not cry.

"What shall we do?" asked Nahla.

"I don't know. Play hide-and-seek?"

The room seemed a good place for the game. It was full of tables and chairs of all different kinds, and there were bars in the corners and along the walls. The lighting was dim, too, which meant lots of shadows.

"Okay," Nahla agreed. "You hide first while I count."

"No, you hide and I'll count." He didn't feel completely safe here. He was worried the Marchonish men might be looking for them. Maybe they weren't done with teasing Nahla. The *Bathsheba* was so big the men would probably never find them, but it was better to be careful. He had to keep his sister safe.

He covered his eyes and began counting. As he counted, he heard Nahla moving around as she looked for a good place to hide. She wasn't being careful to be quiet. He could hear she'd gone to the left-hand side of the room.

"Thirty-four, thirty-five, thirty-six..." They hadn't agreed whether he should count to fifty or a hundred. As they were only playing in one room, fifty would be enough, but if he stopped there Nahla might say he was cheating.

He reached fifty and stoically continued, though he couldn't hear her anymore. She'd found her place to hide and was waiting for him.

"You can look for me now!" she called out.

He took his hands away from his face and rolled his eyes. She'd given her hiding place away, just about. She'd shouted from somewhere on his left, near the hull. Should he make a show of looking for her everywhere else first so she didn't feel bad about being found quickly? He set off.

But someone was comming him.

"Hi, it's me," he answered.

"Hi," said Bryce, sounding relieved. "Where are you?"

When he told him, Bryce went on, "Darius, did you go to see the people from Marchon?"

Before he could answer, Bryce added, "It's very important that you tell me the truth."

His guts seemed to squirm.

Nahla popped up from under a table. "Who are you talking to?"

"Bryce."

"What?" Bryce asked.

"I was speaking to Nahla."

"She's there with you? That was my next question."

"Yeah, she's here. Do you want to talk to her?"

"No, Darius. I can comm her too, remember? *Did* you go to see the Marchonish men?"

The tone Bryce was using, as well as his reminder to tell the truth, was making Darius uncomfortable. A hot feeling spread up from his neck over his face. "I, er…"

"If you did, it's okay. You didn't do anything wrong. No one told you to stay away from them. I thought you were both in your suite, but it doesn't matter. That's my fault, not yours. Only, I need to know if they've seen you."

"Yeah," Darius admitted. "We were spying on them, but they saw us. They…" he swallowed "…they were mean to Nahla, Bryce. Really mean!"

"I can believe it. What else happened?"

His distance from Bryce meant he couldn't feel his emotions, but he heard something in the man's tone. He was trying to make what he said sound unimportant, but in fact it was very important.

Bryce was asking if he'd Cast in front of the Marchonish men.

He wanted to deny it. Mother and Carina had told him many times he mustn't Cast around people who weren't mages. He wanted to explain to Bryce why he'd been forced to do it, how he hadn't any choice, but all that came out was a very soft, quiet, "I Cast Transport."

Bryce's heavy sigh rattled out of the comm button.

"Sorry," Darius added.

"No, you don't have to be sorry. You're just a kid. But it's made things tricky for us. Can you promise me something?"

"Yes, what?"

"That you'll stay right where you are. Some Black Dogs will be there in a couple of minutes."

"Okay, I promise."

"You *and* Nahla, right?"

"Me and Nahla."

"Great. And please don't Cast again, not unless your life depends on it."

"Or Nahla's!"

"All right. Or Nahla's."

Bryce cut the comm.

"We have to stay here?" asked Nahla.

She'd walked over while he'd been talking and must have heard the last part of the conversation.

"Yeah, but we can carry on playing, I guess."

"No, I don't feel like it." She slumped into a seat.

"What else do you want to do?"

"I don't feel like doing anything."

He sat down beside her.

"You know when you were showing me how to use my interface yesterday?" she asked.

"Uh huh."

They'd watched a show together and she'd wanted to know how to find more things to watch.

"I found something I wrote on it before my accident."

"You did?"

He feared what was coming next. Emotions were pouring out of Nahla like a waterfall tumbling over a cliff: sorrow, confusion, and worry.

"I didn't understand it," she said. "How come I wrote it, but now I can't understand it? How's that possible?"

He didn't know what to say. Even if he knew a doctor's explanation for what had happened to her—which he didn't—he felt she was asking something more. How could it be right that she'd gone from being so smart to someone who could barely read?

He didn't know how to make her feel better.

Since they'd come to the Lakshmi Station system everything had gone wrong. Nahla and he had nearly died on Deck Zero and she would never be the same again; Carina and his other siblings had lost their special abilities and they'd all gotten so sick he couldn't bear thinking about it; then the people from Marchon had arrived, and now they knew he could Cast.

The doors opened and light from the passageway lit up the entrance, creating silhouettes of the four heavily muscled figures who stood there.

For a terrifying instant, Darius thought the Marchonish men had found them, but then he recalled his conversation with Bryce.

He also noticed one of the figures had lost an arm.

"Hey, kids," said the one-armed man. "Uncle Jackson's here to look after you."

CHAPTER 31

*B*ryce closed the comm to Darius.

Shit. Shit. Shit.

Jackson had listened in to the conversation and immediately left with Rees and two more Black Dogs to guard the kids. He didn't doubt the mercs would protect Darius and Nahla with their lives, but the situation was getting seriously out of hand.

The group from Marchon had turned from an annoying problem into a real threat. If he hadn't been paying attention to what a Marchonish man said, he might have missed it.

He'd sensed a change in the atmosphere when he'd returned with the mercs to the mission room. There was something different about the way the men looked at them, something hidden behind their friendly smiles and greetings. A menacing intent had entered their expressions.

Jackson picked up on it too. He faked scratching his back to turn to Bryce and whisper, "Something's up."

"Do you think they've guessed our decision?" he whispered back.

"Nah, it isn't that." Jackson faced the group again, his eyes narrowing.

Porcher stepped forward. "We appreciate your consideration of our proposal and are anxious to hear your response."

Bryce had agreed to let the older man deliver the news. If Carina were well, she would probably have handled it, only she was so ill she had him seriously worried. Would she think they'd come to the wrong decision? Maybe not, though she would be pissed off no one had asked her opinion. But what help was her opinion when she clearly wasn't thinking straight?

"I'll get right to the point," said Jackson. "We've given your request serious thought, but the answer's no."

"I see," said Porcher, not losing his fatuous smile. "Are you going to grace us with your reasoning?"

"I guess you deserve that at least," said Jackson. "Two groups on the same ship won't work. We tried it in the past, and the other group ended up taking a spacewalk with no suits. We're not prepared to take the same risk again. That's about the long and short of it, though several of us said they'd be happy to take your women."

"Our women!" Porcher echoed before bursting into guffaws. He turned, amazed and amused, to his companions, who shared his reaction.

A short period followed where the Marchonish men laughed and Bryce and the mercs watched them in silence.

When Porcher's laughter subsided, he wiped his eyes and said sarcastically, "A most generous offer. I can see why you would want our females, but they are not available."

Bryce had a strong suspicion he entirely misunderstood the mercs' motivation. He thought the Black Dogs wanted the women for sex and children, but it had been Van Hasty who had suggested accepting the Marchonish women onto the ship, in order to save them from men who treated them like cattle.

It didn't matter. Only the men were aboard the *Bathsheba*. The women were waiting on their ship and inaccessible. They would probably never learn they'd had a chance to escape their planet, but their men had refused on their behalf.

"So that's it?" asked Porcher. "We leave now and you continue on your journey without us?"

Jackson replied testily, "I'm not sure what else you expect. You came here uninvited and we were gracious enough to allow you aboard and listen to what you had to say. You asked and we answered. The discussion's over."

The tension in the room moved up a notch.

Jackson had anticipated trouble. Every merc was carrying a handgun. A condition of entry for the Marchonish party had been that they were unarmed.

That should have been the end of it. It would be suicide to go up against the mercs considering the imbalance of firepower. But the Marchonish men were surprisingly uncowed.

"What if we refuse to leave?" asked Porcher.

"I can't believe you would be so stupid," Jackson replied.

Still, the men didn't move.

"You're missing out on a great opportunity," said Porcher. "Maybe you should think it over some more."

"We'll escort you back to your ship now," said Jackson.

Porcher's arms jerked up, causing the mercs to reach for their weapons.

He gave a fake yawn and stretched his arms out wide. "No need to get jumpy, boys. We won't outstay our welcome."

Someone muttered, "You already have."

Slowly and lazily, the men who had been sitting got to their feet. The others began to move slowly toward the exit, the Black Dogs stepping aside to give them room to pass.

Some lacked Porcher's faux nonchalance and were grumbling and mumbling while they walked by.

"We didn't have to give up so easy," one of them said.

"Don't worry," his friend replied, "once we get the word out about that kid, they won't be going anywhere."

That was all Bryce heard before the men left the room. But he didn't need to hear any more. Dread rose up in him. There were only two kids on the ship the men from Marchon could have seen, though he hadn't known they were in this section. The last time he'd seen Darius and Nahla they'd been playing happily in their room.

No one would have any reason to 'get the word out' about Nahla. She was only a little girl battling the effects of her accident. But Darius… There was a lot to be told about Darius, or rather one thing in particular. And if anyone outside the *Bathsheba* knew about it, a world of trouble could descend on their heads.

"Wait!" he blurted.

All movement in the room stalled.

"What's up?" Jackson asked. He was at the door, waiting for the last of the visitors to leave.

"I think we were too hasty," said Bryce. "We should talk it over some more."

Jackson frowned. "I don't think so. Everyone had their say and we voted so…"

"You're going to discuss it again?" asked a Marchonish man hopefully. "We don't have to leave?"

"No," said Bryce. "You don't have to go yet."

He pushed through the throng to the doorway, where Jackson was eyeing him quizzically.

He called down the passageway to the departing men, "Come back! Come back in here. We're going to have another discussion about your proposal."

Porcher had been leading his men back to the airlock. His head turned and he called back, "What did you say?"

Jackson said, "Bryce, what the fuck are you doing?"

Ignoring him, Bryce answered Porcher. "You and your men can stay here tonight. We need more time to—"

Jackson grabbed his arm.

"Trust me!" he hissed.

Jackson gave him a dark look, but he released his hold. "Yeah, you can all stay another few hours while we, er, hear some more opinions."

CHAPTER 32

"We have to kill them," said Van Hasty. "What other choice do we have? After we've killed them, we board their ship, kill any other men we find, bring the women here and then blow the ship up. The women don't know about Darius, and if we leave the system with them right away, when they find out it won't matter."

Bryce couldn't help but think her opinion was colored by the gender imbalance in Marchonish culture, but she did make some good points. They couldn't risk knowledge of Darius's abilities to leak to Marchon or anywhere else. Even a non-aggressive society would be very interested in a kid with mage powers, let alone the three militaristic ones on the *Bathsheba's* doorstep.

Yet he still had nightmares over the time they'd spaced the Lotacryllans. He wasn't sure he could do the same thing again or be a party to it in the circumstances. He didn't like the Marchonish men and thought their attitudes were ridiculous, but they hadn't actually *done* anything. All they'd done was put their case for inclusion in what they believed was a colonization expedition.

It wouldn't be right to kill them for something they *might* do.

"I know what you're thinking," said Van Hasty, watching him, "but we aren't in court. We're not judges or a jury. We're talking about the life of a little kid and all the rest of our lives too. It's them or us. You know what the fuckers would do if they got a chance."

"We do," Hsiao agreed, "but how do you know their women won't do the same?"

"Why would they when we rescued them from those pricks?"

Bryce sighed and shook his head. "I wish Jace was well enough to be here."

Jackson snorted. "Jace would want us to invite every bastard in the three systems aboard."

He'd given over guard duty to other mercs, who were currently guarding Darius and Nahla in their suite while the Marchonish men had been taken to the twilight dome to sleep.

"He would try to find a non-violent solution to the problem," said Bryce. "That's what we're missing. There has to be an alternative to killing probably a hundred men and who knows how many women because some of them saw something they shouldn't have. It's so ruthless."

"The black's a harsh place," said Jackson in a tone that made Bryce grateful he didn't add a patronizing 'kid' at the end of his sentence. "You have to be ruthless to survive."

"If I might say something?" asked Justus.

He hadn't taken part in the first discussion, saying he was a guest himself so the decision should be up to the Black Dogs. But now the question had broadened out, he'd been invited to the meeting.

"Go ahead," said Hsiao.

"Whatever we do with the Marchonish, we have to factor in our business on Lakshmi. We aren't done there yet. We haven't upgraded the *Bathsheba's* defenses, and we were planning on re-stocking supplies before we left."

"Why does that matter?" Van Hasty asked.

"Because we're aboard the biggest ship in the sky. The Marchonish group saw us, and we can be sure plenty of others are watching and listening in our direction too. If one of our visitors manages to get word out during your proposed slaughter, Marchon military might turn its attention from its enemies to us."

"So you're saying we should complete our business before we kill anyone?" asked Van Hasty.

"Not exactly, but close."

Hsiao explained, "He's saying we need to finish dealing with Lakshmi before we deal with our problem here."

"That's it," said Justus.

"And what is our business with Lakshmi?" Bryce asked. "Carina hasn't been able to talk much since she got back, but as I understand it no one on the station could help Nahla."

"That's right," said Hsiao. "That's what she told me on the way back before she got sick."

"Damn," said Jackson.

"You need to talk to the doctors about replacing your arm," said Justus.

"That's not a priority right now. I'm left-handed, so it isn't a big deal."

Justus scoffed, "You're planning on going all the way to Earth one-armed when you have the best medical facilities in the sector right here?"

"He's right," said Van Hasty. "Stop playing the martyr and get it fixed. I don't want to fight beside you unless you have four functioning limbs. How are you going to suit up, moron?"

"All right! I'll get a new arm. But what are we gonna do about the assholes in the dome?"

"You know what I think," said Van Hasty. "Nothing anyone

says will change that. I'm going to check on Carina while you guys make a decision."

Her departure brought a pause to the discussion.

Eventually, Bryce said, "There has to be another option than massacring a bunch of unarmed men."

"If there is," said Jackson, "I'm not seeing it. Not if we want to keep Darius out of the hands of the first space fleet that manages to board our ship."

"One child's life against a hundred others?" Bryce asked.

"One innocent life against a load of worthless shitheads," Jackson countered.

"What do you think, Justus?"

"I see both sides. I'm military too, and I've seen more soldiers die in a minute than we're talking about here. But I'm sick of fighting and bloodshed. If there's a way we can avoid murdering those men, I'm willing to hear it."

"I feel the same," said Hsiao. "I can see the necessity, and if we were measuring the worth of one life against another, I would say Darius deserves to live more than anyone we've seen from Marchon or anyone here. The kid has a special gift that could be used to do a lot of good and improve the lives of millions. We have a duty to protect him at all costs. Plus, as we know, if we allow a hair of his head to be harmed Carina will kill us all."

"True," Bryce agreed. "I'd rather face the Marchon, Quinton, and Gugong space fleets put together than her."

"But at the same time," Hsiao continued, "the idea of executing the men just because of something they know leaves a sour taste in my mouth."

"This is all fine and good," said Jackson, "but I'm not hearing an alternative."

"There has to be another solution," said Bryce. "What about taking them with us but marooning them somewhere along our way?"

"Too risky," Jackson replied. "Once they're all aboard, I'm pretty sure they will outnumber us. We would end up not waking up from Deep Sleep."

No one mentioned the idea of swearing the Marchonish men to secrecy. That was plainly ridiculous.

Jackson's comm chirruped.

"Porcher wants a chat," said a voice at the other end.

"Damn," said Jackson. "He must have guessed something's up."

"Maybe," said Bryce. "I'll come with you."

The Marchonish men had spread themselves out in the twilight dome, sprawling on the sofas and deck, making themselves at home in a way that left Bryce feeling uncomfortable. They were already acting as though they owned the place, and Porcher had an arrogant look in his eye as he saw Bryce and Jackson arrive.

"Over here," he said beckoning them closer.

Jackson calmly halted and tucked his remaining thumb into his belt, refusing to bend to Porcher's power play. The Marchonish man was forced to walk over to them. A smile and a scowl struggled for control of his face.

"I was wondering how the talks are going," he said.

"That's it?" Jackson asked. "That's why you made us come up here? You'll find out how the talks went when they're over." He turned to leave.

"That's not all," said Porcher.

"What else do you want?" Jackson growled, turning back.

"There's something else you should know."

"What?"

"Before we came here, we told a lot of people where we were going. Parents who were too old to come along, friends and relations who wanted to stay on Marchon. They'll be waiting for news. If they don't hear from us soon, they'll inform the

Marchon Government, which will be interested in finding out what's happened to its citizens."

"Right," said Jackson. "That it?"

"That's it, for now."

After they left, Bryce said, "You were right. He's guessed this isn't any longer about whether they can join us. Do you believe what he said about the Marchon Government?"

"No. Why would it give a shit about a couple hundred opportunists leaving its system? But it shows they aren't going to patiently wait for days on end for us to make up our minds, and we can't forget about the men they left behind on their ship. I'm going to double the guards on the airlock and the dome door. We need to come to a decision fast."

CHAPTER 33

a shadow fell over Carina, and she opened her eyes. A tall woman stood next to her bed, blocking the light.

"Van Hasty?"

"Hi." The merc dragged a chair over.

Carina winced at the noise of chair legs scraping on tile.

"How are you doing?" Van Hasty asked as she sat down.

"It's nice of you to come and see me," said Carina, thinking if this woman was paying her a visit she must be dying. Van Hasty wasn't renowned for her compassion toward her fellow mercs, or anyone else for that matter.

"No problem." She rested her hands on her spread knees, bent forward, and peered into Carina's face. "You look like shit."

"Thanks." Carina turned onto her back and tried to sit up.

After watching her for a couple of seconds in confused silence, Van Hasty helped her by grabbing her shoulders and hauling her upward. Then she bent her forward while adjusting her pillows and thrust her into them. "Is that better?"

"Uhhh…" Carina felt like she'd just finished Basic again with the Sherrerrs. "What's happening? No one's telling me anything."

"That's what I thought. We have a big problem to sort out. Hsiao and the guys are talking about it now, but you should know what's going on too. It concerns Darius."

"Huh?" Carina sat up straighter. "Is he okay?"

"He's fine, but… Let me tell you what's been going on."

Van Hasty began to explain the events of the last few hours, during which Carina had been wondering why Bryce hadn't been to see her, and why Asher had looked so worried when she checked up on her.

As she listened, her heart beat faster. Before the merc had finished her tale, she guessed where it was headed and broke in, "They know about Darius's ability."

Van Hasty nodded grimly.

"*Dammit.*"

"Yeah."

"What are they going to do?"

"That's what they're talking about. I gave them my opinion and came to see you."

"Thanks, I appreciate it."

But Carina didn't know what to tell the merc. She could barely think, let alone get up and go to the defense of her brother, which was her first impulse.

Since she'd collapsed in the passageway after trying to find out what was happening on the ship, she'd felt sicker and sicker. Moving her limbs was a Herculean task, an industrial compactor had set up in her head, and even thinking about food caused her to retch for minutes at a time.

Parthenia, meanwhile, seemed to have passed out entirely. She hadn't opened her eyes in hours. Carina wasn't sure if Asher or Baxter had given her a sedative or it was the effect of their illness. She couldn't remember if a doctor had given her something. Her memory was hazy as she'd drifted in and out of consciousness herself.

Seeming to sense she wasn't capable of forming coherent

thoughts about the problem, Van Hasty got to her feet. "I shouldn't have bothered you. I didn't realize you were so sick."

"No, stay," Carina said. "Or…call Asher for me."

When the doctor arrived, Carina asked her for a stimulant.

"Why?" Asher looked from her to Van Hasty as if suspecting they were colluding to commit a crime.

"I have to think something through, but I can't. My brain won't work."

"No, out of the question. You're already on the maximum doses of medications to control your symptoms, and you're far too weak. If I give you anything else it could stop your heart or give you a stroke. I don't think you understand how sick you are."

"Oh, I do," Carina replied. "Believe me. But I have to be able to think. Darius is in danger. We all are."

"You mean the group from Marchon?" The doctor pursed her lips and frowned at Van Hasty. "It was very unwise to come here and bother her with this." To Carina, she said, "Other people are perfectly capable of dealing with the problem. Leave them to it and concentrate on getting better."

"Stop bullshitting me!" Carina spat, though her voice was pathetically weak. "I'm not going to get better. You said yourself you and Baxter don't have the first clue what's wrong with me. Only one outcome is possible now. I don't have much time left, but what time I do have I want to spend helping my brother. Give me something so I can think!"

The older woman stared at her, and for a second her stony expression broke, revealing anguish and guilt. She turned on her heel and marched out of the room without another word.

Van Hasty raised her eyebrows.

An uncomfortable pause followed.

Van Hasty said, "Do you think she's gonna—"

The door slid open and Asher returned, holding a syringe

aloft like a weapon. She halted at Carina's bedside. "Do you take full responsibility?"

"Yes, I— *Ahhhh.*"

The doctor had forced the syringe against her upper arm and its contents exploded into her bloodstream. A cleansing wave washed over her. Suddenly she knew how it felt to be completely well again. Her mind cleared, the ache left her muscles, and she no longer felt like a lead weight was holding her down on the bed.

Then her pulse began to pound and her skin was instantly wet with sweat. Her hands began to tremble.

But she could think. At last, she could finally think.

"I might know a way," she said. "Just give me a minute."

"We have to kill them all, right?" said Van Hasty.

Carina glanced at her sister, pale, thin, and asleep on the neighboring bed. "Maybe not."

It took her longer than a few minutes to think up a plan, but when she had it, she felt confident it would work and she hadn't forgotten anything.

She told Van Hasty. As she spoke, the stimulant started to wear off. The lead weight began to descend on her again, pinning her to the mattress. The hammering in her head resumed and the dreadful nausea returned.

Dr Asher had waited by her bed the entire time, watching the figures on the wall interface, tutting and shaking her head.

When Carina had finished her short explanation, Van Hasty said, "I'll tell them. They might not agree, but I'll tell them."

There wasn't anything else she could do. She was descending to the depths of her illness again for what seemed the last time.

As Van Hasty was leaving, Carina asked Asher, "Am I dying?"

"I haven't given up hope yet, and neither should you."

Van Hasty halted at the door. "Everyone dies, Carina. The only win you get in this life is outliving your enemies."

CHAPTER 34

*P*orcher reached out and grabbed Bryce's hand before shaking it forcefully. He did the same with Justus but, moving to shake Jackson's right hand, he hesitated, forgetting it was missing. He grinned and grasped his left hand instead.

He awkwardly nodded at Hsiao and Van Hasty, and then, redirecting his attention to the men, he said, "I can't thank you enough. You've come to the right decision. You won't regret it."

"We have some things to do before we leave the system," said Jackson. "You'll have time to get settled in. The *Bathsheba's* a big ship. There's plenty of room for everyone. I'd suggest spreading yourselves around rather than all of you settling in one spot. It'll help you integrate."

"Right." Porcher paused and smiled uncomfortably. "I think we would prefer our women to remain aboard our ship for now. Maybe when we begin our voyage we will bring them aboard. It will be necessary in order for them to go into Deep Sleep, naturally."

"You...what?" asked Van Hasty. "They can't come aboard?"

Bryce nudged her with his elbow. "We understand you might

be worried about them mingling with the Black Dogs, but you don't have anything to fear on that account. I've lived with the mercs for over a year, and, contrary to their looks, they're very well behaved."

"Thanks for the glowing endorsement," Jackson muttered.

"Nevertheless," Porcher countered, "it would be better for all if our females stay apart from your company for the time being. Speaking as a Marchonish man, I can assure you that's what they want."

Van Hasty burst out, "Well, aren't they lucky to have you—"

"If that's what's best," said Bryce, "we'll take your word for it."

"It is," said Porcher. "Now, if you don't mind, I'll tell my men the good news. Then some of us will return to our ship to begin bringing our belongings aboard."

"Of course," said Justus.

Porcher left with a spring in his step.

"That's *that* done," said Jackson after waiting for him to pass out of earshot. "So we aren't as bad as we look?" he asked Bryce.

"Not quite," he replied.

Jackson cuffed his head, though not hard.

"I mean," Bryce went on, laughing, "you do have a few redeeming features."

Jackson cuffed him again.

"Quit it," said Hsiao. "He was only feeding into Marchonish prejudices. That's right, isn't it, Bryce?"

"Yeah, something like that."

Bryce suddenly remembered Carina, whose idea they were following, and his chest grew tight. The way things were going she might not live to see the outcome of her plan. If the worst happened, how would he carry on without her? Though he would have to for Darius and Nahla's sake.

Jackson's hand descended on his shoulder. "Coming with us to Lakshmi Station?"

"I don't know if I should. I think I should stay here to look after the kids."

"They're coming too," said Jackson.

"They are? But that wasn't part of the plan. Carina wouldn't approve. She would want us to keep them safe."

"That's why we have to take them with us," Hsiao explained. "The people from Marchon know there's something special about them. They saw Darius and Nahla disappear into thin air, so they're going to keep a very close eye on them from now on. It's much better for the kids to stick with us."

"Yeah," Bryce conceded, "you're right."

"Besides," Jackson said, "I'll be visiting medical centers to see if they can shed any light on what's wrong with the mages and to talk to them about fixing my arm. I can ask about treatment for Nahla too. I might still find someone who can help her."

The proposal of bringing the children along on their next visit to Lakshmi was making more and more sense.

"It's a shame the mages are too weak to go to the station," said Bryce. "We should have taken them there earlier."

"They deteriorated faster than anyone expected," said Hsiao sadly. "It's taken everyone by surprise."

Only Jackson, Hsiao, Bryce, and now Darius and Nahla would be going to Lakshmi. Van Hasty would remain behind to keep an eye on the Marchonish men, and they couldn't risk taking any other mercs due to the events of the previous visit. A similar episode might bankrupt them, and they needed all the funds they had to purchase the space weapon Carina had suggested.

* * *

BRYCE HAD HEARD SO MUCH about Lakshmi Station. Hsiao had described the hordes of people and aliens and the huge numbers of shops and facilities. Carina had told him about the friend she'd made, the guide Bongo. Even Darius had chimed in, talking about the range of weird foods on the menu at the restaurant where he'd eaten.

Yet none of it prepared Bryce for his first sight of the station from the *Peregrine's* bridge.

He'd never seen so many starships of so many kinds in one place. There were battleships being serviced, repaired, and fitted out, dwarfing the engineering vessels that flitted across and between them. Huge cargo haulers hung in space, too large to ever enter a planetary atmosphere. Commercial cruise liners floated along, sleek and luxurious, probably heading for exotic destinations. Or perhaps they were simply taking their passengers beyond any government's jurisdiction, where they could push the bounds of legal behavior without fear of repercussions. Private starships built for speed zipped along almost too fast to detect.

And the station itself was vast, easily the biggest man-made structure he'd ever heard of, let alone seen. It was hard to imagine how it sustained itself. How could there be sufficient people in the surrounding area to support it? But then, he reminded himself, three entire worlds contributed to its existence—billions of people, out of which probably only a fraction ever had the opportunity to visit it. Though, from what he understood, hundreds of thousands lived on the station, either permanently or as part of an ever-changing contingent of migrant workers, shipped in from the three worlds and farther afield.

"Where do we dock?" he asked Hsiao, noting what looked like lines of ships vaguely spiraling out from several of the many points of the star.

"It wouldn't mean anything if I told you," she replied, "but it's the same spot we've docked the previous two times. The station authorities seem to want to keep us in one area."

"Is visitor movement restricted inside?"

"Not officially. The last time I was here..." she looked abashed "...we were taken far from the commercial zone. Hours away. And I didn't see any signs prohibiting entry to anywhere. But my guess is most visitors never leave the district nearest their docking point. The place is too big, and you can find anything you might need in just one of the points of the star."

"What goes on in the middle?"

She shrugged. "I'm not sure, but maybe it's where the permanent residents live? The arms dealers, tycoons, business moguls, and so on. They probably don't want to mix with the shoppers and tourists."

"And they don't want to live on any of the planets."

"No, and now we know why."

Van Hasty had returned from Carina's bedside with a horrific story. The war that maintained Lakshmi Station was artificially generated. Billions had given their lives so that others could live in luxury. It was no wonder the party from Marchon were desperate to escape.

Despite the magnificence of the station's appearance, it sickened Bryce to go there. Simply setting foot on it would feel like he was contributing to the injustice. And they weren't only going there, they were fueling the economy by purchasing a weapon.

He'd tried to speak to Carina about her plan before he left, but she'd been too out of it to have a proper conversation. He'd only been able to hold her, tell her he loved her and he hoped she would get better soon. He'd said Darius and Nahla were okay and not to worry, but he wasn't sure she'd understood.

Silently, he watched the station grow larger until the point they were headed toward dominated the view.

Hsiao gave the order to strap in as they were about to dock.

hen Bongo heard Carina and Parthenia were ill, his legs lost some of their tension and his body sagged between them.

"You should have brought them here," he said. "Lakshmi Station has the finest—"

"They're too sick," Hsiao interrupted. "It started after they got back from their last visit."

"You don't think they contracted their illness here, do you?" he asked. "The station managers are usually excellent at maintaining high levels of hygiene."

"No," Hsiao replied. "Some of our crew members fell ill before they returned, people who have never been here."

"Then it's something aboard your ship?" he asked, crawling backward a couple of steps.

"It's hard to explain why, but you don't have to be concerned about catching it. Carina and the others who are unwell are… Well, they're different from the rest of us. Everyone else on the *Bathsheba* is fine."

Bongo crawled toward them. "I'm glad only a few of your crew members are affected. How can I help you today?"

Hsiao told him about the two purposes for their visit.

"Have you brought any samples for the staff at the treatment center to test?" he asked when she'd finished.

"We have," the pilot replied, lifting the refrigerated box containing vials of bodily fluids and swabs from the patients.

"I hope you can find someone to help you," said Bongo. "And I see you've brought the little girl back too. Maybe you'll be more successful this time. However, I can't be in two places at once. I can't take you to medical centers and to arms dealers. Let me ask my cousin if she's free to help out."

Whatever method of communicating the alien used, Bryce couldn't see. Bongo bounced gently two or three times, and then he seemed to be waiting.

Bryce occupied the time by watching the crowds and surveying the myriad of establishments lining the walkways around him. In reality, his mind was tens of thousands of kilometers away in the sick bay of a colony starship.

A figure two heads taller than the tallest person in the surrounding throng came striding toward them. Skin softly scaled, hairless, her pupils vertical slits, she was otherwise vaguely human, though there was no telling what lay under her shirt, pants, and boots.

"Ah, here she comes," said Bongo.

"That's your *cousin?*" Hsiao asked, her jaw going slack.

"On one of my mothers' side, far distant," he replied. "And from a different planet, naturally."

Bryce and Hsiao exchanged a look.

"Scroocher," he hailed her as she neared them.

"Bongo," she replied, leaning down to pat his head, which he didn't appear to mind.

"I'm about to show this young lady and her one-armed companion to several of our best hospitals," said Bongo. "Would you accompany the remainder of the party to reputable starship weapons suppliers?"

"My pleasure," said Scroocher.

Hsiao handed the medical samples box to Jackson.

"*Scroocher*," she muttered as they set off. "This place gets crazier by the minute."

BY THE TIME they reached the fifth arms dealer, Bryce had begun to despair. What they were looking for seemed impossible to find. When they explained to Scroocher the weapon they had in mind, hoping she could narrow down the field of prospective suppliers for them, she leaned her head back.

Was she thinking? Surprised? Comming Bongo?

Bryce had no idea.

Her head returned to vertical. "I've never heard of such a thing."

"Oh come on," said Hsiao. "A place like this? Best weapons technology in the sector? There has to be."

"Wait here," said Scroocher. "I'll see what I can find."

"Where's she going?" Bryce asked Hsiao as the alien disappeared into the crowd. "I can't believe she can't look up whatever she wants on the local net."

"It is strange," Hsiao agreed.

Turning to Darius, who had quietly accompanied them on every failed attempt to secure the specialized weapon, Bryce asked, "Scroocher is a good person, right? Can you tell?"

"Uh huh. She's okay. She's like a fizzy drink, sweet and bubbly."

"A fizzy drink, huh?" asked Hsiao, squinting after the departing alien.

They had to wait half an hour for Scroocher to return, by which time they'd begun to wonder if she'd abandoned them. But then they spotted her scaly head weaving from side to side as she navigated the ever-present throng of visitors.

When she arrived, she scrutinized them for a few seconds as if making up her mind about something. "Will this be your last visit to Lakshmi?" she asked. "If you can find the weapon you desire?"

"Yes," Bryce quickly replied before Hsiao said anything to the contrary.

If Jackson managed to find a medical center that could treat the mages, they might actually end up returning, but it appeared whatever Scroocher had to offer them was contingent on their never returning to the station.

Darius looked up at him, frowning.

Shit. The kid could tell when people were lying.

"Then follow me," said the alien.

Hsiao asked Bryce, "Are you sure—"

"Absolutely. If we get what we want, why would we come back?"

Scroocher led the group to the other side of the concourse and for the rest of the way they stayed close to the wall, passing the entrances to the many and varied facilities. Noise blared from some, odors from others, and some were dark and silent, though people entered and left just the same.

When they arrived at the next stage of their journey, Bryce almost didn't see the exit point. Scroocher halted at an area of plain wall. Looking closer, however, it became clear a door stood there. Exactly the same color and texture as the wall, it was almost invisible.

Checking from side to side, the alien pushed it halfway open, creating a gap only just wide enough to slip through, and motioned everyone into it. Once they were all through, she closed the door. It was only then the lights turned on in the passageway.

Bryce was reminded of the security area he'd passed through when they'd arrived at the station. No decoration marked the walls, and there were only two options for movement: forward or back the way you came.

Scroocher took them forward.

Hsiao gave Bryce a worried look.

He felt the same. They were clearly traveling into the less-orthodox regions of Lakshmi. If it had only been him and Hsiao he might only have felt more alert and wary, but he didn't like the idea of taking Darius with them. Ironically, this was even though the little mage was more capable than either of them of extracting himself from a dangerous situation, as he'd shown with the Marchonish men. Bryce had told him to bring his elixir as a precaution, hoping he wouldn't have to use it.

They left the noise and bustle of the regular areas of the station far behind as they traveled the nondescript corridor. Apart from themselves, it was nearly empty. They saw only one other person: a small, slight man with a long beard. He fast-walked past them. Neither he nor Scroocher acknowledged the other, as if pretending they hadn't seen them.

Bryce counted three plain doors the same as the one they'd entered by, lacking any sign or adornment, before the alien stopped at the fourth. Resting a hand on it, she said, "You never came here, you never met this person, and you didn't see anything, okay?"

"Okay," Bryce and Hsiao replied simultaneously.

"Okay," Darius solemnly echoed.

Scroocher smiled and ruffled his hair.

Then she opened the door.

CHAPTER 36

*I*nside, a bald, fat man sat at a low table. His legs barely fit beneath it, and his gut hung over the surface like a dessert pudding waiting to be sliced up and served.

In each corner sat larger men with... Bryce did a double take.

For the first time since entering the station, he saw weapons.

The men were armed, pulse rifles held easily across their laps. As Bryce's gaze moved from the weapons to the men's eyes, one of them winked.

"Take a seat," said the fat man, sweeping a hand in the direction of low stools that stood between them and the table. They were even lower than the man's chair, designed to put clients at a psychological disadvantage, no doubt.

"Cute kid," he added as they sat.

Hsiao shot Bryce a glance that expressed how he felt too— they were getting in far deeper than they'd intended. He wished Jackson were here. Even one-armed, the merc was better suited to this environment than he was or, he suspected, Hsiao. She was a good pilot, but she rarely saw combat or had dealings with lowlifes.

Scroocher hovered near the door, looking nervous.

"I hear you're in the market for a rather special space weapon," the man asked. "Am I right?"

"Yes," Bryce replied. "I'm—"

"No names!" said the man, holding up a hand in warning.

Bryce continued, "I'm here on behalf of a friend who can't make it, but we'll do our best to describe the weapon she wants."

"Before we discuss it," said Hsiao, "I should check with another member of our party. He's seeking out medical treatment and if he's successful it'll affect our budget."

"No comm in here," the man said. "At least, not any you can access."

It was potentially a big problem. Unless they could speak to Jackson they wouldn't know if he'd agreed to pay some of their funds in return for a cure for the mages or Nahla. A new prosthetic arm for the merc wouldn't make a significant dent in their creds, but they had no idea how much they might have to pay for other treatments, which took priority over space armaments.

"Relax," said the man. "We're just talking, right? We can discuss payment later, if I have what you want."

He poured a drink from a jug into two glasses and pushed them across the table before pouring another one for himself. The liquid was vivid purple and gave off a vapor.

"Sudden Death, right?" asked Hsiao.

The man smiled. "The lady knows her cocktails."

"Only take a sip," Hsiao murmured to Bryce.

He did as she suggested. Just a taste of the drink was enough to make him feel as though he was losing grip on reality. He guessed whatever was in it could be absorbed through the membranes inside his mouth and throat.

"What are you drinking?" Darius whispered, though in fact his voice must have been plain for everyone to hear. "Can I have some?"

The man and his two goons laughed.

"No, sonny," said the arms dealer. "This isn't for you. I see you've brought your own drink. Have some of that if you're thirsty."

Darius looked warily up at Bryce.

Bryce wasn't sure what exactly the look meant. Was he asking if he could drink some elixir to refresh himself? He didn't think so. He'd never seen any of the mages do that. Elixir didn't taste pleasant. You would have to be pretty dehydrated to consider drinking it not for its specific purpose.

Was Darius asking him if it was okay to Cast?

He couldn't imagine why the boy would want to. As a precaution, he gave a slight shake of his head.

The dealer focused on Bryce and Hsiao. "Now we've oiled the wheels, let's get down to business."

Bryce described what they wanted.

The dealer listened attentively. When Bryce reached the end of the description, he said, "Tell me about your ship."

"Is that really necessary?" asked Hsiao.

As they'd already discovered with the Marchonish men, the *Bathsheba* was a desirable prize. The last thing they should be doing was giving details about her to this shady character.

"It's necessary if you want me to supply a weapon to fit her," said the man. "Do you think space armaments are one-size-fits-all? This is complex machinery we're talking about. Are you serious? Do you want to do business or not?"

"We're serious," Bryce assured him. "Just cautious. I'm sure you understand."

He nodded. "A little caution is wise. But in this world you've entered there must also be trust. I'm trusting you just by allowing you to speak to me. If there's no reciprocation, our talk is over."

"We don't want the talk to be over," said Bryce.

Hsiao said, "I'll tell you about our ship." She gave the dealer the rough specifications. "I can send the details later via an encrypted comm."

He listened attentively, his gaze never leaving her face. "I can see where your reluctance comes from, but you have nothing to fear from me. I have no need for a colony ship. There's no better place to be than Lakshmi, and I have more wealth than I can ever spend. I only dabble in semi-legal armaments for the thrill. When you can buy anything and everything you want life loses its edge, if you know what I mean."

"Do you have the weapon we need?" Hsiao asked brusquely.

"I think I do, but indulge me a little further. What you're asking for is extremely expensive, as I'm sure you can guess. Why not use all those creds to purchase a range of armaments? Placing all your bets on only one is foolish, and you two don't strike me as idiots."

"We have our reasons," said Bryce. "Don't tell me you need to know those too."

The dealer held up his hands, palms outward. "That's your concern. Just offering a little friendly advice. So..." He turned to one of his men and nodded. The man got up and left the room by the rear door. "It will take me some time to arrange transportation and a team to fit the device. We're looking at 48 hours minimum to remove the equipment from storage and run checks, then another three or four days to ship and fit it, depending on what the team finds when they arrive at your vessel."

"A week?" asked Hsiao.

It seemed a long time to Bryce as well, but it was only to be expected considering the dimensions and complexity of the weapon.

"Roughly a week," the dealer confirmed, "give or take a day or two."

His man returned bearing a reader.

"We haven't talked about the price yet," said Bryce.

"I have a figure in mind."

"A firm figure?" asked Hsiao. "We don't have unlimited funds and, as I said, we aren't sure what else we might need to pay for."

"Reasonably firm. Naturally, I can't lose money on the deal. Your other expenses are not my concern. I require fifty percent down payment before you leave this room, the balance to be paid upon installation and successful testing."

"I'm guessing there's no written contract," said Bryce.

"If there were, you wouldn't be talking to me. You would be out on the concourse somewhere, listening to a one-hundred-percent-legit dealer telling you they can't help you."

Bryce shared an anxious look with Hsiao. If they agreed to the man's terms, they would be committing a large amount of the *Bathsheba's* crew's remaining money, possibly spending money already earmarked for medical treatment.

"What kind of figure are we talking about?" Bryce asked.

When the dealer answered, he and Hsiao drew in a breath. It was nearly all the creds remaining in the account.

"That's too much!" Hsiao blurted. "We can't afford—"

"Then you've wasted both our time," said the man, rising to his feet.

"Wait a moment," Bryce said. "You said the amount isn't completely firm. Can you give us a discount? We have children aboard, who we're taking to find a new home."

He rested a hand on Darius's head. The boy peered up at him.

"Trying to appeal to my humanity?" asked the dealer, sitting down. "I'm too cynical and jaded for that. But I would like this deal to go ahead. It isn't every day I get to sell such a specialized weapon. I'll knock off five percent."

"Five percent?" Bryce did the mental calculation.

Hsiao sadly shook her head at him. It was still far too much. They needed a bigger buffer in case Jackson had been successful in his endeavors.

"It's too expensive!" exclaimed Darius, no doubt picking up on Bryce and Hsiao's anxiety.

Everyone except those two laughed, Scroocher included. She'd stayed by the door the entire time in silence.

"Is it, young man?" the dealer asked, smiling.

"I'm afraid it is," Hsiao said. "It does look like we've wasted your time."

Bryce was gutted. Carina's idea had been so good, but they didn't have a way of carrying it out, not if they also wanted to buy a cure for the mages' awful disease and pay other medical expenses.

The atmosphere in the room descended into mutual disappointment. The dealer stood up again and motioned to his men it was time to leave.

"I'm thirsty!" Darius announced as he unscrewed the lid of his elixir bottle.

Bryce's eyes widened. "Darius," he cautioned, instantly aware of what the boy intended to do.

"Very thirsty," he insisted and took a swallow of elixir. "That's better."

He closed his eyes.

Darius's actions were so deliberate and odd, the arms dealer and his men stuck around to watch him.

A few seconds was all it took for the Cast to take effect.

The dealer's eyes lost their focus.

"You know, maybe I was too hasty," he said. "Maybe I can give you a better deal. What do you say to a fifty percent discount?"

His men stared at each other, but neither intervened.

Bryce underwent an internal struggle. Darius had created a situation with many pitfalls, yet they would never be able to carry out Carina's plan without the weapon.

"A fifty percent discount sounds great."

CHAPTER 37

*I*t wasn't until after Scroocher had taken them to meet up with Jackson and Bongo, and left them alone outside the treatment center, that he could finally talk to Darius about his Cast.

"What you did back there was kind but not very smart," Bryce told him.

The boy looked glum. "Sorry."

"What are you talking about?" Hsiao objected. "He saved us a heck ton of money."

"For how long?" Bryce asked.

In response to the pilot's puzzled look, he went on, "Carina told me about the Cast Darius did. It has a time limit."

"Ohhh..." Understanding began to dawn in Hsiao's eyes. "How long does it last?"

"It depends on the mental sharpness of the victim. To me, that dealer seemed as sharp as they come. On the other hand, apparently Darius Casts like a hurricane. I suppose that means the effect will last a long time."

"As long as a week?" asked Hsiao.

"Maybe, but I doubt it."

"Holy crap," Hsiao breathed.

Bryce knew how she felt. They'd tricked a dangerous, shady character into a deal that had most likely left him way out of pocket. At some point, he would cease being Enthralled and would wonder what the hell had happened to him. What he might do then was anyone's guess, but Bryce had a strong feeling no one aboard the *Bathsheba* was going to like it.

"Is there any way we can back out?" Hsiao mused.

"I don't see how. As I understand it, while he's under the effect of the Cast the dealer will feel compelled to help us, even if we refuse. Is that right, Darius?"

He nodded, looking glummer.

Bryce continued, "We could ask Scroocher to take us back and try to cancel the agreement, but he's going to put up a fight. He might even force us to accept his services without any payment. If he regains his normal mental state while his workers are attaching a pricey piece of equipment entirely free of charge, he's going to be even madder."

"I was only trying to help," Darius said sadly.

"I know," Bryce replied. "But next time, it would be better to ask before you Cast, okay?"

Darius's shoulders slumped and he didn't reply.

"Still," Hsiao said, "if we can swing it so we get the weapon without seriously pissing off the seller, that'd be a helluva bargain."

"*If*," said Bryce.

She was right, but he couldn't think of a way to do it. There was going to be a reckoning, sooner or later.

The doors to the treatment center opened and Bongo crawled out followed by Nahla and Jackson—Jackson with two arms!

"You got it done already?" Bryce asked.

"Yeah, but there's a small problem."

Two additional figures appeared one step behind him: armed guards.

"Did you order the weapon?" asked Jackson.

"Yes, but—"

"Then we have to leave right away."

"But—"

"It's either that, or we split up now. It's your call."

"We—"

"Are you with this man?" One of the guards approached menacingly, his pulse rifle angled across his chest.

"Why do you want to know?" asked Hsiao.

"Move," the guard said, aiming his rifle at her.

"What the…!"

"Do as they say," advised Jackson. "I'll explain when we get back to the *Peregrine*. Sorry, I had no idea this would happen. The doctors didn't tell me. They assumed I understood."

What followed could only be described as a forced march through Lakshmi Station. The visitors parted before them, gawping at the small party of humans and one spider-like alien being escorted like criminals through their midst.

"Did you find out what's wrong with the mages?" Bryce asked Jackson softly.

"No."

Dread gripped his heart.

"Not yet," Jackson hastily added. "The initial round of tests didn't bring up anything. I've left the samples with a center that offered to test for more obscure diseases."

Bryce didn't think Carina would want to leave the mages' DNA in the hands of strangers. She probably wouldn't have agreed to sending the medical samples to Lakshmi at all. But what was done was done. The Black Dogs' doctors were out of ideas, and if no one found a cure for whatever was ailing their patients, there was almost certainly only one outcome.

"How about Nahla?" Bryce asked. "Any luck there?"

The merc heaved a heavy sigh. "No." His voice quietened to a whisper as he went on, "I couldn't find anyone who could help her any better than our own medics, using therapeutic treatments. She'll have to live with the effects of hypoxia for the rest of her life."

Bryce looked at her. He loved the new Nahla just as much as always—she'd continued to be his non-mage ally in the family—but he missed the nimble-witted girl she'd once been.

The guards accompanied them all the way to the security zone, where Bongo said goodbye, and through the zone. They even waited at the station end of the umbilicus until they entered the *Peregrine's* airlock.

The outer hatch closed and sealed, and the airlock pressurized.

"What the hell was *that* about?" asked Hsiao, removing her helmet.

"Wait until we get inside," Jackson replied, "and I'll show you."

When everyone had stripped off their EVA suits and was waiting expectantly in the *Peregrine's* passageway, Jackson pushed up the sleeve covering his new prosthetic.

It looked extremely lifelike. Bryce hadn't studied the merc's arms in any detail, but he would have guessed the new device was virtually a mirror image of his flesh and bone one.

"It looks the same all the way up," Jackson said. "You can't tell where it joins my body."

Relief and pride shone from his face.

Bryce hadn't realized how self-conscious the merc must have been about his old device. "Cool," he commented, "but why the big fuss in the station?"

Jackson raised his arm and bent his elbow, so his fist pointed at the bulkhead. A rectangular section of his forearm split open, and a miniature gun rose up.

"*Shit!*" Hsiao exclaimed, taking a step backward. "You're permanently armed! Ha! Literally armed."

Jackson grinned. "My humerus is basically a power pack. If it begins to run low, I can charge it up overnight while I sleep."

"So that's why we had to leave immediately," said Bryce.

"Visitors aren't allowed weapons anywhere on Lakshmi," Jackson confirmed. "Not even weapons contained in prosthetics."

"*Especially* not contained in prosthetics, I bet," said Hsiao. "No one can tell you're carrying."

"But they didn't explain before you had it fitted?" asked Bryce.

"They only asked me if I'd completed all my other business," Jackson replied. "I'd ordered the supplies Carina had on her list. They'll be delivered soon. And Bongo said he didn't know of any hospitals better than the ones we'd already visited, so I reckoned I'd exhausted all the options regarding treatment for Nahla and finding a cure for the mages. I told the doctors I'd done everything else I'd come here to do, and they took me in for surgery right away. It only lasted an hour. They said it was a standard operation they perform all the time, on account of the number of wounded military they see."

Hsiao whistled. "You're a cyborg soldier."

The gun retracted into Jackson's arm and the fake skin closed over it.

"Stars," said Bryce. "The surgeons told you it was a standard operation? That means they're turning the soldiers in the Three-System War into cyborgs too."

"It figures," said Hsiao. "Every operation they perform is another stack of creds added to Lakshmi Station's profits."

"You can say that again," Jackson commented. "My arm was pricey, but I figured it was okay because we didn't have any other medical expenses."

"How much was it?" asked Bryce. "And how much did you pay for the supplies?"

When Jackson told him, it only took a little simple arithmetic to realize they'd been right when they'd told the arms dealer they couldn't afford what he was asking.

"How did you guys get on?" asked Jackson. "You said you managed to buy the weapon."

"We did," answered Bryce, "but unfortunately there's a small snag."

CHAPTER 38

*D*arius hated going to see Carina, but at the same time he couldn't help it. He needed to see her.

She looked so sick, so pale and thin and unmoving, it hurt him deep inside. Parthenia looked the same. So did Ferne, Oriana, and Jace in the other rooms. It had been days since any of them had spoken. They slept most of the time, and when they were awake they mumbled and moaned and didn't make any sense.

As if it wasn't enough to see them fading away from life, he could feel it too. In the past, before they were ill, he could have stood in complete darkness with any of them and known who he was with, just by the pattern of their emotions. He'd known Parthenia, Ferne, and Oriana's ever since he was little, and he'd learned Jace and Carina's soon after he'd met them.

But now their patterns were fading, like wallpaper exposed to sunlight over years.

As soon as he returned from his trip to Lakshmi Station, he wanted to see Carina again. He passed through the empty main sick bay area and pushed open the door to Carina and Parthenia's room.

At the same time, another door opened and Dr Asher appeared.

"Darius," she said, approaching him, "what are you doing?"

"I want to see Carina." He couldn't look at the doctor. He had to look down and bite his lip to stop himself crying.

"I'm afraid you…" Dr Asher paused "…I don't suppose it will hurt. Go on in, but be careful not to disturb any of the tubes or wires, okay?"

"Okay."

His eldest sister looked even thinner than she had the last time he'd seen her, just before he went to Lakshmi. The bones of her face stuck out and her eyes seemed to have sunk in under her eyelids. She was attached to two machines by wires, and tubes ran out from under her bedclothes.

The room was silent save for the quiet hum of the medical equipment and Carina and Parthenia's raspy breathing.

Darius sat down at Carina's side.

One of her hands had a thin tube coming out of the back of it, but the other one was free. He held the free one. Though his sister was a fighter her hands were small, not a lot bigger than his own.

"Hey, Carina," he said.

She didn't answer. She was fast asleep.

"I came to tell you what happened at Lakshmi."

No one else had been in to see her as far as he knew, and he thought she would want to hear how the trip went.

"Jackson got a new arm and it's got a gun in it! It's awesome. I kinda wish I had one like it, but I like my real arms too, so maybe not."

He watched his sister, but she didn't react.

"Nahla… Nahla's the same. Jackson tried to find someone to help her go back to how she was but he couldn't." He swallowed. "She's different now. I think she knows it too. I'm not sure she's happy about it. I think she wants to be how she was before. But that's not gonna happen, right?" He paused. "I wish everything was how it was before."

He stared at Carina's limp fingers. "They got the space gun. Bryce and Hsiao, I mean. They met a man, a scary man. You know how Bongo looks like a spider? Well, this man—I don't know his name—he looked like a human on the outside, but he was a spider on the inside. Not a friendly spider like Bongo. He was the kind of spider that bites you in your sleep so when you wake up in the morning you don't know what that red mark is on your leg or why you feel sick. He was like that. But Bryce and Hsiao didn't know, and I couldn't tell them because the man was right there and he had two guards with guns and…" He took a breath and screwed up his face. "I did something bad, Carina! I Cast Enthrall to make the man agree to the deal for the gun. But I shouldn't have because when the Cast wears off the man will be really angry, and then what will he do? What will a man like that do to everyone?"

He swallowed again, hard. "And it's all my fault, just like with Nahla. I didn't Transport us out from Deck Zero when I should have, and now she'll never be better. The Marchonish men were bullying her and I took her away then, but I had to Cast in front of them. That was wrong too. But maybe none of it will matter. Maybe the man selling us the space weapon will do something bad when the Enthrall Cast fades, and nothing I've done will matter anymore."

He bent his head over Carina's hand, and hot tears dropped onto it. "What should I do, Carina? What should I do?"

But his sister couldn't answer him. She'd slept all the time he was talking.

Would she ever wake up?

No one had told him what was going to happen to her and the other mages. All he knew was the doctors at Lakshmi didn't know what was wrong with them. They were going to do more tests, but Bryce didn't seem to think they would find anything.

Bryce's pattern of feelings had changed, but it hadn't faded like the mages', it had grown darker and heavier. His face didn't match how he really felt. He looked normal most of the time, but his fear and sadness was an iron weight always dragging on him.

Darius rested his head on the bed next to Carina's hand.

If she and the other mages died he would be the only one left. He didn't want that. He didn't want to be the only mage. He didn't like being different from everyone else. They all treated him a little bit differently. He could feel a thread of wariness. They knew he could do things they couldn't; that if he really wanted to hurt them he could, very easily. Even Bryce treated him differently. He wasn't the same with him as he was with Nahla.

If he was the only mage, he would feel very alone.

He looked up at his sister's sleeping face. If only she could help him. She'd always helped him in the past. If she couldn't help him, he wanted to hear her voice at least, just a few words to give him comfort. But she was far away and she was journeying farther still.

Taking care not to touch or disturb any of the tubes or wires, Darius climbed up next to her. He laid his head next to hers on the pillow and closed his eyes.

A SHIP-WIDE ALERT had gone out. Darius was missing—again. Bryce couldn't rid himself of the gut-wrenching feeling that another disaster had occurred, only this time it was Darius who would be the victim. Nahla was safe here on the *Bathsheba's* bridge, but Darius had slipped away without anyone noticing.

"I'm sure he's fine," said Hsiao. "He's just wandered off and got distracted by something."

"Then why isn't he answering his comm?" Bryce asked.

Hsiao didn't reply.

"The Marchonish men are on the ship," he said. "We have to watch the kids. We have to know where they are at all times. How did he manage to get out of here without any of us noticing?"

Hsiao had come to relieve Bibik at the *Bathsheba's* flight controls. They had to maneuver to the rendezvous point with the arm dealer's vessel. Jackson and Justus were on the bridge too. Justus had come to find out what had happened on Lakshmi. At some time during the general chatter, Darius had left. It could have been as long as twenty minutes ago.

Bryce's comm chirruped. As he checked who it was, he felt the blood drain from his face.

Dr Asher.

"What's wrong?" asked Hsiao. "Aren't you going to answer it?"

Ever since leaving to go to Lakshmi Station, Bryce had been dreading Asher contacting him. He'd visited Carina to say goodbye, even though she was permanently unconscious now. She'd looked sicker than ever. She was slipping away from him and there wasn't anything he could do about it.

If Dr Asher had something to tell him it could only be bad news, possibly the worst news he would ever hear.

He accepted the comm. "Yes?"

"Darius is here in sick bay."

Relief hit him so hard he almost collapsed.

"He went into Carina and Parthenia's room ten minutes ago," Asher continued. "When I heard the alert, I checked and he's still there. He's asleep on Carina's bed."

"Thank the stars," breathed Bryce. "You're sure he's all right?"

"It depends how you define it," the doctor replied. "Considering everything the poor child has been through, he's far from all right. But, physically, he's fine. Just very tired, I imagine. Do you want me to wake him up?"

"No, I'll come over there and carry him to his suite."

CHAPTER 39

The men from Marchon had been making themselves at home on the *Bathsheba*—excessively so in Bryce's opinion. In the week since they'd come aboard, no one had caught sight of a single Marchonish woman, but the men ranged far and wide across the ship, showing their faces in all the areas the Black Dogs frequented and acting like the place was their own.

The mercs had kept their cool. No one had confronted the newcomers about their behavior yet, but tensions were simmering. It would only be a matter of time before they boiled over.

But today the focus of Bryce's attention had to be elsewhere. The arms dealer from Lakshmi Station had contacted them to say he was on his way with the weapon, accompanied by the technicians and engineers who would fit it to the ship and integrate it with her systems.

The work was already behind schedule. The dealer had implied the weapon would arrive earlier, and the delay had caused Bryce to assume the Enthrall Cast had worn off days ago. He'd thought the man had come to his senses, realized he'd been duped, and pocketed the deposit they'd handed over.

In the circumstances it wouldn't have been a bad outcome, though it would have meant that part of Carina's plan would be unfulfilled. Now it seemed the deal was going ahead, Bryce wasn't sure what to think. Was the arms dealer still Enthralled, or was he no longer experiencing the effects of the Cast and was coming to get his revenge?

They would soon find out.

In the days since departing Lakshmi they'd discussed how to fix the problem Darius's Cast had created, but they'd been unable to come up with a plan.

Bryce waited with Hsiao and Van Hasty at the airlock, ready to greet their visitors. Darius and Nahla were confined to quarters under express orders to not leave for the duration of the weapon fitting process. 'Uncle Jackson' and a rotating team of mercs were their protection from the Lakshmi Station-ites and Marchonish men.

The temptation to have Darius on hand to Cast them out of potential trouble from the arms dealer had been strong, but Bryce had decided against it. The boy's powers had worked against them recently. He couldn't risk more problems. Also, it was clear to anyone who knew Darius even a little bit that the boy was in a terrible mental state. It wouldn't be fair to place any more burdens on him. He needed nurturing, not responsibilities, though Bryce felt inadequate in that regard. There was only one person who could heal Darius, and not by a Cast but by her overwhelming love for him.

By some miracle, Carina and the other mages continued to cling to life, though how much longer they would last was unclear. The medical samples left at Lakshmi Station had yielded no results. The doctors there were just as confused by the mages' disease as were Asher and Baxter. When the seemingly inevitable happened, Bryce feared it would break the boy.

The arms dealer stepped from the airlock. His ship's hatches were compatible with the *Bathsheba's*, so he hadn't arrived via umbilicus wearing an EVA suit. Bryce guessed his vessel was an ancient model, like the Marchonish men's ship, only the dealer's would be refurbished and brought up to date, cherished in the way some people loved old autocar models. A cursory scan had told them the vessel was, nevertheless, bristling with armaments.

The dealer was better dressed than the last time Bryce had seen him. He wore a suit tailored to hide his belly and a wig of thick golden hair to cover his bald pate. Bryce thought he saw traces of make-up on his eyes and lips too. A man and a woman, similarly formally dressed, flanked him.

Bryce looked more closely at the dealer's eyes.

From the hazy, slightly unfocused look, he appeared to remain Enthralled! The length of time Darius's Cast had held was remarkable.

"Welcome aboard," said Bryce.

"Thank you. Members of my team are moving into place on the exterior of your ship. We will also need access to your existing weapons systems, engines, and bow infrastructure. My team leaders will organize the fitting from here."

He didn't mention his companions' names.

"Hsiao and I can show you to the bridge," said Bryce. "Does someone need to go to the bow section?"

"Me," said the woman, raising her hand.

Van Hasty departed with her.

"How long will the process take?" asked Bryce as he set off with the dealer and Hsiao.

"Barring any hiccups, about five hours. But there are always hiccups."

"As little as that?" Hsiao asked. "I thought you said it would take days."

"We made some adjustments before setting out," the dealer explained. "That was the cause of our delay. I thought it would be better to spend as little time out here and away from the station as possible."

"Why's that?" Hsiao probed. "If you don't mind me asking."

Bryce, too, wondered why the man was avoiding spending time at the *Bathsheba*.

"Haven't you heard? The Three-Systems War is heating up. Gugong has swapped sides and is now allying with Marchon. There are rumors a massive attack on the Quinton space fleet is planned. Interstellar space is big, but I'd rather be safe on Lakshmi if and when it kicks off. The speed and firepower of each side's battleships has increased exponentially over the decades, thanks to developers and suppliers like me. The risk is small, but I don't want to become collateral damage."

Bryce had to bite his tongue to avoid giving an angry response. The dealer didn't mind *other* folk being damaged by his business. Hsiao looked sour too.

"What are your plans after we finish our work here?" the dealer asked. "Are you leaving the system immediately?"

"We don't have any reason to stick around," Bryce lied.

"A wise move. Where's the young boy you had with you before?"

"He's playing in his cabin."

"Huh. Sweet kid. I never had any of my own. But there's still time."

How many tens of thousands of children had the man's business made orphans?

They walked onto the bridge. Bibik moved to rise from his seat, but Hsiao gestured at him to stay put. She took the male team leader to a weapons console and sat down with him.

While the pilot was guiding him through the *Bathsheba's* systems, it was up to Bryce to keep the dealer occupied—and to pray the effects of Darius's Cast would last until the work was completed and the people from Lakshmi were far, far away.

"How old is this ship?" asked the dealer. "I don't recognize the model."

Bryce wasn't sure how much it was safe to tell him. "We don't actually know. She seems to have had several owners before us. The database was originally in another language, not Universal."

"That old, huh? I thought so. She's held up pretty well, from what I can tell."

"We've had a few problems, but she hasn't killed anyone yet."

Not quite.

"They don't build them like they used to, not since the Colonization Period. Nowadays, battleships are where the money's at. People aren't interested in settling new worlds. Our ancestors found new homes and settled down. Even now, thousands of years later, most populations haven't exploited the full potential of their planets. There's no pressure to move on, you know? Not like there used to be in the old days."

Bryce thought of the group from Marchon, desperate to escape the home their ancestors had created.

"Can I get you a drink?" he asked, dying to effect an escape of his own. "I can probably program the printer to create any cocktail you want."

"I appreciate the offer, but I never touch a drop of alcohol until a job is done and the equipment has passed all the tests. It's a little superstition of mine."

Shame.

If he could have got the man off his face, they wouldn't need to worry about—

It happened.

The dealer blinked and his pupils contracted, as if bringing everything around him into sharp focus.

Dammit!

Darius's Cast had finally run its course.

"What...what was I saying?" he asked uncertainly.

"You were telling me about your superstition," Bryce answered, clinging to a tenuous hope that if he carried on as normal, the dealer might follow his lead. He might not recall he'd sold his highly expensive space weapon at a huge discount for no reason whatsoever.

"Yeah, that was it. I never...I never..." He squinted at his team leader where he was hunched over the console.

Murmuring could be heard as the man liaised with workers outside the *Bathsheba*.

"How about I give you a tour of the ship?" Bryce asked brightly. "You said you don't know this model. You might find it interesting."

"I, er..." The dealer ran a hand through the golden mop on his head, which didn't budge a millimeter. The wig had to be cemented on. Or perhaps it was real hair, grown within days by a body modification clinic. "I think I would. She's old but a beauty, and unique as far as I know. You're lucky to have her."

The man really was a connoisseur of ancient spacecraft. No one else would have called the *Bathsheba* beautiful.

Hsiao looked over her shoulder as the dealer and Bryce got to their feet. Apparently noticing the panic on her friend's features, her mouth opened to an O. Then her jaw snapped shut. She pointed at the team leader's back and gave a thumbs up. She would keep the man distracted and cut off from the arms dealer for as long as necessary. Or, rather, for as long as she could.

Bryce escorted the dealer from the bridge.

CHAPTER 40

*T*hanking the galactic gods the *Bathsheba* was a vast ship that took hours to tour, Bryce guided the arms dealer to the top deck and twilight dome. Not only was it far from the bridge and the bow where his team leaders were working, it was usually fairly empty.

Except as he stepped inside, he remembered it was one of the areas the Marchonish men had taken for their own. They weren't blatant about their territory-claiming efforts—yet. They used more subtle methods, such as turning silent whenever someone not belonging to their group entered their midst, or pointedly commandeering all the available seats.

It was dumb of them to antagonize the very people who had agreed to help them out of a tough spot, especially before the journey had even begun. But the men had been made arrogant by their culture. They clearly saw anyone who was either female or not from Marchon as stupid and inferior.

Not that the Black Dogs took any notice. They knew exactly what the newcomers were attempting, and they would have none of it. All silences were ignored, and if there was nowhere to sit down, they would fetch more chairs from somewhere else.

In the twilight dome, no struggle for dominance was going on. The place was filled with the Marchonish. They'd discovered the stored drinks behind the bars, and a party was in full swing. Bryce hesitated at the door. Would this be a good or bad venue to draw someone's attention from the fact they were in the process of losing a huge amount of money?

The arms dealer liked to drink. Perhaps he could persuade him to break his superstition.

It was the ideal spot.

The dealer was gazing up at the partially filled-in transparent dome. "That must have looked great when it was whole. What happened?"

"Uhhh…" There was nothing to be gained in telling him about Mezban and her bomb, or the Regians. "A blowout. The structure must have weakened over the years."

"Yeah? Hm." The dealer peered upward, his apparently knowledgeable gaze traveling the struts between the overhead sections.

"Are you sure I can't interest you in a cocktail?" Bryce asked. "What was it you said when we met? Something to oil the wheels?"

The Marchonish men were staring at them. Their tactical silence had fallen.

The dealer frowned. "Who are those guys? And what's their problem?"

"Just some passengers we'll be taking with us when we leave."

"I don't like the look of them. If you'll take my advice, you'll leave them behind, or drop them off at the first asteroid you see."

"Your advice is duly noted," said Bryce. "Now how about that cocktail? It's going to be hours before your team is finished."

"My team… My team that's fitting your—"

"We found some ancient drink recipes in the ship's database.

Unusual combinations you would never normally consider, but when you taste them they're rather special."

"No kidding? Well…"

"I'll mix you something. You don't have to drink it, only try a sip."

Without waiting for a reply, Bryce strode to the nearest bar. A surly man leaned on it. He lifted a lip before asking, "What do you want?"

"Get out of my way," Bryce hissed, shouldering the man aside.

"Hey!" the man protested.

His companions grumbled and edged closer.

Bryce took no notice of them as he hastily splashed random liquors into a glass and finished the drink off with a squirt of soda. He'd never made a cocktail in his life. His concoction probably tasted disgusting, but he hoped to get the dealer drunk as quickly as possible.

If the man's stomach didn't immediately press eject when the drink hit it, this recipe should have the desired effect. When he took it over, the dealer accepted it graciously, saying, "Just a sip, mind. Otherwise it's bad luck."

He lifted the glass to his lips and took somewhat more than a sip.

Instantly, his eyes widened until the whites showed all around the irises. His face turned red.

"That's…" he spluttered "…that's pretty good!"

"It is?!"

"I might indulge myself just a little further." He took a second drink and swilled the liquid around his mouth before swallowing it. He smacked his lips. After smiling like a child caught with his hand in the cookie jar, he slurped some more. "My! You must tell me what's in it."

"It's…er…" Bryce racked his brains. He didn't know the

ingredients. He hadn't read the labels on the bottles. "It's a secret family recipe, I'm afraid. I really can't tell you."

The dealer waggled a finger at him. "There's no need to be mysterious. I won't tell anyone, and you're leaving the system soon, right?" He drained the dregs of the drink.

"I'm sorry, if I told you I would bring down the family curse on you, and who knows what might happen then?"

The dealer considered this response for a second before shrugging. "Oh well, if this is going to be my only opportunity to enjoy your wonderful cocktail, you'd better make me another."

Shit.

"Sure." Bryce took the man's empty glass and set off toward the bar again.

What had he used to make the drink? He definitely couldn't remember. He'd created the chance to render the dealer so drunk he would allow the deal to go ahead, only to fumble it.

"Remind me," said a voice directly behind him.

Bryce jumped in shock. He turned. The dealer had followed him.

"How much are you paying to complete your purchase today?" Despite the alcohol circulating in his system, the man's gaze was clear and hard.

"I'm not sure exactly," Bryce replied. "Let me get you that cocktail, then I'll look it up."

"No more drinks. Look up that figure right now."

"No problem," said Bryce. "Come with me."

The Marchonish men watched with interest as he and the dealer walked to the door.

Bryce's mind was in turmoil. The dealer had clearly realized something was wrong. What would he do when he confirmed he'd been tricked? His battleship was easily a match for the *Bathsheba's* old, outdated weaponry, and he had a large team of workers, probably armed.

The doors to the twilight dome closed, shutting out the curious looks of the newcomers. The passageway stretched out left and right, empty.

What should he do? It would be hours before the dealer's team finish fitting the weapon to the *Bathsheba's* bow. He couldn't possibly put off revealing the deal was a sham for that long. What would happen then? At the very least, they would lose the weapon they wanted and needed. At worse, they would lose the ship and their lives.

They were passing Jace's cabin.

On impulse, Bryce slapped the security panel and the door opened. He'd had access to the man's suite ever since he'd fallen sick. Before he'd lost consciousness, he would occasionally ask Bryce to fetch him personal items.

"What are you doing?" asked the dealer. "What's in there?"

"We can access the computer via the interface here," Bryce replied. "It'll save us time."

The dealer blinked and leaned in. The lights came on, revealing a very ordinary cabin. Bryce's chest ached at the sight of small reminders of his friend, like the empty jug and the beakers from which Jace would drink cha.

"If you're sure..." The dealer stepped over the threshold.

Bryce was one step behind. As soon as they were both inside, he closed the door.

The dealer asked, "Where's the interf—"

Bryce's punch knocked him out cold. He snatched the comm button from the fallen man and searched him for weapons, relieving him of a gun in a shoulder holster before dragging him into the inner bedroom. He closed the door and locked it, and then returned to the passageway and locked the outer door too. Finally, he went into the suite's connections via the security panel and cut off its access to the ship's comm system.

With luck, no one would hear the dealer's hollers or banging. The Black Dogs wouldn't have a problem ignoring him, but the

Marchonish party had no knowledge of the situation. The newcomers' involvement would only complicate everything.

The un-Enthralled dealer was safely out of the way for now. What to do with him next was a question for which Bryce had no answer. Carina hadn't included a duped, outraged, very dangerous man in her plan.

CHAPTER 41

*W*hen he returned to the bridge, he found a holo on display and Hsiao and the team leader watching it.

"The battle's started!" the pilot exclaimed as she caught sight of him.

Streaks of light were speeding across space as the ships fired their pulse cannon. Long beams—particle lances—flashed out, carving into their targets. Tiny flecks representing fighter ships spewed from the bellies of larger craft, spread out, and turned in unison like a shoal of killer fish scenting prey.

The happenstance of the space battle was a welcome complication. It would serve as another distraction to the arms dealer's team, and hopefully it would encourage them to work fast so they could return to the safety of their station as soon as possible.

"How are you doing?" Bryce asked the team leader.

"Oh, uhhh..." The man returned his attention to the console. "I'm waiting for the engineers to give me the go ahead to begin synchronization. From what I've seen, it shouldn't be a problem." He added, "I'm Chi-tang, by the way. I don't hold with all that anonymity nonsense. It's not like you're going to implicate yourselves by giving us up to station security, is it?"

"So the weapon is actually illegal?"

"Oh yeah," Chi-tang replied. "About as illegal as they come, according to the current legislation on inter-system warfare. But my boss likes to stay ahead of the curve, developing new weapons ready for when they become legal."

"But what if they never become legal?" Hsiao asked.

"They always do. That's the way things have gone for the history of the war. The latest tech is one step ahead of the lawmakers, but the law catches up eventually. Whoa! Did you see that?" As Chi-tang had been talking, he'd continued to watch the battle.

Bryce checked the holo. A battleship had been cut clean in two. The halves were floating apart. Inside, rapid depressurization would be wreaking havoc, hurling crew into space, sucking them through hull breaches, slamming equipment into them. All personnel would be wearing EVA suits as a precaution against such an eventuality and the hatches between sections would seal, but the loss of life would be massive.

Chi-tang was staring at the scene, transfixed.

Bryce caught Hsiao's worried look. She had to be wondering what had happened to the dealer, but he had no way of telling her. Neither of them could mention the missing man without reminding Chi-tang of his existence.

Then, right on cue, he turned from the horrific scene on the holo and asked, "Where's my boss gone?"

"I left him in a lounge...relaxing," Bryce answered lamely.

"Relaxing?" Hsiao echoed, her eyebrows lifting as if to say *You couldn't think of anything better than that?*

"No problem," said Chi-tang. "I need to check something with him." He tried to use his comm button to speak to the dealer but, predictably, received no response. "That's odd."

"A malfunction maybe?" Hsiao suggested.

"If it was, it would be for the first time. We don't screw up stuff like that."

"Then he must have mislaid his button," said Hsiao.

"That's more likely. I'll have to go and speak to him face to face. Where is he?"

"In one of our lounges," Bryce replied, "really far from here. I'll go and get him for you."

"No, don't do that," said Chi-tang, alarmed. "He would hate the idea I was summoning him. *I* have to go to *him*."

"Well, I'm not sure where I left him," said Bryce.

"You're not sure...?"

Hsiao's eyebrows rose higher.

"I'll go find him." Bryce strode toward the door.

"No, I..." Chi-tang's focus switched to the console. "Great. An update."

Bryce slipped out quickly.

He jogged down the passageway, trying to get out of sight before Chi-tang finished reading the message and came after him. Hsiao could make up an excuse about not being allowed to leave the bridge and tell the team leader he had to stay there too, for security reasons.

She would think of something.

Hours of the weapon installation process remained. They had to keep the workers from discovering the disappearance of their boss until then.

After that?

Bryce had no idea.

But one thing he did know was he had to apprise Van Hasty of the situation. She was in the bow with the other team leader, who they also had to prevent from trying to contact her boss. He didn't want to risk a comm conversation with Van Hasty the woman might overhear, and he had to do something while avoiding the bridge and awkward questions from Chi-tang. He took a turn and headed forward.

The first people he encountered as he arrived, panting, at the bow were Marchonish men.

Were these the same ones he'd seen in the twilight dome, drawn by the new activity on the ship? Or were these different ones? They seemed to get everywhere they weren't wanted, hanging about like a bad smell.

They drew aside as Bryce approached. He saw someone he hadn't seen for days: Porcher. The Marchonish leader had put on weight in his short time on the ship. A bulging stomach seemed to be a feature of leaders in the region.

"Just the man I want to see," said Porcher, noticing him.

"Oh?" Bryce replied, slowing to a walk. "I'm busy right now."

He carried on past Porcher, but the man followed him.

"Something's going on we weren't informed about," Porcher persisted. "What is it? An adaptation to the ship?"

Bryce ignored him, scanning between the clustered bodies for Van Hasty.

"It's just, if you're doing something to the *Bathsheba* we should have been consulted, as per our agreement."

This comment drew Bryce to a halt. He faced the man. "What agreement is that?"

Entirely without shame, Porcher replied, "Our partnership in the running of the ship."

Bryce said darkly, "That isn't the agreement I remember. There *is* no partnership. We allowed you to join us. That's all."

"I don't recall the exact words, but it stands to reason we're an equal party in the venture, considering there are more of us than you."

"Your numbers don't mean anything, unless we're talking about the extra mouths to feed while you're out of Deep Sleep or the additional chemicals we'll need for the chambers. In fact, stacked up against the *colony ship* the Black Dogs own, your numbers mean a whole lot of nothing."

Bryce fixed the man with a stare, his hands on his hips.

Porcher's men were reacting badly to the conversation, their grumbles growing louder. Porcher held Bryce's gaze for a minute, but eventually looked away, shrugged, and smiled. "There will be plenty of time for negotiations after we set out. As a goodwill gesture, we'll agree to whatever it is you guys are having done to the ship this time. In the future, we'd appreciate some consultation."

Not dignifying this bullshit with a response, Bryce moved away and forced his way through the men who had gathered around them.

Fifty meters farther on, he found Van Hasty.

She was alone, standing next to an open maintenance access hatch, her pulse rifle slung across her back.

"Are those assholes still hanging around back there?" she asked.

"Yeah," Bryce replied.

There was no need for any explanation of which assholes she meant.

"Dammit. I can't get them to leave us alone. They don't take any notice of what I say. Half the time they pretend they can't hear me."

"Have they been interfering in the installation?"

"No, not yet anyway. The engineer's somewhere in there." She nodded at the open hatch. "I haven't seen her for half an hour."

"Good." Bryce brought her up to date on everything, finishing with, "So the longer that woman's in a tunnel and not asking where her boss has gone, the better."

"I'll keep her occupied as long as I can," said Van Hasty. "But don't you think it's time we got things moving?"

"What, now? That isn't what we planned."

"I know, but we didn't plan on locking up a furious arms dealer either. We need to improvise."

Bryce considered for a moment. "You're right. I forgot to tell you the space battle our dealer was worried about has started."

"It has? That could work to our advantage. I'll comm Jackson and tell him to get the ball rolling."

"And I'll message Hsiao and tell her to start building power for the 'test'."

CHAPTER 42

*P*orcher wasn't difficult to find among his buddies. He was 'holding court'. A bunch of men surrounded him listening to him spouting off about changes needed aboard the ship.

Bryce asked the man standing between him and the Marchonish leader to step aside. When he sneered and refused, Bryce took out his gun and pressed the muzzle into his chest.

The man's eyes popped and he backed away, hands raised.

Porcher noticed the commotion. "Hey, what are you—"

Bryce advanced, aiming at him. "It's time you and your men returned to your ship."

"Huh? Why?" Porcher shot a narrow-eyed glance at his supporters, as if to say, *It's happening. You know what to do.*

"The deal's off," said Bryce. "Move."

"Now wait a minute," Porcher protested. "Let's talk this out like men."

"I don't see you moving. You have five seconds."

"This isn't fair! You said—"

"Four. Three."

"Okay, that's enough," said Porcher, his tone hardened. "You asked for this."

There was a flurry of movement. Two men grabbed Bryce from behind. His gun was wrested from his hand.

"I never liked you," sneered Porcher as one of the men handed him Bryce's weapon. "Jumped up teenager, barely out of short pants. It's going to give me great pleasure to—"

Jackson appeared behind him, suited up. Porcher jerked forward as something was thrust into his back.

"What?" Jackson asked. "I'm dying to hear what's going to give you great pleasure. Don't let me stop you."

Porcher grimaced. "Let's not be hasty. I wasn't really going to hurt the kid."

"Back off!" a Marchonish man yelled, pulling a gun from the back of his pants. "Let him go!"

They weren't supposed to carry arms on the ship. It was one of the conditions of the agreement. Not that the mercs had taken them at their word. They were frisked before being allowed aboard. But clearly someone had slipped up. Either that or they'd managed to break into one of the armories.

Another man darted forward to snatch Bryce's weapon from Porcher. "Yeah! Let him go!"

The men edged in, closing the space around Bryce, Porcher, and Jackson.

"Kill them both," someone urged. "Then we take over the ship."

"Nuh uh," said a voice from somewhere at the back. "That ain't happening."

Van Hasty had come up.

"It's the bitch!" a man called out.

A pulse round hissed out. Van Hasty was taking the initiative.

The bunched-up men broke in a confused wave. Some were heading toward Van Hasty and some were running from her.

Bryce was buffeted hard. Something heavy landed at his feet: the Marchonish leader, a smoking hole in his back.

"He killed Porcher!"

Jackson shot the man aiming at him next. At the same time, Bryce ran at the other armed man and knocked him off his feet. He grabbed his gun. When the man wouldn't let go, he kicked him in the head.

"Where's Van Hasty?" he gasped, rising with his weapon back in his hands.

Another tide was passing them. The Black Dogs accompanying Jackson had arrived. They crashed into the Marchonish men.

The fight was brief. Any of the newcomers who didn't surrender immediately were executed on the spot. Most of them weren't dumb enough to put up a fight. As the struggle died down, only six or seven bodies lay on the deck.

The Black Dogs led the men from Marchon away, their heads hung low as reality caught up with them. Van Hasty brought up the rear, her rifle at her shoulder. When she reached Bryce and Jackson, she halted. Gazing down at Porcher's corpse, she said, "Damn. *I* wanted to kill him."

"You don't get everything you want," said Jackson.

"Ain't that the truth. Where to now?"

"A lot of them are in the twilight dome," Bryce replied, "but don't you have to wait here for the engineer?"

"Nah," she said. "I mean, yeah, probably, but the longer she wanders around trying to find someone to talk to the better, right?"

* * *

As THEY PASSED Jace's cabin, Bryce listened for sounds of the imprisoned arms dealer. No shouts or banging could be heard.

Either he'd given up or Bryce's guess at the soundproofing afforded by two doors and a room in between was correct.

Fifteen Black Dogs had already arrived at the dome as requested by Jackson and were waiting outside.

"This should be fairly easy," Jackson told them.

"Aw, don't say that!" Van Hasty protested. "You'll jinx it."

"We only want them back on their ship," Jackson went on. "But they don't get two chances to argue about it."

He opened the doors.

A pulse round hit his breastplate, scorching it, though it must have been fired at some distance because it didn't seem to hurt him.

The Black Dogs had retreated to each side of the open doorway, out of the line of sight of anyone in the room.

"Dammit, Jackson," said Van Hasty. "What did I say about jinxing it?"

The Marchonish men had overturned the tables and chairs and used them to build a barricade. Word had reached them about their forced evacuation.

"Come out with your hands raised," Jackson called out. "You know there's only one way this can end."

"We're not going back to our ship!" came a reply. "We're not going back to Marchon!"

"You're leaving the *Bathsheba*," said Jackson, "dead or alive. Whichever doesn't matter to us."

"Speak for yourself," Van Hasty muttered. "I don't want to scrape their bloody carcasses off the deck."

"We would rather die here like men!"

"Sure," Jackson replied. "Have it your way. You're pretty dumb men, if I'm honest, but if that's what you want." He nodded at the Black Dogs.

They piled into the room, rifles blazing.

Through the flash of rounds, some tentative hands rose beyond the barricade. A pulse hit one, turning it into a macabre torch. The hand disappeared, its owner screaming. Figures were moving in the shadowy room, running, darting into the corners.

Bryce had a feeling the man who had asserted the group's death wish hadn't been speaking for all of them.

"They're giving up!" he yelled. "They're surrendering."

The furniture was already ablaze. Fire-suppressing foam spurted from overhead. The mercs gradually ceased firing. Some men lay on the floor, groaning. Others peeked out from their hiding places.

"We'll go peacefully," someone said. "Just don't shoot."

"Shit," Van Hasty muttered, surveying the smoking, charred scene. "What a mess."

* * *

WHILE THE TWO largest groups of Marchonish men were being rounded up, Black Dogs had been roaming the ship finding the rest of the individuals and giving them their marching orders. Despite their swagger, when it came down to it the men generally did exactly what they were told. Though perhaps that wasn't so surprising considering the proximity of rifle muzzles to their faces.

When the Black Dogs were confident all their unwelcome visitors had returned to their own vessel, they prepared to disable her engine. The group would be stranded in space but they would leave them with working comms. Someone would come to their rescue eventually. Then they could tell whoever they liked about the kids on the colony vessel who could disappear at will. The *Bathsheba* would be long gone by then.

Jackson, Van Hasty, and two merc engineers stood at the airlock, along with a plentiful guard in case the Marchonish men put up a fight.

"Right," said Van Hasty. "So after we kill their engine, that's when we get the women."

"We what?" asked Jackson.

"Are you deaf? We get the women. We can't leave them with those pricks."

"We never discussed this."

"We never discussed it because it's *obvious*."

"Not to me."

"What?!" Van Hasty's voice rose in outrage.

"How do you know they want to join us?" Jackson challenged. "No one's even seen one, let alone talked to any of them."

"Of *course* they want to join us. What's *wrong* with you? Haven't you lived alongside the evolutionary throwbacks controlling them for the past week?"

"And you're so much better, deciding for yourself what these women want?"

Van Hasty frowned at him. "After we kill their engine, we get the women."

CHAPTER 43

hile the expulsion of the Marchonish men had been going on, Bryce had suited up. He decided to accompany the Black Dogs into the Marchonish ship, driven by curiosity as much as anything. No one from the *Bathsheba* had boarded her until now. He wanted to see the other half of Marchonish society the men kept so secluded.

The vanguard of mercs stepped from the airlock onto the foreign vessel.

"What do you want?" a voice called out. The man kept himself out of sight. "We did what you asked. We left your ship. Now leave us alone."

"We have a couple more jobs to finish first," Jackson replied, "before we're done."

"What?" the man asked. "What are you going to do? Porcher's dead and so are seven others. We've paid our dues. Let us go."

"When we've finished our business."

The mercs were advancing into the ship. Bryce was part of the rearguard, walking backward. In here, their enemy had access to their own weapons. The Black Dogs could meet some foolhardy resistance from men whose arrogance sometimes overrode their common sense.

The Black Dogs pushed forward. Van Hasty was on point.

"Bring out your women," she said. "We have a proposition for them."

"Ha!" the mystery man replied. "I bet you do. So that's why you're here. You want to steal them. We should have guessed. That's why you forced us off your ship. You never wanted us. You only ever wanted our females."

"This is the engine room," said Carter via helmet comm. "Blake, Rees, with me."

Three figures split off from the group and disappeared to the side. The rest of the mercs halted.

"We want to speak to the women," said Van Hasty. "Bring them here."

"Like hell," the voice replied. "You want them, you come and get them."

"Leave it, Van Hasty," Jackson said via comm. "It's not worth the risk."

"No, dammit," she replied. "I'm not leaving until I've talked to them."

"Maybe they don't have any women," a merc joked. "Maybe they only exist in the men's imaginations."

"I had a girlfriend like that once," said someone else. "Best woman I ever had. Never complained about anything."

"Quit kidding around," Van Hasty snapped. "You're doing a goddamned public service here."

"Get out," said the invisible Marchonish man. "You're not having our women and that's the end of it."

A tense pause stretched out.

"Van Hasty," said Jackson, "unless you want to search every corner of this ship with hostiles at every turn—"

"Wait," she said before switching to external comm. "I get it. You know what their answer will be if you bring them here. You know they'll leave you in a heartbeat when they see what's on offer. You know you don't stand a chance against real men."

"You said it, Van Hasty," someone commented.

"Shut up, idiot."

"That isn't true!" the voice yelled. "Bitch! You're just trying to manipulate us."

"If it isn't true," she replied, "prove it."

Silence.

Then sounds of movement and muffled arguments.

Bryce had been watching the empty passageway that led back to the airlock. He risked a look over his shoulder, past the Black Dogs to the passageway ahead.

He was just in time to see the first woman appear.

He drew in a breath.

She was heavily pregnant, her swollen belly pressing against the thin fabric of her dress. Aside from her stomach, she was painfully thin. Her eyes were wide and frightened above her jutting cheekbones, and her long hair was an unkempt mess.

The mercs moved uneasily. Van Hasty's enforced rescue mission was no longer such a joke.

More women stepped into view behind her. They differed in stature and coloring, but in their half-starved, fearful state they were alike.

Bryce quickly counted them before he had to look aft again in case of a rearward attack. He'd counted about twenty. Were there more who hadn't come forward? How many had been held back? They would probably never know.

"*Fuck*," Van Hasty whispered. Then over external comm, she said, "We're inviting you to come with us aboard the *Bathsheba*. We can't promise you anything much except food, your own space, and whatever else you might need. We're traveling out of this system, destination undecided. You're welcome to join us, but there will be no going back and you have to decide now, this minute."

Bryce's attention was inexorably drawn to the spectacle playing out behind him.

The pregnant woman's eyes shifted to the side, like she was conscious of being watched.

"You don't have anything to fear," said Van Hasty softly. "We'll protect you."

The woman took a step forward.

"Ava!" someone yelled. "Don't you dare!"

She froze.

"It's okay," said Van Hasty, hoisting her rifle to her shoulder.

The woman took another step.

Van Hasty and the man next to her moved to the side so Ava could pass between them.

"Get back here!" a man shouted. "You're not taking my kid!"

He darted into sight.

Van Hasty fired and he fell.

The women screamed and ducked. Some ran toward the mercs, others sped away from them. More men appeared, firing. The mercs shot back.

Bryce whirled to face the rear. Marchonish men were heading up the passageway. He began shooting.

"Fall back!" Jackson hollered. "Back to the ship! Carter, Rees, Blake, where are you?"

"Coming," Carter replied. "Their engine's dead."

Bryce was pouring round after round into the men blocking their escape. Their enemy was in armor, but the barrage began to take its toll. But Bryce's suit was heating up too. He marched steadily forward, forcing a passage to the airlock.

Someone stepped in front of him. It was one of the Marchonish women, panicking in terror. He thrust her back.

The airlock appeared. The hatch remained open. Perhaps the Marchonish men had some brains after all.

Bryce ran to the airlock and laid down cover up one side of the passageway while his partner covered the other. The rest of the mercs and Marchonish women raced through the hatch. Bryce counted the women.

Five.

Only five out of the twenty or so he'd seen.

Five out of all the women on the ship had managed to get out.

Van Hasty entered the airlock. The passageway was empty.

Bryce and his partner stepped inside and together they ran through to the *Bathsheba's* airlock.

They closed the hatch and Bryce slammed the button to decouple the ships.

CHAPTER 44

*B*ryce burst onto the bridge. He'd run there after taking off his armor, eager to tell Hsiao of the successful de-infestation of the *Bathsheba* and the handful of Marchonish women they'd saved.

Chi-tang turned to look at him curiously.

Shit.

The space weapon.

The dealer imprisoned in Jace's cabin.

The second part of the plan.

"Hey," Hsiao greeted him.

She looked tired and anxious. Her efforts to keep Chi-tang distracted for the last several hours were telling on her.

Bryce gaped as he desperately tried to think of something to say.

"Our visitors left," was all he could come up with.

"Our visitors?"

"From Marchon."

"Oh," said Hsiao. Then her eyes widened. "Ohhh, *those* visitors. That's fantastic news."

"A few of them are staying though."

"They are?"

"Yes. I'll explain later." He faced Chi-tang. "How is the installation going?"

"It's complete," the team leader replied. "We're ready to move on to testing, but I still can't locate my boss. Did you find him? He needs to be here for the test."

"The test? The *test*? Excellent. Hsiao, could you...?"

"I'm on it." She moved to the pilot's console.

"Has everyone from your team returned to your ship?" Bryce asked Chi-tang.

"Definitely. It's far too dangerous for them to be out in the black when we fire the weapon. But my boss has to be here. Where the hell has he got to?"

Bryce shrugged. "Who knows? It's a big ship. He could be anywhere." He comm'd Jackson. "Phase two."

"Copy."

The comm went dead.

Chi-tang's brow wrinkled. "Look, I'm not an idiot. I know something's going on here. What I can't figure out is, what? What are you guys up to?"

Without turning around, Hsiao replied, "It's better you don't know. You seem like a nice person. I don't want to get you into trouble." Then, into her mic, she said, "Strap in, everyone. We're going for a ride."

"I'm probably already in trouble," said Chi-tang sadly as he fastened his safety harness.

"Why's that?" Bryce asked, slipping into the nearest seat and doing the same.

"Because whatever it is you have planned, I'm sure my boss isn't going to like it. And when he realizes I've been here all this time while you did your thing, he's going to blame me for not stopping you."

"How could you stop us?" Hsiao asked. "You don't know what we're doing."

Chi-tang shook his head. "He isn't a reasonable man."

"Then why are you working for him?" The pilot was easing the *Bathsheba* into motion after her weeks of dormancy, trickling power into the engines from the large store the generators had built over the last few hours.

"I don't have a choice." Chi-tang scanned the bridge as if he expected the arms dealer to pop out somewhere. "He paid my school fees. It was the only way I could afford college. I agreed to work for him for ten years once I'd graduated. I was young and stupid and didn't understand what I was getting into. I thought when my ten years were up I would be free to do my own thing. But do you think a man like that will let me leave? I know too much now. I'll be working for him the rest of my life."

Hsiao and Bryce shared a look.

"Hang in there, Chi-tang," said Hsiao. "Things might not turn out how you expect."

She swept her screen, and the *Bathsheba's* thrusters burst into life, slamming Bryce into his seat.

It took a couple of minutes for the acceleration compensators to fully kick in. During that time, it was all he could do to avoid passing out. Chi-tang *did* pass out. His mouth hung open and his head hung to one side. As the acceleration effects eased, his head flopped forward.

"Is the space battle over?" Bryce asked Hsiao.

"Yep. It only lasted a couple of hours, luckily for us. I would *not* have liked to fly into the middle of that. It was a slaughter. I don't know who won, if anyone."

"How long to our destination?"

Hsiao consulted her screen. "Twenty-one minutes eighteen seconds."

"We're that close?"

"We flew a lot closer when we came to the rendezvous point."

"We're going to need Chi-tang awake," said Bryce. "Unless he taught you how to fire the weapon."

"He didn't. We were supposed to receive the instructions after we paid the dealer the remainder of what we owe."

Bryce imagined the dealer, trapped, probably bounced and buffeted by the ship's movement. All comms to Jace's cabin cut, he wouldn't have heard Hsiao's warning.

"Someone's going to be disappointed," he remarked.

"Someone is already severely disappointed."

Chi-tang began to come around a few minutes later. He sat upright and blinked. "Where…? Oh, yeah." He looked worried.

"Now you're awake," said Bryce. "I want to talk to you about something."

"What?" Chi-tang asked cautiously.

"This weapon we're in the process of buying, we need you to fire it."

Chi-tang looked from Bryce to Hsiao. "Why me?"

"Because we don't know how," Hsiao explained.

"But I could run you through—"

"There isn't time," said Bryce. "We'll only get one chance to make the shot. It has to be perfect. So it has to be you. You're the expert, right?"

"Yes, but…" Chi-tang swallowed.

"And in return," said Hsiao, "you can come with us."

"Leave Lakshmi Station?"

"Yes."

"Leave the system on a colony ship?"

"Yes."

He appeared to consider the offer. "No. I'm sorry. I can't deny it's tempting. I don't have anyone in particular I'd be sad to leave behind. My family were killed in a Quintonese attack and my best friend from school signed up as a space marine. He didn't even last a year. But my boss is smart and ruthless. You'll never get away with fooling him. Whatever your plan is, it won't succeed. I can't take the risk."

"Maybe if I tell you what you'll be firing at," said Bryce, "you'll change your mind."

Chi-tang said, "I'm listening."

After Bryce relayed the information, a smile broke out over the man's face.

"I'll do it! That's a brilliant idea. I wish I'd thought of it myself. But you're right, it'll need perfect targeting to do the job correctly."

"Great," said Bryce.

"Less than fifteen minutes to arrival," Hsiao warned.

He unsnapped his harness and leapt from his seat.

Chi-tang was right. The arms dealer was a smart man. The easiest thing to do would be to kill him, but his workers might be more loyal than his team leader, and they were aboard a fully armed vessel. They would be deeply suspicious after not hearing from their boss for so long, and they might decide to inflict some damage on the *Bathsheba* to persuade the Black Dogs to hand him over.

As Bryce waited for the elevator to take him up to the top deck, the answer to his problem came.

Hsiao comm'd him. "Nine minutes."

"I know. I'm nearly there. I figured out what to do with the dealer. Chi-tang is still on board with the plan?"

"He's raring to go."

The elevator stopped and the doors opened.

* * *

THE ARMS DEALER WAS RED-FACED, bruised, and furious. As soon as Bryce had opened the door to Jace's bedroom, the dealer flew at him. Bryce shot low to avoid killing the man. He needed him alive.

The dealer screamed and collapsed, all his anger and energy gone in an instant. He rolled on the deck, clasped his right calf and yelled in agony.

Bryce cursed. He hadn't meant to hurt him so badly.

But when he looked more closely, the damage didn't seem serious. The pulse round had grazed him, burning his pants and skin, but not deeply wounded him. He threw the EVA suit down on the dealer. "Stop yelling and put that on, or next time I'll aim higher."

"You'll regret this," the dealer seethed, but he did as Bryce had instructed, fumbling the zippers and clasps.

"Hurry up," Bryce urged, poking him with his rifle.

In a few minutes Chi-tang would fire the weapon. Then they would only have a short time to get out of range of the dealer's ship.

The man put on his helmet.

Bryce pushed the muzzle of his rifle into his back and forced him out of the cabin. The nearest airlock would do, he calculated. Once the dealer was outside, his men would be forced to decouple from the *Bathsheba* and pick him up, buying them precious moments. He checked the time. Fifty-three seconds remained until they reached their target. The ship would be decelerating quickly now.

The dealer was saying something and gesticulating as Bryce marched him along. He hadn't turned on his external comm, so Bryce had no idea what he was saying.

"I'll kill you for this!"

He'd found the external comm.

"I'll have you tortured until you beg for death!"

They were at the airlock.

Bryce opened the hatch and gave the man a hard shove, sending him through the opening and down, sprawling, onto the deck. He closed the inner hatch and immediately opened the outer one. It was against protocol, but it achieved the desired effect: the fast-escaping air expelled the dealer far away from the ship.

"Five," said Hsiao over the shipwide comm. "Four. Three. Two. One."

There was no need for any explanation. Everyone aboard knew what she was counting down to, with the exception of the rescued Marchonish women.

"We did it!" Hsiao announced. "We hit it perfectly."

No one was around to celebrate with, but Bryce didn't care. There would be time to celebrate later.

What mattered was the rogue planet, the excuse for decades of war, immeasurable pain and suffering and the loss of countless lives, and the source of the ill-gotten wealth of Lakshmi Station's elite, had received a hit from a weapon so powerful it would break it apart, leaving nothing but scattered rocks and a dusty haze.

It was over. There was nothing left for Marchon, Quinton, and Gugong to fight over. Their governments and corporations might scramble to find another excuse, but if the Marchonish would-be colonists were anything to go by, the populations were ripe for change. Hopefully, they had provided the catalyst.

He returned to the bridge.

Van Hasty was there and so was Jackson.

"Did you check on the kids?" Bryce asked him.

"Yeah. They're doing fine, and they were very glad to hear the Marchonish men are gone."

Chi-tang was looking pleased with himself.

"What's happening with our business partner?" Bryce asked Hsiao.

"You mean our soon-to-be-ex business partner?" She looked up from the scanner. "His friends spotted him and are maneuvering to pick him up."

"Then it's time we left."

"That's exactly what I was thinking."

Van Hasty gasped. "Oh shit! What happened to the engineer?"

"She's still on the ship?" asked Bryce.

"She's still here somewhere. Where exactly is anyone's guess."

"She'll turn up sooner or later," said Hsiao, returning to the pilot's seat. Before she could issue the command to fasten safety harnesses, however, she received a comm. She listened, her shoulders slumped, and she gave a little *Oh!*

To Bryce's surprise, she collapsed onto her console and her shoulders began to shake.

"Hsiao?" He got up.

At the same time, Van Hasty noticed her. She reached the pilot first and leaned over her. "What's wrong?"

But Hsiao couldn't answer. She was sobbing her heart out. Deep, gut-wrenching sobs.

Her face a mask of bewilderment, Van Hasty removed Hsiao's comm button and spoke into it.

Bryce was close enough to hear Dr Asher answer. The doctor's words were crisp and formal, but her tremulous tone conveyed her struggle to maintain her composure as she said, "I'm sorry to inform you that Jace died a few minutes ago."

CHAPTER 45

*B*ryce sat with his head bowed at Carina's bedside. He'd told her that her plan had succeeded. Everything she'd set out had worked, he'd said, with a few wrinkles along the way, though they hadn't managed to find a cure for Nahla. Still, she was healthy and seemed fairly happy.

The last part was a white lie. Nahla appeared down, in fact, and so was Darius. But Carina didn't need to know that. Should he tell her about Jace? Bryce doubted she could hear anything anyway. She was clearly near death herself.

He recalled collecting Darius from her bed the other day. The boy had looked so sad even asleep. No one had told him Carina would pass away soon, but he knew. Of course he knew. Bryce wondered how he could even begin to offer the boy comfort when he was broken too?

He remembered the first night they'd met in the tavern on Ithiya. He'd watched her from a distance getting drunker and drunker, drowning a nameless sorrow like so many in that place. He'd followed her out into the street, drawn to her for some unknown reason. He recalled how he'd tried to steal from her to fund the meds he needed to keep himself alive, and how she'd woken and nearly killed him. The memories came flooding in: the journey over the snowy mountains to the Sherrerr fortress; persuading her to trust him on the Sherrerr ship, *Nightfall*, when they'd helped her family escape; her treacherous snake of a brother, Castiel; Sable Dirksen, malevolent and callous; Carina trapped in the battered mech on Ostillon; riding on horses when they left the Matching; sitting with her inside the eye of the space-traveling, sentient creature Darius had incongruously named Poppy.

They'd lived so much in such a short space of time, and now Carina's time was coming to an end.

What hurt him most was that he'd never had the chance to tell her how much he loved her. He'd gone to Lakshmi hoping he would be able to talk to her when he returned, but it was too late. She'd gone downhill so fast. After explaining the plan to Van Hasty, she'd never spoken again.

Dr Asher arrived. Her eyes were deeply shadowed and her face thin and pale. She'd suffered through the mages' illness too. Bryce couldn't imagine how hard it must be to lack the ability to help your patients, to be forced to watch young, healthy people wither away while you, the medical professional, stood by, helpless.

"I think you should call Darius and Nahla in here," she said.

A tight band fastened around his heart and chest. He swallowed and asked, "To say goodbye?"

Asher nodded. "It's advised. It will help them make sense of what's happening, and, eventually, it will help them come to terms with it."

Hardly able to get the words out, he said, "So she doesn't have long?"

"A few hours at most."

"And Parthenia?"

"She and the twins haven't entered the dying process yet, but they probably only have days left. Maybe a week or two."

His world was closing in around him, but somehow he had to find the strength to struggle through. "I'll go and get them."

He forced himself to his feet and out of the sick bay. In a waking nightmare, he walked to the children's suite.

The door opened on familiar furniture. There was the table the family used to eat at together and where Ferne and Oriana would create their unorthodox fashion designs. Across the living space was the door to Parthenia's room, where she would hide away refusing to speak to anyone. That was the sofa Darius and Nahla would sit on when they played cards.

Where were they?

He hadn't checked up on them since hearing the news of Jace's death and hurrying to Carina's side, fearing he might never see her alive again.

Did the children even know about Jace?

Heavy with guilt, he crossed the living area to their bedroom. Opening the door, he stuck his head around it.

Phew!

They were both here. Nahla was sitting on her bed reading her interface and Darius was asleep on top of his bedcovers.

Nahla looked up. "Hi Bryce! Something wonderful has happened."

"Has it? Tell me about it. I need to hear something wonderful."

"I can read what I wrote before."

"You can read what you wrote? What do you mean?"

"After I had my accident," she explained patiently, "I had to learn to read again. But it was hard and I was very slow. I used to ask Darius to read for me. One day I found something I'd written months ago, a translation of the mage documents. I couldn't understand it at all. But I tried to read it again just now, and I can! Listen."

She began to read aloud, fluently and confidently. Her intonation of complex sentences was perfect and her pronunciation of difficult words was correct. Bryce sank onto her bed. As he watched her, the truth dawned on him: the intelligent spark had returned to her eyes. He reached out to touch the interface she held, pushing it down.

She looked up, confused. "Did I read it wrong?"

"No, you read it perfectly. Could you do something for me? Could you walk to Darius's bed and back?"

She strode the ten steps swinging her arms.

Her limp had gone.

The old Nahla was back.

"This is a miracle!" he exclaimed. "You're the same as you were before. I wonder how it happened. What have you done since we returned from Lakshmi?"

"Nothing much. Just the usual. Except I had to play by myself because Darius wouldn't play with me. All he would do was lie on his bed and mope. How are Carina and the others? Are they getting better? It's boring staying in here with only Darius to talk to."

Bryce regarded the sleeping boy, and his elation over Nahla's miraculous recovery turned to despair as he remembered the awful news he had to convey.

Darius was lying on his back, his elixir bottle in his hand. The cap was off and from its position the bottle was empty. He must have drunk all the contents.

That was strange. Why would he need to do a lot of Casting?

A creeping horror bled into the edges of Bryce's mind. He looked at the sleeping boy more closely. For someone in a deep sleep, his chest was barely moving.

Was it even moving at all?

He thumbed his comm button. "Dr Asher? Please come to the children's suite immediately." He ran to Darius's side and listened to his chest. After two seconds of agonized waiting he heard one beat of the boy's heart.

Darius had saved Carina's life once, bringing her back from

the edge of death. It was something only Spirit Mages could do, Carina had told him, but it was at the risk of losing their own lives. Had Darius Healed Nahla's brain, reinvigorating the dead cells, returning her to her original, highly intelligent state? And had he thereby put his life in the balance?

Just when Bryce thought his world could not become any darker, a new darkness descended. If Darius died, he couldn't see a way to go on.

Footsteps sounded in the outer room. Asher had arrived in record time.

But it wasn't the doctor who walked into the bedroom, it was Hsiao. Her grief over Jace's death still marked her features, but she managed a wan smile.

"I've left Bibik in control of the ship. I thought I would offer Darius some more flying lessons to help cheer him up."

"He's...He's..." Bryce struggled. The words wouldn't come out.

"Stars, Bryce, what's wrong?"

She sat down beside him and put an arm over his shoulders.

"I think he might have done something really stupid."

"Huh?"

"I think he might have sacrificed himself for Nahla."

"What do you mean, sacrificed himself for me?" asked Nahla, looking up sharply.

He couldn't hide it from her. She was too smart. She would figure it out anyway.

"You know Darius is a Spirit Mage and the rest of your brothers and sisters are Star Mages?"

"Yes, of course. They don't talk about it much, but I do know that."

"Well, do you remember that time we went to the Matching, and Sable Dirksen had the place set alight?"

"It isn't likely I would forget something like that, is it?"

"Hold on," said Hsiao. "What did you say about Spirit Mages and Star Mages? What's the difference?"

"Spirit Mages are far more powerful," Nahla answered. Then her expression grew troubled. "Did Darius Cast for me? That's why I'm better?" She leapt up. "Is he going to be all right?

Asher ran in. "What's the— Stars, no!" She bent over Darius and lifted his eyelids. "He's out cold." She pulled a handheld scanner from a bag and placed it against his chest before running it over the rest of his body. As she read the display, a little of her tension visibly eased. "He has a steady heartbeat and respirations, but they're worryingly low. Let's get him to sick bay. You can tell me what happened on the way."

Bryce lifted the boy into his arms.

Hsiao grabbed Nahla. "Why are Star Mages called that? Is it something to do with stars?"

"They aren't really sure, but it's believed they might derive their power from stars, while Spirit Mages derive theirs from the energy of the people around them."

"It was the star!" Hsiao yelled, so loud Bryce and Dr Asher paused in the doorway.

"The star at Lakshmi Station is abnormal," Hsiao continued. "It doesn't fit in any of the categories. It sends out all kinds of weird stuff. The star must have been affecting the Star Mages like a poison. First it killed their ability to Cast, and then it got to work on the rest of their bodies. Oh no! No! If I'd realized earlier, I could have saved Jace!"

She collapsed onto the bed, but Bryce could do nothing to help her. He had to get Darius to sick bay.

CHAPTER 46

They committed Jace's body to the universe the mage way, placing wood, water, iron, and earth with it. Unable to supply a real fire, they would cremate him in a blast from the *Bathsheba's* thrusters in the same way Carina had burned Ma's body all those months—years?—ago.

She clung to Bryce's arm as the ceremony took place, for physical as well as emotional support. By the time the short speeches were over, she was at the end of her strength.

Waking up had seemed like a miracle. After that last boost to her metabolism by the stimulant, her descent into her illness had been rapid. She could vaguely remember closing her eyes for what she thought would be the last time.

Then when she'd opened them again, it had been three weeks later. The Black Dogs had successfully carried out her plan, ridding the ship of the Marchonish would-be invaders, and possibly putting an end to the Three-System War. What was more, the *Bathsheba* was now fitted with a weapon so large and powerful it should deter the most intrepid space pirates.

She wondered what Bongo had made of the news the planet had been destroyed. Did he guess she had something to do with it? Bryce had said his cousin had been there when they negotiated with the arms dealer to purchase the weapon. He had to know he'd been indirectly responsible for the destruction of the planet. She hoped the knowledge brought him some satisfaction.

She was certainly happy about it. She was grateful to Parthenia for changing her mind about it being none of their business.

They had also gained seven new passengers while she'd been unconscious—eight if you counted the baby born this morning. But they had lost one very important, very loved crew member, who Carina would never forget. They would miss his calm, gentle presence and wise advice.

The airlock doors opened. Six mercs carried Jace's wrapped body through the hatch carefully and respectfully. They gently placed him on the deck, saluted, turned, and marched out.

It wasn't quite the usual mage funeral, but Carina guessed Jace would have approved anyway. He and the Black Dogs had grown friendly over their time together, despite their opposing philosophies on life. But then again, Jace could make a friend of anyone, and who could have known him and not loved and respected him?

The airlock hatch closed.

Carina closed her eyes and slumped against Bryce's side.

"Hey," he said softly. "Come on, let's find you a seat. I said you didn't need to stand. Everyone would have understood."

"I know, but I wanted to." She allowed him to lead her to the nearest room, where they found somewhere to sit down.

"I wanted to stay," she said weakly. "I should have stayed to the end."

"You're only missing the final part. It doesn't matter. Jace has gone. That was just his shell we were saying goodbye to."

"I know," she whispered, hunching over as tears spilled from her eyes.

Bryce pulled her close. "I don't know what to say to make you feel better. I'm going to miss him too, so much. But at the same time I'm glad there aren't five more bodies in that airlock."

"I'm glad the rest of us survived too. I really am, though it might not look like it. Especially Darius. He came so close."

"You *all* came so close. Asher told me you only had a few hours left and that's why I had to go and get Darius and Nahla to…" He took a deep breath, paused, and pressed a finger and thumb to his eyes. When he'd mastered himself he went on, "Things could have turned out a whole lot worse. If we hadn't happened to leave the vicinity of that star in time, you wouldn't be here now."

"If only we'd left earlier," said Carina. "If only I'd figured out the star was having an influence on us. Hsiao told me there was something weird about it when we arrived. I didn't pay any attention. I was still angry at her over what she said about Darius at the meeting. I didn't think about the star at all after that. I still don't know how it affected us, but Hsiao must have been right."

"Right or wrong, I don't care. You're on the mend, thank the stars—though not the one powering Lakshmi Station."

Oriana peeked into the room. "There you are! We were wondering where you'd gone."

"I needed to rest a little," said Carina, "that's all."

"You'll feel better soon. Ferne and I are nearly back to normal. Dr Asher said it's because we're the youngest. Our bodies resisted the effects of the star longest. That's why Jace was the first to…" Her face twisted up and she hung her head.

"It's okay," Carina said.

Parthenia also appeared and sat down next to Carina, resting her head on her shoulder. "Let's not ever fight again, okay? I can't even remember the last time I spoke to Jace and now he's gone. I'll never get another chance to talk to him."

Parthenia appeared to be holding herself together, but the

death of their friend had to be hitting her particularly hard. Jace had helped her and Darius when they were lost in the forest on Ostillon. He and Parthenia had always been close. In some ways he'd been the father she'd never had, though who her true father was, Carina remained unsure.

"I'll never fight with you again," she said. "I promise. You're right. You never know when it might be the last time you see someone you love."

"I'm going to hold you two to that," said Bryce.

Oriana lifted her head and wiped away her tears. "Is there any news on Darius?"

"He should be out of sick bay next week," Carina replied. "Dr Asher said he's making good progress."

"She also said he should never attempt to do the same thing again," Bryce said, "so it's up to us to keep an eye on him. I'm certainly never taking my eyes off any of you."

"That could get old fast," said Carina.

"You're just going to have to put up with me."

"Have you met any of the new people yet?" Parthenia asked.

"No," Carina replied. "Maybe in a few days when I'm feeling better. I noticed Jackson has a new arm."

"Oh yes," said Oriana. "You should get him to show you what it does."

"Um, arm things?"

"More than that, but I won't spoil the surprise."

Nahla wandered in reading an interface. "Hey everyone. I looked something up and I thought you would be interested to know."

Seeing her little sister had returned to normal had been one of Carina's greatest joys on waking up—until she found out the reason why. But it was good that she was better. "Okay, spill the beans."

"Lakshmi is the name of an ancient goddess," said Nahla, "who bestowed wealth and prosperity on her worshipers."

"No kidding?" said Bryce. "That makes a lot of sense."

"Are you talking about Lacks Me Station?" asked Ferne, also appearing at the door.

Oriana groaned. "I'm so glad we're leaving that place behind. I won't have to listen to you mispronounce the name all the time."

"We never even got to go there," Ferne complained.

"You didn't miss much, believe me," said Carina. "I'm very, very happy to be leaving it too. And I guess now we have our ability to Cast back and we're mages again, we should continue with our plan to go to Earth."

"I think that decision requires a meeting," said Bryce.

"Yes," said Parthenia, "and don't leave me out this time."

Carina hugged her. "Don't worry, you're invited."

The ship suddenly dipped. The three children who were standing stumbled and Parthenia clutched her sister in surprise.

"What was that?" Ferne asked from the deck. "Is Bibik at the controls?"

The *Bathsheba* swerved upward and then jerked right.

"What's going on?" Oriana complained.

Hsiao's voice came over the shipwide comm. "Strap in, everyone, quick as you can. A strong gravitational field is pulling at us. The computer can't identify the source."

"Stars," said Carina, "can't we have a smooth, trouble-free passage for once? Is that too much to ask?"

CARINA'S STORY CONTINUES IN...

GALACTIC RIFT

Sign up to my reader group for a free copy of the *Star Mage Saga* prequel, *Daughter of Discord*, discounts on new releases, review crew invitations and other interesting stuff:

https://jjgreenauthor.com/free-books/

(If you don't receive an email, check your spam folder.)

Printed in Great Britain
by Amazon